THE BOOK OF A
THOUSAND SINS

WRATH JAMES WHITE

DEADITE PRESS
205 NE BRYANT
PORTLAND, OR 97211

AN ERASERHEAD PRESS COMPANY
WWW.ERASERHEADPRESS.COM

ISBN: 1-936383-14-4

Printed in the USA.

CONTENTS

He Who Increases Knowledge

I never believed in God and if I had I'm quite sure my response would not have been to prostrate myself before him and offer myself up as his eternal slave. I doubt that I'd have been so awed as to renounce all reason and autonomy to become his unquestioning, submissive, yes-man; and offer him my throat to crush beneath his heel and my backside to kick like one of his many mindless cattle. The very notion offends me. I might have sought to study him, after he'd been captured and caged. Run him through a few IQ and physical dexterity tests before vivisecting him and examining his organs through a microscope with thin slices of his brain laid out on slide trays. Worship? No, I would want to own him; claim his power for myself. Pretty soon, I was hoping there really was a god, actively searching for him. If such a being existed, there was hope that I could usurp its power.

It was this search for God that led me into the sciences. I studied everything from bio-chemistry and quantum physics to astronomy, psychology, and socio-anthropology. I sought him in petrie dishes, in electron microscopes, in radio telescopes, in chemical and mathematical equations, in ancient crypts and burial mounds, and in the minds of men, but he eluded me. I then took all the traditional routes. I went to churches, mosques, temples, and synagogues. I went to sights where miracles were said to have taken place. All I found were more deluded sheep following a shepherd who was nowhere in evidence. Until the day I was led, as if by fate, to a whorehouse in Mexico.

A man I'd known for some years had come to me with a tale I'd heard many times from many men but had never found so thoroughly convincing as I did upon hearing it from him. He told me that he'd found heaven . . . between the thighs of a woman. He told me that he'd touched God.

Big Willie was 6'5" 235lbs of muscle-bound lady-killer. Every common epithet used to describe a notorious womanizer applied to him easily. The same women who called him a no-good-dog still called him every night. His friends lived vicariously through him, recounting his infamous exploits while seated on bar stools and knocking back 40ozs. "Pimp" and "Player" were titles he wore with pride. It made no sense to me at all to hear him talking like this.

"I found an angel. Her pussy is paradise!"

"Okay, so which deluded little slut might this be?" I asked, not just skeptical, but downright hostile. I had listened to stories of his various conquests since our days in high school together and I no longer found them amusing. I felt as if he told me these things merely to feed the jealousy he knew I already had for him. My entire sexual history was barely a weekend in his life. But then, I'd never heard him lavish such praise upon a woman after he'd already slept with her. Generally he would become obsessed with some woman or other but then once he'd had her he would immediately loose interest. Once she was demystified and revealed as a mere mortal, his disappointment would become immediately apparent. I often wondered if perhaps Willie was looking for God too, but just taking a different approach in his search, seeking him in the flesh. Perhaps Willie sought the goddess?

As unusual as it was to hear him talking about a woman like this, I did not regard his comments as anything more than the inevitable downfall of any man, even an unrepentant pussy hound like Willie. I assumed that he'd simply fallen in love—that this man for whom

5

passion was a sport had finally found his competitive equal. It was only when he began to elaborate that my curiosity was piqued.

"Man, I'm tellin' you, this ain't what you think. It ain't like I'm in love or nothing. I'm tellin' you, this woman's pussy is like the gates of heaven! I was fucking her and man I was like teleported straight to paradise! I saw the face of God! I could feel the entire universe!"

"In some bitch's pussy?"

"Yeah!"

"Well, what a fool I have been! Here I was looking in churches and books and all the time all I had to do was find the right piece of tail!"

"Bro, I'm not bullshitting you. Her pussy is like some kind of portal to another plane of existence! It's true! She works in this whorehouse in Tijuana and everybody down there knows about her. She's like a legend! They even pray to her! Women send their husbands to the whorehouse to fuck her as part of a religious ceremony. They call it getting "the blessing". There's even some big controversy with one of the local churches down there because they want to take her out of the brothel and put her up in the church, make her a saint and put her up on the altar. They want to make her part of the communion! But the brothel owners don't want to lose her because of the money she brings in."

"You have got to be full of shit."

"Bro, I ain't even creative enough to come up with some shit like this if I tried. You've got to come down there with me and see for yourself."

So I went. On the slim chance that it was true I had to go see. I knew it was ridiculous, but I was intrigued. We lived in Los Angeles so it was only a short drive to Tijuana. We jumped in the Mazda Civic hatchback and made a run for the border with images of the sainted whore dancing through our minds.

The den of holiness and iniquity where the holy slut lay on a bed with legs akimbo, was a dingy little place that featured a live sex show in the basement in which women demonstrated one of the acts that had made the city famous, fucking a donkey. The upstairs lobby was littered with last ditch whores who wreaked of infection and disease. Many of them were missing teeth and had black eyes or busted lips and a profusion of other scrapes and bruises, mostly on their knees and elbows. Many of them were smoking crack pipes and shooting themselves up with heroin right there in the lobby as they sat on battered lice-ridden couches waiting for the next trick. They all had vacant eyes and hopeless expressions like prisoners at a death camp. This was the end of the road for the world's oldest profession. The place where whores came to die. I could only wonder what the hell had brought Willie here.

Willie could have any woman he desired. He had a way with women that went beyond his rugged handsomeness or chiseled physique. He knew all the right lies to tell. Women looked into his soft brown eyes, followed the movement of his heart shaped lips, and believed every word that came out of him. Willie could make a woman feel like the most beautiful woman on the planet. Yet for some reason he had chosen to pay for sex with prostitutes that would have made the elephant man lose his appetite. The only thing that struck me more oddly than Willie having been there was the site of the long line of respectable looking gentlemen of every age from sixteen to ninety waiting to get into a room somewhere in the back of the establishment.

Every now and again a man would step out of the room and genuflect with one hand while zipping his fly with the other, then the next man would cross himself and enter for his turn. Everyone in the line seemed to have a look of solemnity and piety and many of them carried bibles. This was some weird shit.

"Willie, how the hell did you find this place?"

"A cab driver brought me here. I told him I wanted some pussy and you know, I thought he'd bring me to a dance club or something. He tells me that he knows where there's some pussy like nothing else in this world. So I said, well fuck yeah! Take me there! Next thing I know we're darting through dark alleys at like 80 miles an hour and we wind up here."

"Okay, so why didn't you just turn around and leave when you found out what the place was?"

"Do you want to leave?"

I looked at the long line of men waiting to get into the room. They looked more like they were waiting to enter a confessional than a whore's bed. My curiosity was roiling like a furnace. No, I didn't want to leave. I wanted to uncover the mystery. I had to find out what was behind that door.

Another man came out with his eyes glazed as if in a religious rapture. I grabbed him and asked him what he'd seen. His eyes stared straight up at the ceiling and did not even turn my way. When he didn't reply I shook him and repeated my question in Spanish. His eyes swam slowly towards my face, pupils as wide as marbles.

"¿Qué viste?" <"What did you see?">

"¡Vi a Dios! ¡Vi la eternidad!" <"I saw God! I saw Eternity!"> he replied.

"¿Quién es ella? ¿Quién es aquella mujer allá adentro?" <"Who is she? Who is that woman in there?"> I asked.

"¡Es la puta de Babilonia! ¡María Magdalena!" <"It is the whore of Babylon! Mary Magdalene!"> he replied again, nearly swooning as he spoke in a tone that could only be described as reverent.

The whore of Babylon, the woman who'd been afflicted with seven different demons whom, according to the bible, Jesus had exorcised with a mere touch. The woman who'd watched as Christ was executed and who'd been the first to witness his resurrection, over two thousand years ago. These peasants believed that she was still alive, or had been resurrected herself, and was now throwing her legs up for money in the filthiest brothel in Mexico.

I searched his eyes and the eyes of those who stood around me, mumbling prayers and clutching bibles and crucifixes to their chest as they waited to be perhaps the one-hundredth man that day

8

to fuck the same ho, and I could see not one shred of doubt in them. Whatever lay beyond that door, it had convinced them all. This was either the crowning example of man's absolute superstitious idiocy or the most profound leap of faith I'd ever seen. More than likely, it was both. I kept thinking about a quote I'd heard years ago: "The world holds two classes of men—intelligent men without religion, and religious men without intelligence." I'd seen nations, entire cultures comprised of the latter. It should not have surprised me at all to find a brothel filled with them.

There was no way I could have left at that point. I let the man go and watched as he stumbled past me, out the doorway, and off into the shadowy street, already growing dim as the sun set and twilight slipped into darkness. He shouted something as he staggered down the street with his head pointed heavenward. Loosely translated it was something like: "I have been saved! I have seen God!" Whatever it was that Willie had experienced in that room, between that woman's thighs, it was not, it seemed, an isolated occurrence.

What he had told me about the locals treating the place like a house of worship was by far an understatement. Even children walking by stopped and crossed themselves. As the man who'd just left the tiny room made his way down the street people rushed out to touch him for good luck. How a prostitute could become an object of worship was completely beyond my comprehension. I had to know what it was about her that could cause such a reaction in these people and even in my own friend.

I'd spent nearly every year since high school chasing miracles and messiahs around the country. I dropped out of UC Stanton one year before achieving a doctorate in Science and Philosophy just to pursue my quest for God and have never regretted it a single day. I have seen bleeding statues of the Virgin Mary. I have seen infants worshipped as the resurrected Messiah. I have seen stigmatics bleeding with the wounds of Christ. I have seen Buddhist monks levitate and voodoo priests possessed by demons. Still, this was the most bizarre religious experience I had ever had and it had not yet even begun. Ignoring the *I told you so* look on Big Willie's face, I took up my place in line and watched as the men kissed their crucifixes and hugged their bibles while waiting in line, in a whorehouse, to pull a train on a living saint.

Nearly an hour had gone by before it was my turn to enter the little room. The man who'd gone before me was kind enough to hold open the door for me. The first thing I noticed upon entering the dingy little room were the candles. White candles by the dozens filled the room casting shadows everywhere. The second thing I noticed was the smell. The overpowering odor of semen and stale pussy hung in the air like a fog and fired in my nostrils like a mentholated nose drop, causing my nose to run and my eyes to water almost immediately. The source of the malefic stench lay unmoving on the bed with her blank weeping eyes, white with cataracts, staring vacantly at the ceiling.

She was little more than a skeleton with wrinkled and mottled flesh wrapped loosely about her brittle bones. Her hair was all but gone save for a few white follicles clinging stubbornly to her crinkly liver spotted scalp. Her mouth was a hollow crater devoid of teeth and with gums that had shrunk back against her jawbone. Her withered breasts drooped like two empty bladders from her chest and were draped on either side of her ribcage. Her ancient thighs were a maze of varicose veins from which shriveled skin sagged loosely like gooseflesh. Between them was a raw and angry gash, a worn and shriveled vagina that looked like an infected hatchet wound, leaking a steady stream of semen from the countless dozens of men who had visited her this day, if not from the hundreds and possibly thousands who had visited her over her lifetime. Her labia hung like dried and wrinkled curtains of jerked beef from the ghastly orifice that so many men had come to worship.

I stepped closer to the bed and leaned over the impossibly ancient woman who looked more like a mummified corpse than a living person. I whispered softly to her some stuttering greeting. There was no reply. I raised my voice slightly and shook her bed.

10

Still, she did not move or respond in any way. Her skin looked as dry and brittle as an autumn leaf, yet when I reached down and pinched her on the thigh, it felt tough and oily like a wallet I'd once owned made out of eel skin leather. She still gave no indication that she was even aware of my presence. The woman was catatonic. Her brain was completely gone. I lifted one of her tiny hands and felt for a pulse. It was faintbut present and you could see her bird-like chest rising and falling ever so slightly as she inhaled and exhaled. At least she was alive.

How could Willie have fucked this half-dead thing?

I looked back down between her thighs and could see a faintlight emanating from the hairless slit. Her vaginal fluids seemed to have a chemical luminescence. I tried to approach the experiment with clinical detachment, but the unctuous cocktail of fluids still weeping from her loins made the very thought of entering her a repulsive and abhorrent prospect. Still, I had come for revelation, to capture God in a bottle, and if this was the vessel he was hiding in than I had no choice but to go in after him. If all those other guys could do it than so could I. In the interest of science, I dropped my pants and mounted her.

I wasn't really too fond of missionary position, but I thought it might have been somewhat blasphemous to bend her over doggy-style. I took myself in hand and masturbated to semi-erectness, imagining tit-fucking Tyra Banks while Pamela Anderson licked my balls and tried my best to ignore the putrescent odor emanating from the brainless vegetable I was about to fuck. As soon as I squeezed my near flaccid penis into her I knew what Willie had been raving about, what all those superstitious peasants had been so awed by. I was awed by it too. My manhood surged, growing massively erect as all the blood from my body seemed to suck down into it. My very consciousness seemed to have relocated to the tip of my swollen cock. But there was no way I could have been conscious. I had to have been dreaming. Because what I was experiencing was beyond anything imaginable.

Entering her was like falling from a great height. No, it was like hurtling through space at the speed of light. I saw worlds rush by as my dick slid into her sopping wet snatch. My head was filled with images that belonged to nothing on or in sight of earth. It exploded with colors that I'd never seen before and that I could not describe to you now. It was just like Willie had said. I'd entered a dimensional doorway and I was as far from earth as the sun is from the nearest quasar. The harder I pumped into her the faster the universe flew by. The experience was exhilarating. It was like fucking on the head of a comet! My body was on fire with sensation. My every nerve ending was electrified! Soon I found myself at the very end of the universe, looking at it from some perspective beyond space, outside of existence. What I saw was astounding.

An amorphous semi-organic organism that seemed to be composed of living energy, stretching to infinity in all directions, so impossibly vast that the entire universe nestled within it. As I watched, entire galaxies emerged from it and others dissolved down into it. Planets formed and life emerged while other planets winked out of existence and were re-assimilated back into it, broken down and recycled into new planets. It was like a program stuck in an infinite loop of wanton destruction and recreation.

I somehow found myself in some type of telepathic connection with it or rather I became aware of the connection that had always existed. I was in touch with its mind and there was not a single discernable thought. It was all thought merged into a screaming cacophony of white noise, an endless riot of thought with no order or cohesion. The voice of the entire universe in one inarticulate stew, incomprehensible except for one powerful drive—survival, continuance! But it was not concerned with the survival of any one person, or species, or world, or galaxy, but simply that something survive, that something continue, that life in some form continue to exist. Endlessly it recycled one species and created another from its ashes, an endless continuum of emergence, evolution, and inevitable extinction leading back to the emergence of new species, new planets, new solar systems, and galaxies. This was the very force of creation, the source of all life. I had found God and it was all voracious appetite and mindless creation. Not a being but a force. A force that could not be pleaded with or appealed to. A force that did not share any of the concerns of mankind. A force that could never be captured in a book or in a laboratory or in any one man's mind or heart. This was the face of infinity and no finite being would ever be able to fathom but the smallest iota of its depths.

Suddenly I understood man's place in the universe. We were not the favorite children of a "Supreme Being" in whose image we were created, we were just one finite part of an infinite creation. We were grains of sand in a vast beach among countless billions of beaches. All of man's religions appeared as childish and ridiculous fairy tales and flights of presumptuous vanity compared to the reality of this.

I don't remember screaming, but I must have, and the screams must have been terrifying, because Willie came rushing into the room calling my name and looking at me as if he were afraid I was going to drop dead on the spot. I turned to look for him in the doorway, but all I could see was a vast sea of stars. Then the orgasm came thundering through me with the force of an exploding sun and my entire being nearly flew apart.

My body convulsed so violently that Willie had to grab me and hold me down to keep me from breaking my own back as cataclysmic explosions went off in my head and shook me to my soul. I was abruptly jerked backwards through time and space, back to the filthy little Tijuana whorehouse where I lay weeping atop the withered husk of a two-thousand year old vegetative prostitute whose pussy was the gateway to truth, with my seed running down her inner thigh and my tears running down her cheek.

I had found God. I had seen the mysteries of the universe revealed. And I wished that I had been smart enough to have left well enough alone.

I looked about me at the men who still stood in line, holding their ridiculous religious trinkets, and wondered why none of the other men who'd come into this room had been so struck by what they'd seen. Then, when I looked into their vacuous exaltant faces, I knew the answer. They'd had their faith to shield them from the truth. They'd gone into that room already knowing what they'd find and no matter what they experienced their answer would always have been the same: "I have seen God!" Their God. The Christian God. There was nothing else they would ever have allowed themselves to see. Faith had blinded them to even this awesome experience. I had gone in unprotected.

I reached out and took the bible from a man's hand who stood waiting to enter after me. I kept think about what the philosopher, Arthur Schopenhauer had said nearly a century ago—"He who increases knowledge, increases suffering. Man has but two choices, to be a happy animal or a suffering god." I should have listened. I did not want to know what I now knew. I did not want to suffer. I wanted to believe. I wanted to become one of the mindless sheep, to be a happy animal, unaware of the absolute insignificance of every breath I inhaled.

I cracked open the bible and began to read as Willie helped me out of the brothel and back into the hatchback. I read passage after passage as we traveled back up the road toward Los Angeles. I read about Adam and Eve and the Garden of Eden. I read about Moses and the Ten Commandments. I read about the birth of Christ and the Resurrection, and I began to laugh. All I could see were those planets being ingested into that mindless pitiless mass. I knew now what had sent the old prostitute into that mindless fugue. She had seen the truth. It didn't even matter if she was really Mary Magdalene or if she was actually two thousand years old or not. I would never be able to believe in anything again. The truth had set me free.

Don't Scream

I disappeared inside of her. Thrusting my engorged cock into her puckered anus with all the violence and passion of some erotomaniacal savage bent on the rape and destruction of her, but it was she who was destroying me. I pulled her hair and smacked her ass. She scratched my back and bit my shoulder, met each thrust with her own, growled in my ear and drew the scalpel across my nipple once again. I hated how much I loved it.

"Oh my god that feels so good! Arrrgh! No! Oh God that hurts!"

I had become a favorite joke of the emergency room nurses. I no longer tried to explain the bite marks on my cock or why I needed to have my testicles sewn back on twice in three months. The electrical burns on my ass from the cattle prod, the cuts and slashes on my back from the razor-barbed cat o' nine tails, the cigarette burns around my anus, it wasn't worth lying about. They knew that I was a sick puppy with one hell of a sadistic playmate. They probably thought I was a male prostitute who specialized in rough trade.

"Don't scream." She said pressing a finger to my lips. I knew she was about to hurt me.

I turned my back to her, baring it to her whip. She alternated between cracking the cat o' nine tails across my tight muscular buttocks and jacking me off, bisecting my nipple with the scalpel, and swallowing my cock whole. She pulled me down between her legs and smothered me in her juices. I lapped them up like the last meal of a dying man. When she finally pulled me inside of her, I was broken, defeated. My ego dissolved in the sweet nectar flowing from the lubricious folds of flesh enveloping my swollen member. Each thrust took me deeper into a self-destructive ecstasy of salacious sensations as if I were alone at sea being sucked down into a whirlpool.

My body went wild as electric tendrils of ecstasy radiated upward from my cock and fired through my nervous system. Her nails rent the skin on my back, shoulders, and throat to cheesecloth. Her teeth finished the job the scalpel had done on my nipples as she bit one of them off, masticated and swallowed it. She smiled, her teeth stained crimson. I screamed and died inside of her.

"Don't scream." She repeated breathlessly, silencing me with a kiss before biting down hard on my lip and tongue and lapping tenderly at the resultant blood.

Every night went like this. She took and I gave. Then she walked back out into the yard and dug her way back into the grave where I'd left her.

Our sex life had never been this adventurous when she was alive. Going to hell has a way of loosening a woman's inhibitions. Maria had always been such a self-righteous cunt before the thirty-six stab wounds I put in her chest and stomach on our seven-year anniversary when she'd refused to perform oral sex for the 365th time that year. I got head anyway, gagging her with my cock as she drowned in her own blood and eventually my cum.

Her eyes bulged in their sockets as I raped her esophagus, rolling around in her head as if seeking an exit from the nightmare she'd suddenly found herself in. The whole mess of semen and gore came bubbling up out of her mouth as she gargled and coughed, trying desperately to give voice to her horror, as she squealed out her last strangled breath.

"Shhh," I said, " Don't scream." Then I covered her mouth and pinched her nostrils closed, watching as she suffocated and drowned in her own blood.

I dragged Maria's corpse out into the yard and started to dig. I didn't want her to have a shallow grave. I didn't want anyone to ever find her. I didn't want Maria coming back to haunt me. I wanted her gone and forgotten. I dug through hard soil and sedimentary rock using a shovel, a pick, and a sledgehammer at times. I eventually dug a hole six-feet long, three-feet wide, and six-feet deep. Then I dug deeper.

There was another layer of rock and I had to take the pick and finally the sledgehammer to it to break through. I hit a pocket in the earth, an underground cave or something. Suddenly all the dirt began to collapse down into it as the hole grew wider and deeper, an avalanche of earth falling into some vast underground void. I could feel myself being pulled down into it as well, as if there was a great vortex beneath me sucking me down into a vacuum. Dirt and rubble cascaded over me in a great wave, knocking me back and nearly sending me careening down into the abyss below. I cried out for help as if Maria would suddenly reawaken just to save her murderous husband. I screamed as I found myself drowning in a whirlpool of free flowing earth. My mouth filled with soil and rock and for a moment I lost consciousness.

I was only out for a brief second but when I regained consciousness I was completely buried, entombed in the ground and sliding deeper and deeper into the hollow pocket of earth at the bottom of Maria's makeshift grave. I couldn't breathe. I clawed at the earth trying to climb my way out of the ground, but the loose dirt slipped between my fingers and dropped me further into the ever-widening hole beneath me. Then, just shy of tumbling headlong into the vast aperture beneath me, my fingers found purchase in the earth and I pulled myself out of the hole, barely escaping living internment. I scrambled free as more dirt fell away and my little hole became a great chasm in the earth.

There was a smell of decay that wafted up from that hole like the putrescence of a thousand corpses. I staggered from the assault and covered my face with my t-shirt. That's when I heard the screams.

Cries of pain and terror more horrible than anything I'd ever heard echoed from within that hole. I leapt backwards away from the pit, my entire body trembling, urine dribbling down my thigh, hair standing on end. There were people down there in the earth somewhere and they were in agony and I'd nearly joined them.

I listened to the screams for a long moment wondering what to do. I knew that I had done something far worse than killing the frigid bitch I'd made the mistake of wedding. I had dug something far more than a simple grave. As the screams seemed to grow nearer, louder, more terse and shrill, swirling around my head like a maelstrom, I began trying to fill the hole again. At first the dirt just fell and kept falling before I started tossing some of the larger rocks back into the grave to plug the mouth of that underground cave. Finally I blocked the hole enough to where I could pile some of the dirt back on top of it. Then I went to throw in Maria.

Maria had always been a stunning beauty. Half Puerto-Rican and half Filipino. She was slight of limb but with a large, round, voluptuous ass and huge breasts. A body like a porn star. Her hair swirled down her back in long curly black locks like strands of liquid night. Her skin was a natural tan like fresh pastry. Her dark smoky eyes were fanned by long luxurious eyelashes giving her a sultry appearance as if she'd just had an orgasm or smoked some really good weed. Unfortunately she had been raised by strict Catholic parents who'd taught her that sex was a sin. I'd admired that at first. She had wanted to wait until marriage to have sex. So we did. Seven years later it felt like I was still waiting.

She'd never warmed to the idea of sex with me. Anything other than missionary position was completely out of the picture and even then it was a rare treat that she merely tolerated rather than enjoyed. I grew to resent and eventually to hate her for her frigidity. I would seethe in rage as I lay beside her at night masturbating to fantasies of raping my own wife all while trying to be quiet enough not to wake her. It was pathetic. But now it was over. I'd finally done it.

18

Before I threw Maria into the ground, I rolled her over, removed the rest of her blood-soaked clothing, and anally raped her, something else she'd never let me do in life. I punched my cock up into her lower intestines, tearing through her rectum, until blood ran out of both ends. Then I threw her in and watched her fall all the way to hell.

I guess she thought she'd go to heaven after such a righteous life. I mean, she was such a good Christian, suppressing all carnal desires and forsaking all earthly rewards for the promise of paradise. It must have been quite a shock when her vain, pious, judgmental ass wound up careening through inferno.

I'd always suspected that The New Testament and the Old Testaments were two entirely separate and unique documents referring to two entirely separate and unique gods. There's Elohim who was the destroyer of Sodom and Gomorrah, the god who drowned the earth and saved only a boat full of his creations, who killed the first born sons of Egypt, who relished the idea of sending those who did not love and obey him to suffer eternal torment at the hands of the first of his creations to betray him. Then there was Yahweh who sacrificed his only begotten son so that man would not die but would know eternal life so long as they believed in him. No way these were the same cats. Of course you couldn't have told Maria that. She found out though. When hell spread it's fiery wings and embraced her, and her soul sizzled and burned as she screamed for that merciful god she'd always read about, the one who was supposed to forgive her petty sins. The myth. And found only the fiery wrath of Elohim.

She had been proud of her own piety. A sin. She had been judgmental of those less Christian than her. A sin. She had refused the love of her husband. A sin. And Elohim did not forgive. She had cried out for Yahweh and found that he had no power in hell. She had cried out for Jesus only to see him burning beside her. So in the end she had cried out to the only god that would listen.

19

She was unwilling to suffer like a good Christian and so she forsook God and clawed her way out of hell in defiance of God's justice. She didn't talk about it but I imagined that Satan himself had helped boost her out of that pit, happy to see the love of God die in the eyes of one so pious. He had helped lift her out of hell and back into my bed.

That first night, when I felt the blistering heat of her flesh slide up against me as I lay alone in my cold bed, I leapt up and nearly killed myself tripping over my own shoes in the dark. Maria followed me out from beneath the covers, a voluptuous silhouette shimmering like a ghost in the half-light of the moon and stars, casting its luminescence between the sheer window coverings. I turned on the light by the side of the bed as she rose with the sheets spilling off her body like Aphrodite rising from the sea foam. She was filthy, covered in grave dirt. Her hair and nails had grown long from the year she'd spent in the ground. But her body had lost none of its luster. She still looked like a wet dream with proportions like those pubescent teens drew on bathroom walls.

She was completely nude. Her large breasts, with the large dark nipples like Hershey's kisses, pointed straight at me. She was breathing hard and she ran her hands slowly over her opulent bosom, squeezing her over-ripe mammaries and pinching and pulling on her nipples. My erection leapt to life even as the fear shook me to my soul. She reached out for my rapidly solidifying flesh and I stepped away from her even as I thrust my hips forward into her grasp, fear and lust competing within me. My legs trembled.

"Shhh," she whispered through a lascivious grin, "Don't scream."

The irony of having the last words I'd ever spoken to her thrown back at me as an introduction was not lost on me. It was proof positive that she still remembered that I was her murderer. I screamed despite her warning.

Maria grabbed my cock and I froze. I could not remember the last time she'd even acknowledge its existence let alone caressed it so lovingly.

20

She dropped to her knees and my body tensed as she opened her mouth and slurped on my engorged penis, sliding its entire length down her throat past her epiglottis and into her esophagus. She grabbed my ass and pulled me deeper into her mouth until her lips were buried in my pubic hair. I thrust slowly three or four times as her tongue swirled around my throbbing erection then I sped up my rhythm and aggressively fucked her beautiful mouth. She did not gag once. She didn't even appear to be breathing. Her teeth scraped my tender foreskin and there was a brief moment when I feared that she would bite down and castrate me, a fitting revenge for what I had done to her. Then I ejaculated in wild jerks and fits and I was past caring. If I had to die than this was certainly the way I wanted to go.

What felt like half my bodily fluids erupted into her throat and she hungrily devoured the warm deluge of semen, lapping up every ounce. She gripped my diminishing erection in her hand and licked the last drops from its wilting head. In seconds she'd stroked me back to full erection.

Maria looked up into my eyes and smiled with her lips glistening with saliva and semen. A predatorial rictus ripped across her face that turned my blood to Kool-Aid, then she sank her teeth into my shaft and tore off my foreskin. I screamed but my erection never waned. She raked her fingernails over my ass, down my thighs, and across my scrotum, tearing into my wrinkled nutsack. I screamed over and over again. My genitals were a bloody ruin when she dragged me to the floor and mounted me. She rode my abused manhood hard, hammering out orgasm after orgasm while slapping me hard across the face and clawing at my throat with her overgrown nails.

She began to strangle me as the rhythm of her hips increased. Spots danced before my eyes from the blood loss and oxygen deprivation. Then an orgasm that resembled an epileptic seizure racked my body and emptied me. I passed out and woke up alone again but with obvious evidence that this had been no dream. I dragged my ass to the ER to get my cock stitched up and anesthetized before the wounds got infected and they had to amputate.

The next night she was back, carrying the shovel I'd used to bury her. I rushed to embrace her and she beat me to the floor with the wooden handle. Cracking it across my head and back until I crumpled at her feet and curled up into a fetal position, whimpering and crying. She slid down to the floor with me and wrapped her warm flesh around me, kissing and caressing the bruises and contusions she'd left all over my skull and on down my neck and spine. I responded to the sensuous wet heat of her mouth as it slid over my wounds soothing each injury with her probing tongue, lapping at the blood that flowed from the welts and abrasions. My manhood swelled urgently and I felt ashamed, like a ridiculously loyal dog that licks the hand that smacks it. She left trails of hot saliva down between my shoulder blade as she kissed sucked and licked her way down my back. My entire body tensed and vibrated with want. When I felt that slick serpentine tongue squirm its way into my anus I had to concentrate to keep from ejaculating right there. Then she kissed her way back up my spine to my neck. I could feel her hot breath in my ear and then the handle of the shovel wedged beneath my chin.

She pulled tight until the handle bit into my throat and choked off my windpipe. She continued to kiss and suckle my ear even as she strangled me. I clawed the air and tried to scramble free of her but she held on tight and I couldn't throw her off. I stood up and she wrapped her legs around my waist and clung tight to my back still tugging on the shovel handle. I gasped once more before I fell over and nearly passed out. I woke up to the most excruciating invasion. Maria was stretching my anus wide with the shovel handle; ramming it in so hard and fast that splinters lodged in the soft tissue of my rectum and it partially prolapsed. My stomach cramped and I felt my organs shift as she put her shoulder into it. I felt something give and the shovel slid in deeper and lodged there. Blood sprayed from my mouth and drooled down my chin and I knew that she'd done some serious internal damage.

"Don't scream," she whispered into my ear as my eyes rolled back into my head and the most shrill cry of horror and anguish raked the night air.

"Shhh!" she said more firmly, but I had already strained my vocal chords so that I could no longer utter more than a hoarse squeak.

"Don't scream," she said again as she ran a hand through my hair then seized my bruised throat and held me still while she bit my ear off. I tried to scream again, my voice box seized and the chords in my neck strained in silence.

"Shhh!" she commanded again, still petting my head like I was some frightened pet. She waited until I had stopped screaming before she pulled me down on top of her. She would not let me go until I'd satisfied her. So, like the obedient dog that I was, I slid my semi-erect penis between her lubricious thighs and into that infernal pit. I fucked her with the end of that shovel still broken off in my ass where she'd left it.

I spent three nights in the hospital and underwent a psychological evaluation. Of course I didn't tell them that my dead wife had come back to life with the sexual appetite of a serial killer and was fucking me half to death every night. Despite or perhaps because of my refusal to explain the excavation tool lodged in my anus, the admissions nurse was arguing hard to have me committed to an asylum where I could no longer injure myself. As a compromise they put me under 24 hour suicide watch and then released me when my insurance ran out. I went back home that weekend, back into the arms of my beautiful dead wife.

And we lived happily ever after. Except there was something wrong with her. Something beyond the violent and ravenous sex-drive. Something that was leeching its way into me. Everything about this was somehow not right. I was fucking the woman I'd murdered or rather she was fucking me, fucking me right into the grave beside her.

Each night she undid me, and each morning I rushed to the Emergency Ward to get put back into some semblance of my original condition. Eventually my sex drive began to wane. I needed a break from her. To heal from the wounds and to replenish my own desires. After years of relative abstinence I was now thoroughly oversexed, chafed and spent. My erections were painful. My orgasms were streaked with blood. I spent each night cocooned in a kaleidoscopic whirlwind of indescribable agony and pleasure. Taking such abuse each night was draining me. But she would not leave me alone and I could not resist her. When I tried, it ended badly.

"Not tonight. Maria I need to rest. My work is suffering. I'm like a zombie at the office. I keep waking up later and later. The guys at the office are starting to notice the welts and cuts also. I told them I was in a Kung Fu class but they know something isn't right. We have to stop for a while."

She replied with a growl and a slap that knocked me to the floor. My jaw popped and unhinged. My eyes teared up and I rolled over on my back with my arms crossed over my face as if to ward off further blows. Maria seized both of my arms and pinned them to the floor with hands that felt like heated vice grips. Then she pressed her damp sweaty sex to my face and ground it against my mouth as I screamed in pain and fought to free my head from between her thighs. I was smothering and my jaw was in agony but she would not free me until I gave her the orgasm she demanded.

"Shhhh! Don't scream," she hissed and I obediently choked off my cries and did as she commanded, lapping at her clitoris which was still littered in topsoil from her climb back out of the pit. My jaw was a riot of pain by the time she came. Then she forcibly wrestled an unwanted orgasm out of me, nearly tearing my penis right out of my groin in the process. I limped to work the next day with my jaw wired shut and my bruised and swollen penis bandaged to my leg.

"David. Can I see you in my office?"

My supervisor was the type of private anti-social despot that only talked one on one with his employees on the day they were terminated. I packed my things before I even entered his office and walked out halfway through my exit interview. I didn't care about my unemployment benefits or what I needed to do with my 401k and my health insurance benefits. All I could think about was Maria.

I started locking my doors and windows at night. I even put a deadbolt on the bedroom door. Still, she came. Tearing through the drywall to get at me like some hellish beast. I considered hanging up crucifixes and perhaps even a garland of garlic and wolf's bane. She was killing me.

I started praying at night, clutching the bible tight against me and begging the Lord not to let her rise again from the grave. Sometimes I would recite the Lord's Prayer even as she rode my erection and milked me of my seed. I tried to read the bible but fatigue and exhaustion had lead to a bizarre presbyopia in my vision and I could not bring the blurred pages into focus.

The first few nights she had been careful to leave only superficial wounds that could be repaired with a few sutures or stitches, a little ice, painkillers, and some anti-inflammatories. Now Maria would re-open wounds the very next night after they had been stitched closed by the conspicuously annoyed and disgusted ER nurses and she didn't always leave behind the pieces she'd ripped or cut off leaving no opportunity for reattachment. I was looking more and more like some unfortunate accident victim in need of plastic surgery. Soon I was too ashamed to leave the house. I sat in the dark with the curtains drawn tight trying to find a way to defend myself against Maria. I had to get away from her.

I stood in the mirror cataloguing my injuries. Both nipples were missing along with both testicles. They had been chewed up and swallowed. I think she had even forced me to eat one of my own nuts. I vaguely remember swallowing something with the texture of veal.

I was missing most of my left ear and even part of my cheek had been bitten off along with most of my bottom lip. Chunks of flesh were missing from my chest and neck where she had cut or eaten away at me. My ass-cheeks were a minefield of gauges, avulsions, and deep cuts that were now growing infected without the proper time to heal.

Somehow Maria had come back the exact opposite of the woman that I had stuck in the ground. In life she had been repressed and nearly asexual. I had always wanted her to be more adventurous and uninhibited; more willing to try new things. Now, I had gotten what I wanted. She had no inhibitions any longer. She would do almost anything. Anything she thought of she immediately performed regardless of its effects on me. At first it had been heaven. I'd felt like the luckiest man in the world. But now . . .

I saw Maria walk up behind me in the mirror. I felt her hands slide over my back followed by her mouth and tongue and then her teeth. I tensed in anticipation of the pain. I looked back into the mirror as her hands crawled from my back to my chest and the scalpel in her hand slid into view. She had opened me up from my collarbone to my solar plexus before I'd noticed. I was in hell.

It struck me like an epiphany, like a revelation. I remembered it all now. Yes, I had killed Maria. I dragged her out into the garden and dug a hole and the hole had started to widen, to collapse in on itself as the ground swirled beneath me and funneled down into some deep underground chasm, but I hadn't crawled back out. I hadn't raped Maria's corpse and thrown it into the earth. I had died down there, imprisoned in tons of rock and dirt. My eyes widened as the full implication of what I was thinking hit me. I had died and gone to hell or was this heaven? My every desire but yet my every fear.

"No! No! Nooooo!" I yelled as tears rolled down my face and I shook my head as if I could make it all go away just by denying it.

Maria was still cutting on me with the scalpel and now had me opened up from abdomen to mid-chest. I looked down and realized with horror that she had started cutting much lower than my abdomen. My penis was gone. I felt a burning sensation rip across my throat as she plunged the knife into my carotid artery and then ripped it across my neck all the way back to my opposite ear, neatly slicing through my larynx and choking off the scream that had come roaring out of me when I'd realized that this torment would go on forever. My penis reappeared in her hand then disappeared again and reappeared once more sticking out of the enormous gash in my throat.

"Shhh!" Maria commanded, "Don't scream."

I could hear sirens coming and could see the red and white lights of the ambulance as it screeched to a halt outside my door through the gaps in the Venetian blinds. I hadn't called an ambulance and I doubted that my neighbors had either. No matter how shrill and agonized my screams, they would have called the police before assuming I was in need of medical attention. Of course they would save me, stitch me back together, no matter how grievous the injury, so that Maria could take her time undoing me night after night, again and again, forever. My pleasure and my punishment.

Maria kissed my ragged lips as blood poured from them and the look in her eyes was like nothing I'd ever seen in them before her death. Not hatred or even love but pure animalistic lust. I closed my eyes as her kisses descended down my body soothing the wounds she'd created and I wondered again if this was heaven or hell but was certain that it didn't matter either way.

Resurrection Day

"Bring out your dead! Or we'll come drag they asses out! Either way they're going to burn!" The voice shouted through the megaphone over the angry mob of anti-ressurectionists and the crackle of the flame. I heard them just outside my door, pounding to get in. They were pissed off and scared and they wanted their sacrifice. They wanted to offer up another soul in the hope that it would appease the gods and return their world to normal.

I hated to admit it, but I was glad that they had come. It wasn't right, him being alive. It wasn't fair.

A red sun burned through my blinds bleeding fiery tendrils of crimson light and casting dark shadows around the room. The Colt 45 and MD 20/20 hangover made the world stagger and lurch and my stomach roll as I raised my head from the pillow. The light stung my eyes and intensified the throbbing ache in my temples.

It was Easter Sunday, and usually that meant getting up early to go to church with the family. Not that I was all that religious myself, but it was tradition. However church was a highly unlikely proposition that morning.

I had just hit the snooze button and rolled back over to resume my dreams, when a loud and persistent ringing jarred me awake again. Dazed, disoriented, and with my head still pounding like a bass drum, I woke up to my Grandmother's panicked phone call.

"What? Are you serious?"

At first, I thought she was joking. Except Grandma is no comedian. Maybe she was trying to teach me some kind of lesson for missing church? Whatever it was, she had to be wrong. There was no way what she was telling me could be true.

"I'm telling you they're here! Right outside my door! You've got to get over here!"

The choking sobs interspersed between her frantic words convinced me. At least they convinced me that she *thought* she was telling the truth. My Great Grandfather and Great Grandmother were at her front door. They were alive again after twenty years in the grave. It made no sense. Immediately my mind went to images plucked from the scores of horror movies I'd watched in sticky-floored theatres, peeking out from between butter soaked fingers. Hollywood had long ago driven home the lesson that when the dead walked the earth it was always a bad thing for the living. I imagined snarling vampires thirsty for blood or rotting zombies pounding on my Grandmother's door hungry for human flesh. There had to be another explanation.

Of course there had been signs. There was no way to avoid noticing the drastic increase in the local vermin. Roaches and rats blanketed the streets by the tens of thousands and the sky was filled with clouds of knats, flies, mosquitoes, and bees. Even the dog and cat population had exploded, which was the only thing keeping the rats from consuming us all.

One day Mr. Hightower next door walked up and down the street with a couple gallons of kerosene dousing the teeming throngs of vermin before lighting them all on fire. It was the only thing that seemed to work. He'd tried driving his truck over them two or three times a day but somehow it never seemed to make a dent in their numbers. So he began doing his kerosene trick every morning. I hated the caustic stench of burning rat flesh but I hated the rats themselves even more so I never complained and neither did anyone else. The city hadn't done anything about them so we were happy someone was taking action.

I never saw the sudden infestation as anything more than another tragic consequence of ghetto life. Who could have ever envisioned something as impossible as mass resurrection?

"They're on the porch right outside my door! I can see them through the peephole!"

It had been over two thousand years since the last resurrection and that one had spawned a religion. I guess those things are all a matter of where and when. Someone comes back to life in Jerusalem we call him God. Someone comes back to life in G-town and we call the police or run for the shotguns and the wooden stakes.

In the bible it all seemed so wonderful and miraculous. No one had thought to mention all the damned flies and cockroaches or the goddamned rats! What was happening in my little neighborhood was just creepy.

I could here a loud banging coming through the phone and the sound of a doorbell. Then I heard Poppa's voice loud and forceful, just the way I remembered it, not faint and ethereal like a ghost or the moaning echo from the grave of a mindless zombie. It was Poppa all right. And he did not sound too happy about being locked out of HIS house.

"Now, girl I done tole' you, I ain't got my keys! Now open this door and let me up in there. Ya hear?"

As the undisputed patriarch of the Johnson family, Poppa wasn't used to being disobeyed and I could almost hear Grandma's resolve shatter like a pain of glass in a hurricane. I heard a metallic tinkling sound and I knew that she had taken the chain off the door.

"Grandma! Grandma! Are you okay?"

"I don't know baby. They look alright. I think I'm going to open the door."

"Don't open the door!"

"But I don't want Poppa mad at me. It's been twenty years and I don't want our reunion to begin with an argument."

"Grandma! That's not your father! They are dead. Long dead. Do not open that door!"

I heard my Grandmother's screams coming from the other end of the phone and my skin crawled with goosebumps. Every hair stood on end.

"What happened?"

"Now Uncle Joe and my brother Paul are out there too."

"What the hell is going on?"

"I'm going to open the door."

I started to protest when a knock came at my door. My first thought was who the hell would be visiting me at nine o'clock in the morning? My next thought was to wonder who I knew that was dead and knew my address?

I threw on a robe and rummaged around for my shotgun, remembered that I'd pawned it two years ago, and settled for my rusty twenty-five caliber Beretta. I was pretty sure it wasn't enough to stop a zombie or a vampire, but it made me feel better anyway. I grabbed a steak knife out of the kitchen for added back-up. The doorbell began to ring insistently, in chorus with the knocking.

"Who the fuck could that be?"

I went to the door, and saw my friend Rick standing on the front porch. My "Missing and presumed dead," friend Rick, whom I hadn't seen in five years.

"Come on, Bro. Open up the door! I know your ass is home."

He was a little dirty. Grave dirt no doubt. But the sunlight was beaming directly onto him and he wasn't bursting into flames. So he couldn't be a vampire. Could he? I wasn't sure. That sunlight thing could've been a myth. There were no signs of rot or decay and his skin held none of the ashy gray or putrescent green pallor of death. It had an almost healthy glow to it.

Aliens! Aliens that have taken the forms of our dead friends and relatives! That's the only thing that made sense. This had to be some kind of invasion. Of course, there was always the possibility that I was still drunk, and that this was some type of schizophrenic intoxication. Maybe I was still asleep; one of those heavy drunken sleeps that are nearly impossible to wake from. I stared out the peephole at the dead man on my porch and prayed that I was still drunk and not insane.

"Get the fuck off my porch, muthafucka!"

"What? What you trippin' on, man? I thought you was my boy? Now you gonna do me like this?"

"I was your boy, until you died. Now what the fuck is you doin' up and walking around instead of lyin' in a grave?"

"Dead? Did you go to my funeral mutherfucker? 'Cause I just woke up lyin' in the god damned woods bare-assed naked! I had to steal these fuckin' clothes just to get here!"

Of course I hadn't gone to his funeral. Not a real funeral anyway, just an informal affair between some of the homies. His body had never been found. Like I said, he was "Missing and *presumed* dead". No one was really sure what happened to him.

"Come on, Bro. My mom won't let me in. That's why I came to your house."

"Your mom don't live there no more. That's Mrs. Watson's house now."

"Then . . . then where's my mom?"

"I don't know, Bro. She upped and left like a year ago. I don't know where she went."

Rick collapsed against my porch railing. At first, I thought that whatever dire magic had reanimated his corpse, had fled him and he was dying once again. Then, I felt guilty, as I realized that he was crying. I opened the door, still holding the knife and the Beretta of course, but concealed beneath my bathrobe.

"Come on in, Bro."

I stared at him for a long uncomfortable moment before I remembered my grandmother, all by herself with a herd of dead people at her door.

I picked up the phone and chills raced the length of my spine as the dial tone whined in my ear.

"Wait here, man!" I dashed upstairs and shrugged into a t-shirt in jeans. I dialed my grandmother's number again but there was no answer. Taking the steps two at a time I sprinted downstairs and out the front door.

"Fuck! Oh fuck! Come with me, man!"

"What's up bro?"

"I think something's wrong with my grandmother!" I already had tears in my eyes as I imagined that kindly old lady being torn apart by an army of the undead.

I grabbed my coat and started sprinting through the street, with Rick close behind. It looked like there was some type of party going on. There were people everywhere. At first, I assumed it was a block party, or maybe somebody had an accident and they were all waiting for the police to come. Then I started to recognize faces. Faces that all looked wrong, out of place.

The first thing I noticed was the bizarre clash of styles. There were far too many suits with butterfly collars, bell bottom pants, and purple and pink shirts with frills and ruffles. Far too many afros and pork-chop sideburns. It was like the whole block had gone retro. It looked like a pimp convention and my neighborhood just wasn't that hip. The other thing was that everyone seemed to be dressed up. I knew it was Easter Sunday, but I'd never seen that many people at church. Something really fucking weird was going on.

Dirty Ed waved at me, smiling wide, with dirt between his teeth and bloody fingers from where he'd clawed his way out of the grave. He looked like shit, but then he'd always looked like shit, even before he'd gotten his ass shot breaking into Mr. Pratt's house to steal his VCR. I waved back at him, but kept running.

"Hey Skip! Wait up!" I heard Rick yelling at my back. "Hey, wasn't that Dirty Ed? Didn't he get shot a few years back? I mean, we went to his funeral together? How the fuck can he be alive?"

I didn't reply, because I'd gone to Rick's funeral too. It was just a little neighborhood ceremony with some of the kids we'd grown up with, who knew that Rockmond had shot him and dumped his body somewhere, even if the cops refused to investigate. We'd poured out a 40oz, cried, told stories about the old days, and smoked a fat blunt in his honor. Then we prayed and lit a candle down by the old clubhouse where we'd all first met.

I also didn't answer because I was already looking at Sharon, who'd overdosed on crack last year and was now sitting on her porch cradling the premature baby who'd died a week before she did. I didn't answer, because Big Moose was coming right at me with that look on his face like he used to get when he was about to steal my sneakers or take my bike on a joyride. Only I could tell he was confused, because I was bigger than him now and the last time he'd seen me I'd been a twelve year-old kid. That was the day before his big dumb ass got shot by the cops while trying to rob the fucking supermarket. He took thirty-six bullets, wounded two police officers, and killed another. He had a closed casket funeral. People still talk about him around the neighborhood. He was a legend, and now, apparently, a living one.

I was completely out of breath by the time I reached Grandma's house. Her front door was open, and I immediately thought the worst. I was not at all prepared to see her sitting there with Poppa and Nana and Uncle Joe and Cousin Charlie and Aunt Rose and Cousin Jake. They were all lounging in the living room, laughing and sipping tea and coffee and listening to gospel music on the radio, like one great big family reunion. Except all of them were supposed to be dead. I'd been to all of their funerals. Cried over all of their graves. Yet here they were.

"Is that little Skip? Come give your Aunt Rose some sugar."

I remembered how much I hated that when I was a kid. Walking into a room full of old relatives and getting slobbered on and my cheeks pinched 'til they went numb. The thought of kissing her now almost made me want to scream. I looked around the room in a mild state of shock, ignoring Aunt Rose's outstretched arms.

Rick caught up with me, busting into the house like he lived there just as he had when we were kids, when his family and mine were almost interchangeable; when he'd been like the brother I'd never had; when he'd still been alive.

"Hey Grandma!" he said leaning over to give my Grandmother a kiss on the cheek. And of course he did not see anything wrong with all of them being there. How could he? He was wrong too; something else that shouldn't have been.

I looked around at the assemblage of ancestors and could see nothing unusual, nothing sinister or evil, no indication that they had any intention of drinking our blood or eating our brains. If it hadn't been for the stench of grave dirt, the tattered clothing and shredded nails, you would have thought that they'd just been out of town on a vacation or something and not on the wrong side of eternity.

"Uh, Hi Aunt Rose. Hi Cousin Charlie, Cousin Jake, Uncle Joe, Uncle Paulie, Poppa, Nana."

My eyes started to tear up. I didn't realize how much I'd missed them all. I ran to my Great Grandfather and Grandmother and cried in their arms. For a moment they looked confused as if they couldn't figure out who I was; couldn't rectify the boy they'd known with the grown man weeping in their lap. Then they softened, reacting to my pain, and they began to weep as well, showering me with hugs and kisses. I didn't care how they'd come back to us. I was just glad they were there.

It felt like Thanksgiving. We all sat around my Grandma's house cooking, eating, drinking, and reminiscing. More friends and relatives, long dead or long thought to be dead dropped through. Neighbors came by to introduce us to their dead parents, grandparents, or in some cases their children. We sat comforting Mr. Hightower who had shot his father dead again when he'd seen him banging on his screen door.

Mrs. Lucy was in a very difficult position. Uncle Joe had to sit in between her resurrected husband and the man she'd married after his death to keep them from killing each other. They glared across the room at one another, gesturing threateningly. Apparently they'd been best friends before the funeral.

It was funny how difficult it became to keep track of who was dead and who was really alive. I mean, they all were alive, but some of them shouldn't have been. What was even weirder, was that after sitting there laughing with a guy who still stank of formaldehyde, listening to him tell jokes about how he'd seen you running down the street without a diaper when you were two-years old, it was hard to remember that none of this should have been happening. Somehow it didn't feel so weird. The more dead people came crowding into my grandmother's house the less surprising it became. Pretty soon we just welcomed them with a big hug and introduced them around to the other guests as if they had just been out of the scene for a while and only needed reintroduction.

Someone turned on the television and everyone went silent. Apparently what was happening in our little neighborhood wasn't an isolated incident. Somehow I didn't think it was.

"All over the country the deceased are returning to life. In the most unusual occurrence in recorded history hundreds of thousands of the recently departed returned to their loved ones this Easter Morning. Scientists and physicians alike are baffled by the apparent mass resurrection. One noted physician who had the opportunity to examine some of the miraculously reborn had this to say . . ."

A very shocked and confused looking young doctor stumbled in front of the camera stammering nervously. There was a haunted and incredulous look on his face that told anyone observant enough that he had no answers even before he opened his mouth.

"Well, I have actually examined over a dozen of the . . . uh . . . resurrected, and I can find nothing at all unusual about them. They all appear to be in perfect health. They don't even show any evidence of the injuries or afflictions that lead to their deaths."

"Do these . . . uh . . . um . . . reawakened individuals pose any kind of threat to the living? I mean is there any evidence at all that they might not be completely . . . safe?"

"Not at all! You mean will they suddenly start decaying or drinking blood or something? As near as I can tell they are perfectly normal. If it weren't for the fact that some of them have been dead as long as twenty-five years I would see no reason to hospitalize them at all. As it stands we are keeping them in the hospital for observation for a few more days while we wait on the result of a few toxicology tests."

All the laughter stopped. Everyone stood shocked in Grandma's living room. Many of them hadn't really believed that they had indeed been dead. Now, after hearing it on television, they were having a difficult time denying it, but an even harder time accepting it.

My Great Grandmother burst out in tears and Poppa took her in his arms and held her tenderly. He looked frightened and lost. I looked from one pair of eyes to the next and in each there was that hollow-eyed fear and confusion. Everyone had been trying to ignore the question of his or her miraculous revival. But there it was laid back on the table. The room no longer looked like a celebration. Now it looked like a funeral. Mrs. Lucy's ex-husband Tony was the first one to speak.

"But how? How is this possible?" He looked at Mrs. Lucy and then at her new husband who lost all his hostility and looked back at Tony helplessly.

"How did I die, bro? How long have I been dead?"

"You fell asleep behind the wheel of your car like three years ago. Went right through a metal barricade and into Wissahickon creek. I did the eulogy at your funeral, man."

The questions started to fly and soon the party began to dissipate as the neighbors left to answer their questions in private. I was sad to see them all go. That meant we had to resolve our own issues now. Rick shuffled uncomfortably from foot to foot staring down at his ruined Stacy Adams and no doubt wondering how he was going to get a new pair of Air Jordans. The tension rolled in like a wave and stayed there like tepid water filling the air with a dank morbid humidity.

Uncle Joe walked into the kitchen and came back with a bottle of Tangueray.

"So, we're all dead huh?" He said with his voice full of false bravado as he took a long swig from the shapely green bottle. "I guess the question now is does anyone have a joint? Cause this is some heavy shit and I should at least get high before I have to deal with all this."

His bottom lip trembled and tears welled up in his eyes as he spoke. I'd have cried too if I was wearing a blue tuxedo with bell bottoms and a butterfly collar. Joe died back in '76.

We sat for hours talking to our dead loved ones. Soon the conversation turned to practical concerns. Where would they stay? How would they support themselves? Once those essential questions were answered we dove eagerly back into the more obtuse speculations. How had this happened? What was it like being dead? That question seemed to bring the entire conversation to a screeching halt.

"I don't know. It's like one minute I was in my bed. I felt a pain in my chest. The next minute I was clawing my way out of a grave. Who picked out that cheap ass pine coffin anyway? I guess I should be thanking you. If you had gotten me oak like I wanted I might still be down there." Uncle Joe said, still trying to make light of the whole thing.

Aunt Susie started going on about a flock of angels lifting her aloft and everyone rolled their eyes and groaned. It was fairly obvious that she was full of shit.

They were all lying. Every one of them. Something in the haunted look that crossed their eyes at the question of the after-life, told me that they knew more than they were telling.

We left there with everyone taking home a dead person for the night. I took Rick, mostly because he was the only one that I wasn't one hundred percent positive had recently been lying in a grave. Also because I had no idea where his parents had moved to and he had nowhere else to go. Living corpse or not. He was still my best friend.

Rick and I sat up on the couch most of the night watching old sitcoms and laughing about old times. A rerun of Mash started and the solemn theme music caused us both to slip into a deep retrospective silence. Rick was the first one to break it.

"You know I was lying right?"

"Lying about what?" I asked.

"You know what. You always know when I'm lying. I could never keep anything from you."

I didn't want to hear what he was about to tell me, didn't want to think about it, but curiosity got the better of me.

"What you sayin', man?"

"I'm sayin' I remember. I didn't at first. But when you started telling me about how you guys had all assumed that I'd gotten my ass murdered, and how you threw a little funeral for me, it all started coming back to me. I remember lying in that shallow grave out in the woods, insects and animals tearing me apart, my muscles and fat liquefying under my skin. I remember all that shit."

"You mean you were still conscious? While your body was rotting away?"

"I was trapped in there, man. My mind was stuck in that prison of decaying meat. I don't think I lost consciousness until my brain had completely turned to liquid and leaked out through my ears and nose."

"That's horrible, Bro!"

"Yeah, but that's not the worst of it though. The worst was when I finally left my body. There wasn't no heaven, no hell, no reincarnation. I just disappeared man. I felt myself leaking into the earth and my thoughts dissolving and scattering everywhere. Then there was nothing, Bro. Nothing. Until I woke up yesterday and dug myself out of that little hole that Rockmond and his crew tossed me into after they put like thirty or forty hollow points in my ass. Yeah, nigga, I remember that too. I remember the way every bullet felt as it tore through my flesh and pulverized my muscles and organs, shattered my bones. Are those niggas still around? 'Cause I owe them some pain!"

"Fuck those fools man! Do you realize what you just said to me, nigga? You just described your own death, Bro! I mean your sitting here on my motherfucking couch tellin' me about how you got shot tha fuck up and tossed in a hole in the woods to rot!"

I got up from the couch and began pacing back and forth staring at Rick like I had no idea who the fuck he was. It was the look that white folks gave us just before they clutched their purses tighter or locked their car doors when we passed by. I felt guilty, but I couldn't help it. I was scared to death.

"Hey, I thought I could tell you anything?"

"Yeah, man but damn! I mean, that shit is deep! How the fuck am I supposed to sleep now with a fucking corpse sitting up in my crib? Damn!"

"I ain't no fucking corpse, Bro! None of us are. Look at me man! I've been fucking resurrected! Whole and unscathed. Fool, I'm probably in better shape then your ass!"

"Yeah but you're still a fucking corpse and I'm sleeping with my fucking gat by my side. You try to eat my brains or suck my blood or some shit and I swear I'll cap your ass with the quickness!"

Rick laughed as I walked out of the room eyeing him suspiciously. I wasn't kidding either. I loaded an eight shot clip filled with hollow points into my little Beretta and tucked it under my pillow. It wasn't exactly a nine-millimeter but it would do in a pinch. I hoped.

****

More people knocked on my grandmother's door in the following weeks. Family members so old that only Great Grandpa and Nana recognized them. By the end of two weeks, my Great Grandfather's Great Grandfather had come back. Grandma didn't complain but her house was getting over crowded and I was waaaaay too freaked out by it all to invite any of the dead people to come live with me. Our family took care of their own though, and we found homes for them with other relatives.

I watched the news every night. The world was going nuts. It had only been two weeks since Easter and all over the world, nearly half the people who'd ever died had come back to life. The murder and suicide rates were astronomical, but so were the number of resurrections. Then someone figured out how to keep the dead from coming back.

It took many attempts before the answer was uncovered. Someone would murder a spouse or a recently resurrected parent only to find that person back on their porch in the morning. Finally someone realized that cremated bodies didn't seem to revive. People took to cremation like whores to cock. Immolated corpses were literally littering the streets. Apparently some people didn't want to see their dead parents again. Some widows weren't exactly happy to see their late wives and husbands again. Many suicides weren't too pleased to be back either. Murder victims were almost a safe bet to be killed again. After all, if someone had hated them enough to murder them the first time, they would most likely not be too happy to see them walking around again, especially once the Supreme Court declared that the resurrected could testify in their own murder trials.

Predictably, the normal religious groups started their usual racket about the "End of Times," "Judgement Day," and "Armageddon." They got lots of mileage out of it with living corpses sitting beside

41

their loved ones in the pews; the ones that hadn't already banned the undead from church. Even the smallest storefront churches were bringing in millions of dollars in donations. There was probably not an empty pew in the entire country, perhaps not in the entire world.

Scientists, industrialists, nuclear physicists, even cult leaders began to come under fire from those who accused them of causing the resurrections. The phenomenon was blamed on government experiments, industrial accidents, sunspots, homosexuals, Catholics, and nuclear wastes. But the truth was that no one knew. Somehow death had been defeated. And it wasn't just humans. Nothing died anymore. The insect and pest population grew to unbearable proportions. The prevailing opinion was that heaven and hell was filled and was literally bursting open; regurgitating its contents back onto the earth. Of all the theories that was perhaps the scariest one.

The homeless rate grew astronomically as destitute dead wondered the streets in a daze. There were a few episodes of vampirism and even cannibalism. Scientists immediately rushed in to study the captured perpetrators as fear and panic began to spread only to find that the "Vampires" were just confused and psychotic reborn who assumed that they must be undead monsters or else what were they doing crawling their way out of graves?

An ingenious mortician began marketing an escape proof coffin and became an instant millionaire until the screams of the prematurely interred became so loud that mourners complained about the monstrous din and civil rights groups launched protests over the abuse of the undead. The coffins continued to sell but now with a recommendation to bury your loved ones at ten feet rather than the standard six, so as not to disturb the sensitive. Once the graveyards quieted down the protests lost steam and died out as well. No one minded that their dearly departed would awaken in an inescapable coffin so long as they didn't have to hear their anguished screams and no one had yet figured out what rights the dead possessed if they did indeed possess any at all.

So, while the Supreme Court battled over the rights of the resurrected they continued to be denied jobs, housing, drivers licenses, health care, to be used in medical experiments, excommunicated from churches, immolated, and entombed alive.

I tried to imagine what it must be like to awaken in that coffin, slowly suffocate after hours of struggling to escape, only to reawaken and repeat the process again, over and over. I turned toward Rick and shuddered as I recalled his tale of being conscious during his body's entire process of putrefaction. If it was true than there could be no fate worse than death. No fate could be more horrible than months upon months of living decay.

The increased population meant more competition for jobs as well. Anti-resurrection groups sprouted up everywhere lobbying for the exclusion of citizenship rights to the recently undead; most importantly the right to work. Other groups like the KKK and even a few "Right to Life" organizations were taking a firmer stance. They were kidnapping and cremating the reborn.

Even those who had initially been happy to see their deceased loved ones again soon changed their attitudes once the reality of feeding, clothing, and housing their new expanding families set in. Some of the very people who had shown up at Grandma's house that first Easter morning were now turning relatives out on the street and joining anti-resurrection hate groups.

When Uncle Joe disappeared one night after a house party and little Sue, my Aunt Tracy's resurrected still-birth, disappeared from her stroller while on a trip to the mall, fear and anger gripped the entire family. Little Sue had been one of the biggest bright spots in this whole resurrection business. As soon as Tracy had heard that the dead had started coming back to life, she'd immediately driven out to the Rosemont Cemetery and began digging for Sue's tiny coffin. She'd only gotten three feet down before she heard the screams. Grandma had guessed where she was going and had sent Rick, Uncle Joe, and I out to help her. We'd unearthed the tiny casket and found Tracy's beautiful baby girl crying softly inside. She was our miracle baby. And now both she and Joe were gone.

"What the fuck is going on, man? Why are they killing everybody?" Fear had started eating away at Rick. I could see it aging him, breaking him. He had started chain smoking, drinking forties of malt liquor like it was spring water, and I suspected that he'd started smoking crack again. That's what had gotten his ass killed in the first place. He'd been dealing for a thug named Rockmond on consignment and had smoked up his entire stash. When it had come time to re-up he didn't have a dime of Rockmond's money. So Rock did what any self-respecting street entrepreneur would do and peeled Rick's cap back with about thirty hollow point rounds. Now Rick was back to his shit again.

Rick was afraid to leave the house. Dirty Ed had turned up burned half to death. He said that a group of neighbors had come after him with a fucking flame-thrower and Moose had been burned alive by his own parents! After that Rick just sat at home playing Play Station and smoking weed all day. The fear of immolation was a great excuse not to go job hunting.

The ghettoes exploded. Once the population reached its breaking point the reaction was as dramatic as it was predictable. The commodities of existence were much sparser in the overcrowded slums then in upper-class neighborhoods. They, least of all, could not afford the strain of the increased competition for survival. Rick and I sat on the couch watching CNN as the reborn were dragged out of their homes and set ablaze in the middle of the street. There were disturbing images of lynchings. Whole streets lined with bodies that hung from the streetlights and slowly burned to cinders. The rumors were that the Ku Klux Klan was responsible. But everyone knew that many of the victims had been murdered by their own family and friends. There was a horrifying video being shown over and over on the network news stations of a mother and child being burnt alive in the middle of the street in North Philadelphia. The camera would zoom in on their screaming faces as the flesh melted from their skulls and then slowly pan out to include the faces of the woman's husband and oldest son as they doused the corpses with more gasoline, their eyes ablaze with fury.

"That's some fucked up shit, man." Rick exclaimed, staring at the screen in wide-eyed terror.

I didn't say anything. I just kept watching.

There were scenes of the reborn being herded into houses at gunpoint and then the entire house set ablaze in one great funeral pyre. Every night Rick and I watched it on television. It was getting to be an addiction. I could see the worry creeping into his eyes.

"You'd never do me like that, right? You're my dog, right? These people is crazy. I know you got my back though."

I'd give him a pound and sometimes a hug. But I never responded. There was too much on my mind. Sometimes after watching the news we would go to the window to watch similar scenes unfolding outside our own door. That's when Rick's agitation would reach a fever pitch.

"Man. We've got to get out of here! We need to go somewhere where nobody knows me. These motherfuckers are crazy out there! You think they'd come for me? You don't think they'd fuck with me do you? I mean I grew up in this neighborhood. I went to school with all of these niggas, played basketball with them, kicked ass and chased pussy with them. They wouldn't come fuckin' with me would they?"

As I stared down at the streets and took in the shootings, the rapes, the dismemberings, all culminating in the inevitable cremation, I was reminded of the overcrowded rat experiment. The one conducted by sociologists back in the fifties to study the results of overcrowding on the human psyche. The experiment began with a few rats in a pen wide enough so that each rat had just enough space and just enough food to support itself. Then they watched as the rats began to multiply within that space and the space that had been adequate for one was soon filled by two, three, ten, twenty. The rats went insane. They began killing each other, eating their young, and stealing the young of other rats, even gnawing at their own flesh. They repeated the experiment with monkeys and the results were even more extreme; rape, incest, infanticide, patricide, cannibalism, necrophilia, and worse took place once the monkey cage began to swell. All the things I was seeing outside my window. I turned back to the news. It was less depressing.

The newscaster was hyperventilating. Rick was sweating and fidgeting and human nature was showing its worst.

Everyone was surprised when the suburbs started going ballistic. The middle-class bourgeoisie had been killing their reborn all along, quietly burning bodies in their basements or in abandoned lots and cemeteries. Once the news broke about the hundreds of corpses found torched in one neighbor's house the whole thing came above ground and righteous moral patriots began walking door to door dragging the resurrected out of their homes and burning them alive along with any loved ones that resisted.

I could hear them outside my own door now. I could smell the acrid stench of burning corpses. The sky was black with smoke from all the fires.

"Bring out your dead!"

Rick cringed as he heard the cry. He began to cry and beg me to hide him as the mob pounded at the front door.

"Tell them I wasn't dead! Tell them I was in jail or something!"

I looked out my window and saw my Grandmother and my Uncles among the posse. My Great Grandfather and Great Grandmother were already outside tied to stakes burning slowly. Aunt Rose, Aunt Susie, Uncle Paul, and Cousin Charlie hung from streetlights with a dozen other neighbors lit up like roman candles. I looked through the peephole and watched as their eyes sizzled in their sockets and then exploded with audible pops and drizzled down their charred and disintegrating faces. I looked at Rick and slowly opened the door to let the posse in.

"No! Don't! Don't let them take me! Help! Help me, man!"

His screams were terrible as they captured him and tied him up with extension chords. They tossed his body onto a stack of chairs and newspapers and doused him with kerosene. He kept looking at me with his eyes filled with questions as they lit the pyre and he began to burn. Even as he screamed in mortal anguish his eyes stayed fixed on me. He wanted to know why I had betrayed him. Why I hadn't fought for him? But the truth was that it had never sat right with me that he could fuck up his life so bad; sell drugs, become a drug addict himself, get murdered by rival drug dealers, and then come back and sit on my couch eating Doritos, playing video games, and just kicking back like everything was cool, while I worked hard every day. It didn't bother me so much that there wasn't a heaven, but there had to be a hell. There had to be something to make people want to live a good life.

"Sorry, Bro. But it's better this way."

Life had to have consequences . . . and so did the afterlife.

The Myth of Sisyphus

There were dreams and bleak crushing absences of dreams in which pain was the only confirmation of Todd's continuing existence. Each claustrophobic inhalation affirmed his survival. He was alive. Tendrils of crushing agony crawled up from between his shoulder blades, along his spine, and fanned out across his trapezius and deltoid muscles, up his neck to his skull. Every muscle throbbed and ached. Even his lungs burned as they struggled to breathe the dense humid air.

Todd slipped in and out of consciousness, from the darkness of sleep to the Stygian blackness of his reality. He shivered, immobilized in the crushing pressure. Flashbulbs went off in his head as shock, hypothermia, and oxygen deprivation fought each other for the right to claim his life.

He dreamt of stupid things. Weddings, birthdays, funerals, holidays. He dreamt of food, sex, dancing, and beverages. Fruit juice, soda, wine, and coffee. Todd was dehydrating and starving even as he fought to keep from drowning. He was freezing in the muddy effluence that rushed over his face and past his nostrils, fantasizing about warm baths and dry clothes. When he awoke, he almost screamed. He wanted to cry out in terror, to yell for help. His horror intensified however, when he realized that he could not scream. His mouth was underwater.

The ridiculousness of his predicament did little to take away from the horror of it. Todd was wedged face first in a thirty-inch metal drain-pipe that ran horizontally along the bottom of a storm water wash basin before continuing under the city for miles. He was a City Building Inspector who'd been out inspecting the retaining walls along the top of the basin when the torrential down pour had begun.

It was as if a damn had burst somewhere in the heavens. Six or seven inches had fallen in less than an hour. Tiny projectiles of chilling H20 pounded the earth like a meteor shower. Four or five inches in the first fifteen minutes alone. They would later call it the one-hundred year flood, because it was the most rain to fall at one time in Las Vegas in over a hundred years. But Todd didn't know that. All he knew was that he had only three more walls to inspect before he could go home for the day. So, he made one wrong decision. He decided to stay ten minutes too long.

The thunder had sounded like cannon-fire as lightning churned the earth yards from where he'd stood leaving the scent of sulfur in the electrified air. Then the rain had come, bulleting to earth so hard it began to sting his skin, like a swarm of angry bees attacking his flesh. His feet sank deep into the drenched earth as he walked the perimeter of the wall, slowing his progress. The mud sucked his shoes down so deep that pulling his feet out to take each step began to hurt his knees. He had decided to turn around and go home when the wash overflowed.

Todd hadn't even noticed how fast the water-level had risen. The wash basin had never been intended to handle that much water in such a short amount of time and it couldn't drain the water fast enough. The entire basin filled and overflowed. The ground on which Todd stood was suddenly submerged and he was swept off his feet and down into the wash.

"Help! Help me! I can't swim!"

But there was no one to hear him. He had gone out there alone. All of the construction workers had already gone home, fleeing the storm. Only he had been foolish enough to brave the rains.

The violent currents dragged his body under, slamming him hard against the walls of the basin, nearly drowning him as it filled his mouth, eyes, and nostrils with mud and sewage. He was flipped and rolled by the roiling storm waters as they rushed towards the drain pipe, carrying him along at a relentless velocity. Despite the beating his body was taking, Todd had enough clarity of mind to take a deep breath before he was pulled beneath the waters and down into the drain pipe at the bottom of the wash.

The mouth of the pipe yawned wide like the voracious maw of some serpentine predator preparing to swallow him whole. But, Todd was too big to swallow. He slid in on his back and lay face up with his body lodged halfway into the pipe. His shoulders were too wide to allow him to go any further so he was wedged in tight, submerged beneath hundreds of gallons of rainwater and mud.

The water continued rushing past him into the sewer and Todd held desperately to the little oxygen remaining in his cramped lungs. He knew he had only a few minutes before he'd have to take another breath and would gulp water and sludge down into his lungs and drown. The knowledge of his impending end quickened his pulse and stole more of his breath as claustrophobia set in.

Todd struggled uselessly to extricate himself from his narrow prison. His lungs burned like he'd swallowed smoke and ash. They were being crushed by the press of the metal pipe against his arms and torso, the pressure of the water above him, and the struggle to retain the little oxygen he'd managed to gulp down before going under.

Water rushed by him with such force and momentum that he could feel it pushing him deeper into the pipe, wedging him in tighter. Again, he wanted to scream.

That's when the flash bulbs had started going off in his head as oxygen deprivation murdered his brain cells. He was losing consciousness, suffocating. Then, suddenly, the water drained away and he could breathe, just barely. A pocket of air formed at the tip of his nose and he inhaled dank steaming air. Todd's mouth and the rest of his face were still submerged, so he kept his lips and eyes shut. Only his nose protruded just above the waterline.

The air was foul and thick. Still, even this small amount of rancid oxygen was a blessing. Until then he'd almost resolved himself to the idea of death.

It had been the end of the day on Friday when he'd fallen down into the culvert and slipped face first into the drain-pipe. That meant that no one would be out here again until Monday. He had to survive the entire weekend in the pipe, unable to scream.

At night he froze, the frigid rainwater leeching away his body heat as the temperature dropped below sixty outside and what felt like thirty down in the pipe, drenched in tepid water. During the day, when the sun rose and the temperature crept up to eighty or ninety degrees, it felt as if he were boiling alive. He was thankful that it was September and not June or July when the Nevada heat would climb towards one hundred and twenty degrees. If it had been the summer he knew he'd be dead already. But, then again, it didn't rain like this in July.

The humidity made the dry desert heat feel like a tropical heat wave. But that wasn't the worst of it. The worst was not being able to move, feeling like he was being squeezed through the polluted intestines of some impossibly large beast. He was trapped and he was going to die.

Todd wasn't sure if anything was broken, but everything hurt. The trip down into the drainpipe had bruised and battered him. But pain was something he was used to. Life was pain and as long as he suffered he could at least be assured that he remained among the living.

Todd could remember few days that did not end in some catastrophe. From the day both his parents died in the fire that claimed their house, to the day he was raped by a few of the larger boys at the orphanage, to the day his scholarship was revoked for poor grades and he was kicked out of college, to the day his wife left him for a younger man after emptying his bank account, he had known nothing but misery and disappointment with only brief moments of happiness sprinkled in.

Each individual mishap was an exceptional occurrence to be sure, but misfortune in general was the rule for him. That's what had led him to become what he was. His anger at the constant pain of his life is what led him to his first murder. He just couldn't stand to see another person smile at him. The naïve happiness of those who'd never suffered a day in their lives was an affront to him, so he'd decided to introduce pain into their lives.

If he made it out of this drainpipe he knew exactly what he'd do to his next victim. A slow torture buried alive or stuck in a barrel as it slowly filled with water. He couldn't imagine that anything he'd done to any of his victims was worse than being stuck in a drainpipe for days. Life always had a way of outdoing man's own capacity for violence and cruelty. God is the supreme sadist.

Todd had now been stuck in the drainpipe for three days and two nights. When he slept he had nightmares of grinning demons dragging him down into hell through a long narrow tunnel. When he awoke they were still there with him, pulling at him, trying to drag him deeper into the drainpipe. He could feel their claws digging into his flesh as they tugged at him. Sometimes he even heard them laughing at him, taunting him.

"You stuck fat boy? One too many trips to Fat Burger eh? You're lucky though. It's much worse down here. I'll show you as soon as you lose enough weight for me to pull you through. It won't be long now. You're already starving. Soon you'll be down here with us."

Todd wanted to scream so badly his entire body would tremble, but his mouth was still underwater. Instead he thrashed violently in the pipe abrading more of his skin on the rusted metal and still not managing to budge more than an inch.

More days went by and the demons grew more and more hideous and more insistent. Tugging on him and gibbering madly in his face. Laughing and raging as they raked their claws over his wrinkled flesh.

"Hungry fat boy? Still haven't lost enough weight? You thought your life was bad before, wait until we get you down here with us. We're going to make what you did to those women look like euthanasia. Because we won't let you die. We're going to torture your fat ass forever!"

Todd had learned to tune them out. He could almost ignore them completely as long as they weren't touching him. But their scaly claws were always worrying at him, pulling and yanking at him.

"Why hasn't anyone found me yet?" Todd wondered.

He must have been stuck in that pipe for over a week. Surely one of the construction workers or one of the other building inspectors would have noticed his legs sticking out of a drainpipe.

"Not if the whole basin is still underwater," Todd realized with increasing hopelessness

"But they'd notice that the water wasn't draining and they'd send someone down to investigate wouldn't they? But how long before they did that? They wouldn't send a diver down there in scuba gear. They'd wait for all the water to evaporate and then fix the problem. That could take another week or more."

Todd began to struggle. He pushed and squirmed with renewed desperation and the last of his waning strength. Somehow he managed to move backwards a few inches out of the pipe. His face submerged completely now. If he didn't escape now he would drown. His struggle became even more frantic. He opened his eyes and peered through the murky water and thought he saw a demon

53

with a face like an eel and claws like a lizard scampering towards him staring at him with intelligent anthropoid eyes and grinning as it reached out for him to pull him back into the pipe.

"Where do you think you're going fat boy? You're coming down here with us."

Todd thrust with all his might and suddenly he was free of his prison. He'd starved off just enough weight to allow him to squeeze out of the pipe. He swam desperately for the surface as slimy taloned fingers clawed at his backside trying to hook their nails into his flesh and pull him back under. His head broke the surface of the murky water and Todd stared at the sky for the first time in eight days.

He was out of breath and weak from dehydration and malnutrition. He called out, but his voice was weak and barely audible. He'd used the last of his vigor escaping the pipe. Todd floated there on the surface of the water trying to summon the energy to climb up the side of the wash to the street above. That's when he felt the first drops of rain strike his face. Then the heavens opened once again.

"Fuck! Another storm," Todd groaned in a hoarse whisper.

Todd forced himself to swim to the edge of the basin using nothing but sheer will power. All he could think about was how many people he would make suffer for this latest injury life had dealt him, how many ways he would make them scream. He had just reached the edge of the basin when he felt the hands on him. He looked back and the demon with the eel face was behind him trying to pull him back.

"Come on fat boy. You're coming down here with us. No more lonely housewives or teenaged runaways for you. You're the victim now. You belong to us."

Todd struggled up the rocky embankment in near panic as more demons broke the surface of the water and came for him. Some of them looked like humans with animals parts grafted to them for unnameable reasons. Antlers and rhinoceros horns protruded from their backs along their spines, others had thorns and teeth sprouting from odd shaped craniums like military armament. Some were covered in scales and some with fur. Some had multiple arms, tentacles, or fins. Still others had mouths filled with rows of shark like teeth and while others were toothless except for two saber-like tusks. They were all coming right for him determined to drag him back down into the water.

None of the demons worried Todd nearly as much as the rain, which was now pelting the ground and reducing the earth to slippery mud as Todd struggled to climb. Lightning cracked and thunder roared like a nuclear explosion as the rain intensified. Water rushed over the side of the embankment like a new river had been formed and soon Todd was slipping back down into the basin.

"No. No! Nooooooo! Hellllllllp!"

Todd slid back down into the water just as a whirlpool had begun to form. The demons seemed to number in the dozens as they rushed to envelope him, their slavering faces and unctuous bodies pressed against his, noxious breath steaming in his face. They were all over him as suction from the drainpipe dragged him under like excrement being flushed down a toilet. Todd took one last breath before he went under. He could still hear the demons laughing and celebrating as he went hurtled back towards the drainpipe. Seconds later he was wedged in tight again. He lifted his head searching for the pocket of air and found it once again with the tip of his nose.

He had suffered more bruises and now it felt as if his ribs were broken. He was deeper into the pipe this time and the new rainfall meant that it would take even longer for the water to evaporate meaning no one would find him for weeks. By then he'd be a corpse unless he could escape. Todd began to struggle again.

"Why me?" Todd complained, *"Why does this bullshit always have to happen to me? When do I get to catch a break?"*

Todd's life reminded him of that Greek myth about the guy who is sentenced to hell and his punishment is to roll a boulder up hill everyday only to watch as gravity inevitably carried the rock back down the hill at the end of the day. The man made peace with his situation by accepting that it was no different than everyday of his life had been. Everything we did in life was inevitably undone yet still we toiled each and everyday of our lives. Every moment of triumph or joy was inevitably followed by moments of defeat and despair yet still we fought and struggled for that ephemeral happiness. So, Todd had struggled for that happiness everyday of his existence and so he watched each and everyday as his efforts ended in failure. Still, he continued to roll his boulder up hill. Still, he would continue to fight for every breath until hunger or exposure finally claimed his life.

"And each time you will fail. Each time you'll wind up right back here in this pipe."

One week he'd been stuck in there without food or water.

"How long can someone survive without eating or drinking?" Todd wondered.

He was so weak he could barely keep his eyes open but sleep was the enemy now. If he closed his eyes now he'd never open them again. He had to get out of there. He began to struggle again and he could feel the demons latch on to pull him back down. Even still, he somehow managed to free himself. This time he didn't even make it to the edge of the basin before he was pulled back under and back down into the pipe, this time feet first so that he could stare back up at the sky from the bottom of the murky water.

"Fuck you! Fuck you! You can't keep me here!" Todd screamed in his head as he struggled once again to free himself from the pipe.

Todd knew now how it would go. Somehow he just knew. No matter how many times he escaped, the demons would pull him back or the rain would come, but he'd never get out. He would never get out of this damn drainpipe, because this was his punishment in hell. The demons were not hallucinations. They were real. And he hadn't been stuck in here for the last week. He'd drowned when he'd first fallen into the basin. But he didn't care because he would still win. Todd was determined. He'd find a way out of this and he would get his life back and he would torture, and rape, and kill until the memory of all of this was gone from his head. No matter how many times they pulled him back under he'd keep pulling himself out until he finally escaped. Except now Todd was slipping deeper into the pipe.

The sky disappeared as Todd began to slide. He was exhausted now, his muscles spent, too weak to resist the tremendous suction from the water rushing around his body forming a vacuum pulling him down into the sewer. After more than a week in the pipe he was now slim enough to be pulled through the narrow aqueduct. Hands seemed to come from every direction, groping at his flesh, latching onto him and tugging, squeezing him deeper into the pipe. The metal scraped his skin raw as he was towed downward. He could hear the demons laughing and gibbering, celebrating their victory.

"You're going to hell now boy. No mercy for you fat man. Now you'll know what all those girls you raped and murdered felt like. Now you're going to know what it means to be in hell!"

Todd was drowning. He gasped and struggled for air as he was dragged along by the rushing water. His lungs burned for oxygen. The pipe seemed to stretch for miles. He could feel the sides of it contracting against him as if it was breathing and each contraction squirted his helpless form down further into the sewer. The demons released him as a new larger set of hands latched onto his feet and pulled. The sides of the pipe felt warmer now and even more slippery than before as if coated with filth and slime, reinforcing the idea that he was sliding through the bowels of some tremendous beast about to be expelled from its rectum. Even the thick sewage seemed to have warmed somewhat. He could hear his own heartbeat thundering around him, only now it seemed somehow slower and much louder as if the pipe had its own separate heartbeat. Todd's consciousness began to fade as oxygen deprivation murdered more of his brain cells. The deeper he went the less he could remember about how he had gotten into this predicament or even who or what he was.

It felt as if his body were changing too. The pipe got smaller and smaller the deeper he went and Todd's own body seemed to be diminishing as well. Reshaping itself into whatever form he would wear in the afterlife.

"Perhaps I am shedding my mortal trappings of flesh and bone, shrugging off this mortal coil so to speak, so that my soul can enter hell?" Todd wondered.

Finally, one of Todd's feet burst free and he could feel it dangling in space. His other foot slid out of the end of the pipe next and then his entire lower half up to the waist. Next came his torso and then his head slid out last, gasping for air and struggling to breathe.

"It's a breech birth! She can't breath! Clear her airway."

Todd felt fingers in his mouth sweeping back and forth removing the sewage he'd sucked in while struggling to breathe. Then he felt a thud on his back and he belched out all the water he'd inhaled and let out a wail. An oxygen mask was strapped onto his face and Todd took his first lungful of clean oxygen since the eternity ago that he'd fallen into the wash.

Todd didn't know where he was or even who he was. He looked down at the smooth hairless slit between his legs where his penis had been and realized he was no longer even a man. Something in the pipe had changed him. He looked back at the pipe he'd emerged from and saw a bleeding maw surrounded by dense pubic hair and two tree trunk sized legs held up in stirrups. He screamed again.

"Now you'll know what all those girls you raped and murdered felt like. Now you're going to know what it means to be in hell!" The demons had said and only now did Todd truly understand what that meant.

"Here's your new baby girl Misses Wilkins. She's going to be just fine. She's very pretty too. You're going to have your hands full keeping the guys away from this one."

Now Todd knew what it truly meant to be in hell.

A Dialogue Between a Priest and a Dying Man

Father Martin O'Reilly drove himself from the airport stopping briefly at a supermarket deli to pick up some meat on his way to the federal prison. He pulled up outside the gate and stared at the twenty-foot walls topped with razor wire then down at the newspaper under his arm. The sensational headline splashed across the front cover in 24 point Times Roman read: "Terrorist Crashes Fight! 7 Dead!" Father O'Reilly tossed the paper back onto his seat before shutting his door and walking into the building. He'd had enough of headlines like that.

After submitting to a cursory search from a bored and disinterested looking prison guard in rubber gloves, he followed another soldier to the heavily guarded prison hospital. There were FBI agents and military personnel everywhere. The old priest introduced himself and showed his ID and visitor's pass and was immediately escorted upstairs by two FBI agents to the floor where Sharod Abdin's upper torso lay on respirators and monitors, slowly dying. He had been blown apart by the same weapon he'd used to attack the Capitalist devils he believed to be his enemies, a twin engine private plane packed with a nitrogen based fertilizer soaked in gasoline. In other words, a two-ton Molotov cocktail. Somehow the impact had thrown the terrorist free of the plane just before the explosion. He'd been badly burned but not incinerated. Now he was pumped full of morphine and luckily most of his nerve endings were fried. When they started to heal he'd be in screaming agony. Morphine would be little or no help. Unfortunately, Sharod Abdin wasn't expected to live that long.

The old priest greeted the two guards outside the terrorist's door. One of them was obviously FBI and the other was a Military Policeman from the National Guard. There were National Guardsmen everywhere.

"Captain O'Reilly . . . uh . . . I mean Father. Which one do I call you?" asked the MP as he stared from the gold bars on the priest's shoulders to the white collar around his neck.

"Either one is fine."

"I didn't expect to see you here for this one. These Muslims don't seem to like priests much."

"A man of God is a man of God. If he doesn't want me here then I'll leave, but he did reach out to me once. Perhaps he'll do so again. Maybe I can even get some information out of him to find out who his accomplices are."

"You think he'll confess to you?" The FBI agent asked hopefully.

"I doubt it, but like I said. It's worth a shot. Make sure no one enters this room until I'm done. And that includes you. If I'm to get anything out of him before he dies I can't be disturbed."

"Yes Sir! Uh . . . Father, Sir." The MP stuttered as he stepped aside to let the old priest pass. Father O'Reilly blessed them both as he stepped between them and opened the door to Abdin's room.

"Excuse me Father?" The FBI agent asked, placing a hand on O'Reilly's shoulder and gently turning him back around. "What's that under your arm?"

Father O'Reilly followed the agent's gaze down to the package with the blood-stain soaking through the brown paper wrapping and leaking out onto the floor. He looked back up into the agent's eyes and smiled warmly.

"That's my dinner. My sister lives here and she's going to cook up some chitterlings for us tonight. I haven't had good Southern food in a while. You should come join us."

"Uh, no thank you. When you go in there and smell that guy I don't think you'll be too anxious to eat that either. He smells just like barbecued pork."

"Nothing could make me lose my appetite right now."

"You sure you don't want me to come in there with you father?" The National Guardsman offered. The soldier was turning colors imagining the old priest eating pig's intestines after spending an afternoon with the deep fried terrorist.

"No, I'll be fine. I don't want anyone in that room but me. Not anyone. If he thinks he's being interrogated he'll clam up and take his secrets to the grave with him. It'll go much smoother if it's just him and I. We have history. Besides, he's pretty harmless now. And hey, I'm Irish. I know all about handling terrorists."

The two men laughed as the old priest closed the door behind him. The MP looked visibly relieved not to be accompanying him. He would have probably regurgitated the minute he set foot through the door.

The innocuous looking Federal agent turned towards the soldier with a derisive sneer.

"It's funny how that works huh? He's willing to go interrogate that bastard and use his status in the church to secure information that he'd never be able to get otherwise, just to further his own military career. But if we asked him to do that for us, how much do you want to bet he'd pull that shit about not violating the sanctity of the confessional?"

"Well, this ain't exactly a confessional?" The soldier offered.

"Like that shit would matter?"

"Hey, the Captain is alright. He did get that Jeremy Leary guy to confess last year. That sniper who shot all those guys outside the federal building in Pittsburgh? Got him to give up his accomplices and everything."

"Yeah, but he was Irish *and* Catholic. This towel-head will probably spit in your Captain's face as soon as he takes one look at that collar around his neck."

61

The agent rubbed his chin and looked down at the spot of pig's blood that had dripped onto the floor from Father O'Reilly's package.

"You ever hear of an Irish Catholic eating chitterlings?"

"Captain O'Reilly spent a lot of years stationed down in Kentucky with all those hicks, coons, and rednecks. Those country sons of bitches will eat everything but a pig's ass. Looks like he assimilated a little too well."

The FBI agent continued to stare at the blood on the floor.

"Yeah, he must have."

The moment Father O'Reilly saw the dying terrorist he completely understood why that MP had looked so ill. The man who lay strewn across the bed like a piece of fetid meat looked terrible. The terrorist's legs were gone and one of his arms had been amputated at the elbow. The fingers on his one remaining hand looked as if they had been fused together. Half the hair on his head had been singed off and every visible inch of skin was covered in 3rd degree burns. He was covered by a big plastic oxygen tent supplied by two huge tanks at the side of the bed to help his wounds heal faster. They had performed a tracheotomy on him and a tube stuck out from the hole in his throat attached to a respirator. Father O'Reilly covered his face from the sweet smoky stench of burnt flesh. It smelled like rotten pork on an open fire.

"What are you doing here? I did not call for a priest. I'm a Muslim!" The dying man croaked. His nose and lips had completely melted away leaving his face frozen in a perpetual grin. All the fat beneath his face had liquefied and boiled away so that his crinkled skin clung tight to his skull. The priest's stomach roiled at the ghastly site of him.

"You can speak. That's good. I was afraid this was going to be a soliloquy."

"I do not wish to speak to you." Abdin growled in a hoarse whisper. His throat had no doubt been scalded as well from the heat of the explosion. The tube sticking out of it probably didn't help either.

"Yeah, well I told these guys that you did. I told them that you'd spoken to me several times in the days before your big stunt and that you were interested in converting."

"Converting? I would never join your heathen religion!"

"I know. But it was the only way I could get in here to speak with you?"

The priest continued to look over the dying man's flame ravaged torso. He reached out for the nurse's call button, which was wrapped around one of the bed-rails and unwound it, allowing it to drop back behind the bed.

"Whewww! You certainly did a number on yourself. What the fuck were you thinking flying that little twin engine into the side of Madison Square Garden? Were you expecting to do the kind of damage your misguided brethren did to the Trade Center? Couldn't get a real plane huh? You know, you killed the Heavyweight Champion of the world? I bet you're proud of that though aren't you?"

Sharod Abdin's raw shriveled flesh wrinkled even more as the ragged remains of his eyebrows knitted together. A clear liquid oozed from the blisters on his face.

"What the hell kind of priest are you?"

"I'm just your average servant of god here to perform last rights on you, for all the good it will do. You'll be rotting in the earth being devoured by maggots and worms in a few hours. No way you're going to survive this."

"You think you scare me? You think I am afraid to die? I go to join Allah in heaven!"

The priest pulled out a White Owl cigar and bit the tip off of it. He reached up and yanked the smoke alarm out of the ceiling then lit it up and inhaled deeply.

"Cheap fucking cigars. It doesn't pay very much to be a priest. I bet you smoke those expensive Cuban cigars huh? It's a damn shame."

He took another long draw on the cigar and blew the smoke out at the terrorist as he leaned closer, forcing himself to look right into the man's tortured visage. He saw Abdin's eyes widen as he neared the oxygen tent with the lit cigar. One spark and the whole tent would go up in flames.

"So you think you're going to heaven huh? You think you're going to collect your harem of wives and sit at the right hand of Allah?"

"I have done the will of Allah!"

Father O'Reilly leaned back and eyed the dying terrorist curiously. He turned and walked over to the barred window and looked out at the setting sun as night drew first blood, fiery red blood, in its battle to wrestle the day from the sky.

"Yeah, so you said. You know you killed 7 people in that little stunt of yours? Injured about 35 others."

The terrorist continued to breathe heavily as the respirator inhaled and exhaled for him. Father O'Reilly paced back and forth and Abdin's eyes stalked him around the room. The old man was up to something. If the priest had come to kill him than Abdin was more than willing to meet his maker. He'd proved that when he'd crashed his plane into the stadium. Maybe the old Jesuit *was* here to try to convert him to Christianity, a final victory for the capitalist dogs. Abdin imagined them placing an audiotape of him begging Jesus for forgiveness on the evening news. He chuckled.

"Americans are so arrogant." He thought, he would never renounce his god for the anemic pasty-faced devil these heathens worshipped. If that was the old man's plan than Abdin was ready for him

"I know you won't really care about this. But, I care so I'm going to tell you anyway and you're going to listen."

Father O'Reilly stopped to check Abdin's expression to make sure the man was paying attention. The terrorist glared at him murderously. Satisfied, Father O'Reilly continued.

"There was this little boy sitting there at front row; a big fight fan. He was also an exceptional artist. He was drawing pictures of the fight, hoping to get the champ to autograph one of the pictures once the bout was over so he could hang it on his wall. Then your plane came hurtling into the building and he was struck in the face by a piece of flaming debris. Scorched both of his eyes. He'll never see again. I mean, you lost your legs, but this talented kid will never see again! Your eyes look okay though. You wouldn't happen to be an organ donor would you? Maybe I'll scoop those out of your skull before they feed you to the worms."

"What the fuck do you want old priest?"

"I want to tell you what you're about to go through when I pull the plug on this little machine of yours. See, that little boy was my nephew and you ruined his life. For what? So that you could be some kind of martyr for some fucked up ideology that had nothing to do with an innocent ten-year old who just wanted to watch his hero fight?"

The priest's voice lowered to a growl as he leaned down closer to the dying terrorist his teeth clamped down on the cigar and his eyes went flat and dead. "In my book that makes you one evil sonuvabitch and I just cannot suffer a sonuvabitch like you to live."

"Pull the plug old man! I was prepared to die when I woke up this morning and I am prepared to die now! So go ahead! Pull the plug!" The electrocardiograph monitor spiked as Abdin's pulse-rate jumped to 140.

"Calm down before you have a heart attack. You have no idea what death is. Your deluded little fanatic ass believes that there's something waiting for you after all this is over, but there isn't. Believe me, I know. This life is all there is. Religion is one big lie and you're just another sucker and perhaps the biggest of all."

"Your religion is a lie. Mine is real! The word of Allah is truth!" Abdin hissed, that lipless smile looking even more grotesque and sinister than before. His eyes glowed with that peculiar mixture of madness and intelligence that were necessary ingredients in making

65

terrorists of this sort. You needed a madman to crash a plane into a building, but you needed an intelligent man to get it out of the airport and avoid being shot down long enough to get it to the target. Father O'Reilly shook his head in disgust as he looked down at the half-baked zealot whose eyes still shone with the rapture of faith.

"And your god tells you that you're going to heaven after killing all those people?"

"Yes."

"You really believe that there is consciousness after death?"

"Yes."

"Let me ask you something Abdin, how is consciousness achieved?"

"What?"

"How exactly are you conscious of my presence here in this room? How do you know I'm here?"

"Because I'm looking right at you!"

"Yeah, that's right. Because you can see me, you can hear me, you can smell me . . ." The priest reached underneath the plastic and poked his finger into one of the blistering scabs on Abdin's chest, causing the man to wince in pain. He was so close that his cigar was almost touching the plastic tent. Abdin stared at the lethal glow even as the priest dug his finger into his wound. That pain was nothing like what would happen if his cigar burned through the plastic. The priest grabbed hold of the scab on Abdin's chest and ripped it off. The terrorist screamed. ". . . And you can feel me."

"You son of a bitch!" The terrorist panted out of breath as his nerves cried out in agony.

"These are sensory perceptions. Senses that are all destroyed at the moment of your death or at the very least, once your flesh rots off the bone . . .

"You can't see without eyes. Just ask my nephew. You can't hear without ears. You can't taste without a tongue. You can't feel without nerves and skin and flesh. That's why I grabbed your chest instead of your missing legs. All of these things will rot away with the rest of your body and then what will you see with? What will you smell with? What will you hear, feel, taste with? How will you be conscious then? Extra sensory perception perhaps? Maybe there's some mysterious sixth sense that will somehow materialize after you die? Yet we find no evidence of a sixth sense anywhere. Even those people who claim to have it speak of it in terms of their five senses. They have visions. I worked in a home for the blind for many years and I can assure you that people who have never seen before have no visions. They cannot even imagine what the world truly looks like, just as you cannot imagine a color that you've never seen before or a sound that you've never heard. The blind do not have visions and the deaf do not hear voices. At best any sixth sense would be merely an augmentation of your existing senses which, being dead, you would no longer possess."

The old priest began to pace again.

"So there you would be, alive but unconscious, a vegetable of sorts. Oh, but perhaps this afterlife is like some of the Eastern religions believe, an eternal dream state? But see the problem with dreams is that they require memories and you wouldn't have any. Did I forget to mention that? You see when you die your brain rots and everyone knows that that's where your memory is housed. That's why a blow to the head, a high fever, consciousness altering drugs, can all screw up your memory. Furthermore they can screw up your entire consciousness. Now how could that be possible if the consciousness where some non-physical spirit? How can you physically affect the non-physical? How could a blow to the head render you unconscious and even wipe out your memory if the soul and not the brain were the seat of consciousness? Why is it that we can link the damaging of brain cells to the loss of both memory and consciousness if the brain were not a necessary and vital part of your consciousness? Obviously that is not the case. When your brain goes so goes your memory and all other type of consciousness for that matter."

He leaned in and put his hand on the oxygen tube sticking out of Abdin's throat leading to the respirator beside his bed. This time Sharod Abdin's eyes followed the hand. He was nervous, scared. His faith was not nearly as strong as it had been minutes ago. The old priest smiled at him and then pinched the plastic respirator tube closed. Abdin immediately began to gasp for air. His injured lungs tried to work, but they were far too badly scalded and could not inflate without artificial help. Without the respirator he would asphyxiate, suffocate in a bubble filled with the purest oxygen available. His face turned blue and his hand clawed the air while his ragged stumps waved helplessly.

"Oh, I'm not going to kill you. Not yet."

"Pleeease!" he wheezed out between clenched teeth as he struggled to breathe with his scorched lungs.

"Please what? Please spare your worthless life? Please kill you? You haven't figured out yet that I'm not here to give you any mercy? I'm here to bring you the truth before you die."

The priest let go of the tube and Abdin's breathing slowly returned to normal. The wounded terrorist's eyes were wild with fear now. Father O'Reilly breathed another cloud of cigar smoke at the tent.

"So, let's look at this afterlife of yours. You are a disembodied spirit without the ability to see, feel, taste, smell, or hear, no way at all to experience anything new and no memory of ever having experienced anything in the past. Remember what I said about not being able to imagine a color you'd never seen? What if you'd never seen or experienced anything? How could you dream then? Dreams of an eternal blackness without form or substance or sensation? Does that sound like heaven to you?"

The Priest leaned in close again and Abdin winced, as it appeared the cigar was headed straight for his face. The old man stopped just before the cigar touched the plastic.

"Hey, but maybe those New Age freaks are right and life is just this eternal energy that's a part of everything and last forever. That could very well be possible, but so what? That energy is not you. That sounds like that mindless disembodied spirit with no memory and no consciousness. Your self is created by your perceptions of the world, shaped by your own unique perspective. The perspective of a murderous hate-mongering fanatic in your case. The fact that you are a certain height, a certain weight, a certain race, a certain sex, all go into shaping your identity. If I were to remove all of that would you still be you? Think how drastically your perception of the world and your sense of self would change if I were to put your consciousness in the body of a short, fat, American female? You think you'd still somehow retain your identity? Even if I was to remove all memory of you ever having been anyone else? Would you still be the same person or would your entire identity, your entire self, be destroyed?

"I mean even in your current state you are still you, because you remember what it was like to be whole. But what if I took all those memories away and you woke up like this with no memory of ever having been anything else but this hideous malformed thing lying in a hospital bed with tubes sticking out of it? Do you still think you'd be the same evil twisted fucker you are today without all the experiences that made you this way?

"Now how about if I didn't put your mind into another body but just set it adrift in the ether without memory and without senses, without consciousness, essentially without you; as dead and lifeless as a stone? Would that mindless, deaf, dumb, and blind thing still be Sharod Abdin? No, Sharod Abdin would be gone forever. Well, that's death pal! That's what happens when you die. That's why no animal on earth has any desire to shrug off this mortal coil except for man who alone has the imagination capable of self-delusion. And that's what you have to look forward to."

The priest smiled. Abdin looked terrified now. He could see the pall of death lowering over him. And it was not the promise of heaven, not even hell or eternal slumber. It was annihilation. The elimination of all that he was, had ever been, or could ever possibly have become. For the first time he had doubts, he had fears, his faith had faltered and fell, shattering against the reality of oblivion.

"But what about becoming one with the infinite? I have heard many Asians speak about it; uniting with the all, becoming one with the universe?

"Yeah, like a drop of ink in an ocean. Essentially your mind would go through the same process as your body, disintegrating to reintegrate with the larger body. Pretty nice cozy way to describe the extinction of the self. You become part of the all! Digested by the earth or the universe to be recreated as new things that of course would not be you. See you are a specific thing with a specific definition, specific hopes, specific dreams, specific memories and experiences, a specific way of perceiving the world and interpreting those perceptions. Without a body, without a consciousness, and without a memory you would not be you, but something entirely separate and unique from you. What you are describing is akin to melting down a shiny new Ford and making silverware out of it and still trying to call it a car. Sure all the same material is there, but that car is gone. Man is more than just the sum of his parts and I assure you that while all the chemicals and minerals and perhaps even the spark of life that animated your worthless carcass may continue on, once this deep fried meat casket your consciousness is wrapped in right now ceases to inhale and exhale, Sharod Abdin will be no more."

Abdin shivered with a combination of fear, confusion, and righteous anger. The things Father O'Reilly was saying to him made sense, but they couldn't be true. Allah would not abandon him now. He reached out and found his faith again and wrapped it tightly around himself. Protecting his mind from the torturous truth. "Don't think. Believe!" He told himself. And with that he pushed all the doubts out of his head.

"You lie old man. Allah will protect my soul from death. He is almighty! None of the things you call impossible are beyond him!"

"Yeah, I had a feeling you'd feel that way. God will protect you huh? Even after you have sinned against him?"

"I have never sinned against the word of Allah!

"Oh no? Isn't it a sin to ingest swine?"

The priest unwrapped the parcel he'd been carrying under his arm. Inside it lay the partial intestines of a pig.

"You ever have chitterlings before? Pig's intestines? You have to clean them real well before you eat them because they're usually still loaded with feces."

The priest cut a small hole in the IV bag and dumped the intestines inside. The bag turned brown; clouded with blood and fecal matter.

"No! Noooo! You can't do this!"

Abdin began to thrash about on the bed as the murky pork infected liquid made it's way down the IV tube and into his veins. O'Reilly held the dying man's one good arm down so that he couldn't yank out the IV until the pig's blood had entered his system.

"You have damned me! You have corrupted me!"

"Not so eager to meet your maker now are you? Not with your veins full of pork."

"Please. I cannot die like this. I must be cleansed." Abdin was in a panic now. Terrified for his suddenly very mortal soul.

"Yeah, I thought about that. You living forever as a hideously scarred freak, disgusting even to yourself. I thought it would be fitting for you to know a little bit of the pain Tracy is going to feel going through the rest of his life without eyes. Then I heard that your wounds were mortal. That you wouldn't make it out of this hospital alive even without my intervention and the thought of you dying with a smile on your face believing that you were going to meet your maker. . . . Well, I just couldn't allow that. I had to make sure that you knew every minute that your life ticked away just where your death would take you. I had to make sure that you felt that fear."

Father O'Reilly squeezed the respirator tube shut and Abdin once again began to choke and flop around on the bed like an overturned cockroach.

"Do you feel the fear now Abdin? Do you know that you are about to die? You see, you pathetic little moron, this life was all you had, your only chance at happiness and you threw it all away on some bullshit ideology, for a God and a heaven that does not even exist. Well my friend, eat shit and die!"

The terrorist who had so callously taken seven innocent lives and forever altered dozens of others, screamed for his mortal soul and the guards rushed into the room just as Father Martin O'Reilly pulled the tube out of his neck and threw the murderous zealot into cardiac arrest. The guards grabbed for the priest too late before he shoved the butt of his cigar into the tube and jumped back into their arms as the oxygen tent exploded. Abdin was on fire. His flesh sizzled and ran like butter as the ultra-hot oxygen-fed flames consumed his living flesh. Without the smoke alarm inside the room, the sprinkler system came on too late. By the time the flames were extinguished there was little left of the terrorist. The priest watched the heart monitor flat-line as Sharod Abdin ceased to be.

"Ashes to ashes you son-of-a-bitch!"

The Sooner They Learn

Pain is the nervous system's primary indicator that we are doing something that might compromise the integrity of our bodies. It prevents us from destroying ourselves. To not know pain is to not understand what it takes to survive and succeed. Darrell was an educator, a teacher of pain. He had a warehouse of agonies concentrated within him that he needed to share, to diffuse amongst all those who had yet to know it. Those who needed to learn.

The boys walked past Darrell followed by the pungent aroma of tobacco. They were perhaps only eight or nine years old. Way too young to be smoking. The larger of the two boys held out a pack of Newports to his shorter friend as he coughed and choked on the coffin nail dangling from his own lip. He was obviously not used to smoking. Perhaps he could still be saved? Darrell began to follow the two boys, listening to their conversation, looking for the perfect opportunity to issue his sermon.

"Hey Sam, take a hit off this." The larger boy said, shoving the pack of Newports into his friend's hand.

"Naw, Joey. You know I don't smoke. Besides, my mom would kill me if I came home with my breath smelling like an ashtray."

Sam tried to hand the smokes back to Joey who snatched them from his hand.

"Damn Sam! You's a little bitch! I thought you was down? I was going to pick up some weed later. I suppose you wouldn't smoke that neither?"

"Hell no! My mom would beat the hell out of me if she smelled that shit on me!"

"I can't believe what a little punk you are. You scared of your mom? The bitch is like in her fifties! What the fuck is she going to do? I'd smack the hell out of my mom if she tried to talk some shit to me. I do whatever the hell I want!"

Joey took another long draw on his cigarette, smoking it down to the filter, then dug into his pack of Newports and pulled out another, looking around to make sure the other kids in the playground were watching so they could see how cool he was. Darrell sat across the playground on a park bench watching Joey with a tear rolling down his cheek and an anger building within him that seemed to spill from his emotion filled eyes into the air around him.

"Another child that we have failed." He whispered, wiping away the tear with the tattered sleeve of his mangy plaid fur coat.

"That kid knows nothing about pain." Darrell thought. "He knows no consequences for his actions. It's all fun and games to him. I have to teach him." Darrell knew all about life, all about pain. He knew that it built character, made you strong, taught you discipline. He knew that it was something every child needed to know about.

Darrell freely acknowledged that he had failed his own children. He had let the world take them and it had broken them like kites in a hurricane. He watched them spin out of control into the maelstrom of drugs and crime until their shattered fragments had fallen headlong into the abyss, one in the grave and the other in prison. It was his fault. He'd been too permissive, too liberal. He'd allowed them to make up their own minds, make their own mistakes, hadn't set down enough rules, hadn't taught them about consequences and repercussions. Linda and Jake had grown up thinking the world revolved around them, that they were invincible. Now they were lost and it was Darrell's fault. He had failed them. But there were many other children in the world and he would not fail them. He would teach them all.

Darrell rose from the bench and stalked out of the park after Joey.

"The sooner they learned." He mumbled as he closed the gap between them.

Joey's eyes burned from the thick miasm of tobacco smoke that choked the room. He coughed repeatedly and started to retch. The unmistakable click of the hammer cocking back on the revolver aimed at him by the fearsome old man sitting in the corner, immediately silenced his coughing fit. Quickly, he put the cigar back to his lips and sucked down more smoke.

He looked over at the huge disheveled old man sitting beside him. Joey's frightened bloodshot eyes pleaded with him, but the old man's eyes were ruthlessly silent. Joey coughed again and Darrell leaned over and placed the cocked and loaded .38 caliber Colt revolver directly to Joey's head. The boy winced as he felt the chilling bite of the metal pressed against his temple; still he continued to dry heave. He had regurgitated all that he could and his throat was now raw with the acid burn of stomach bile and the caustic fumes raking at his esophagus as he was forced to inhale more of the pungent smoke. The boy's body began to hitch with sobs as tears raced down his cheeks.

Joey wanted to beg Darrell to let him stop but held himself back. He had begged the old man just minutes before only to be snatched out of his seat by the jaw and dragged within inches of the man's enraged countenance, which had twisted into a horrible scowl.

The old man stared into Joey's eyes looking as if he was about to bite his face off, then he spun the barrel on the revolver and dry-fired the gun against the boy's temple. The hammer had fallen on an empty chamber with a dull hollow click and Joey felt his anus clench up and his testicles rise up into his stomach. A violent trembling shook his entire body and Joey had nearly feinted. He had seen the old man put three bullets into the revolver. He knew that the chances of him surviving another round of Russian roulette were not good.

The old man took the cigar from the boy's lips and pressed it into his own palm where it sizzled as it scalded his flesh.

"You stop smoking again and this is going in your eye." He said in a voice that was hoarse and raspy as if he had just smoked six boxes of cigars himself. Joey put the cigar back to his lips and sucked down more smoke.

Joey had never felt so sick or scared before. He swooned and his stomach rolled as he sucked on the huge cigar. It no longer felt cool. It no longer made him feel like a man. Six empty cigar cartons lay on the floor amongst the butts and ashes of nearly a hundred cigars and six more cartons sat waiting for him. Joey felt like he was going to die. If the cigar smoke didn't kill him then he knew Darrell probably would.

Darrell was a child's nightmare. He was the real boogie man. Draped about his neck was a necklace of severed Barbie doll heads, pacifiers, and the miscellaneous limbs of broken action figures. The moth-eaten fur coat that Joey had originally thought was plaid was in fact fashioned from the hides of fur toys, Teddy bears, stuffed rabbits, and big purple dinosaurs. Most of them still had their little glass eyes intact and they stared out of that bizarre collage of artificial pelts as if beseeching you to rescue them. Some of the fur looked real however and were in the perfect shape of small dogs and cats. Some of these still appeared to have their skulls intact, though minus the eyes. It looked like some last minute attempt at a homemade Halloween costume or the place where childhood dreams found their death.

He was a huge man; well over two hundred pounds with a hard athletic build. He had a head full of gray hair that was wild and unwashed. His skin looked like some type of hard wrinkled leather. Cold gray eyes stared out from the weathered landscape of his face without emotion except when they flashed brilliant with rage.

Joey had passed him numerous times in the playground as he sat on the swings. They jokingly called him the Boogie man and made up stories about him kidnapping and punishing bad kids. Joey had noticed the haunted look in some of the other kid's eyes when he made boogie man jokes, but he had always laughed it off thinking they were just little punks scared of a fairy-tale. Now he knew that he wouldn't be making jokes like that again. Now he knew the stories were real.

Joey finally fainted just short of finishing his last box. Darrell stepped back dropping the pistol from the boy's head to allow the limp body to fall to the concrete floor. He left the door open as he left. When Joey awoke he'd realize that he'd been only yards away from his own house in his dad's tool shed. He'd crawl into the house and try to sleep off the whole experience. He wouldn't tell his dad what happened though. They never tell. They knew they deserved it.

There were no more good parents, Darrell thought to himself as he lumbered off down the street. The kind who knew when a child needed a trip to the woodshed and a belt or a switch pulled from an old tree lain across his backside 'til the welts ran with blood. The kind who knew how to pinch you until your flesh turned purple for giggling in church during service, while daring you to make another sound.

Nowadays the child ruled the parent. They threw tantrums when they didn't get what they wanted and parents gave in just to keep them quiet. Didn't they know how easily quieted the child was who knew that a scream would immediately bring a slap across the face? Didn't they know that one day these kids would have to learn that the world did not bend to their wills and may even roll right over them leaving their broken bodies behind? There were no more good parents to teach these lessons. That's why they needed Darrell.

It was already getting dark when he left Joey's back yard. The shadows had locked arms to form battalions of night that laid siege to the entire town. Darrell locked arms with the shadows too. They were his friends. His allies. He moved among them easily. Few people even noticed him as he traveled among his tenebrous troops. He was just another penumbra in an army of darkness.

The couple making love in the Cadillac Escalade parked by the curb didn't notice him either. Darrell would have likewise paid them no attention if it hadn't been for the fact that he saw the school books in the backseat of the car as he passed.

"Children," Darrell hissed in disgust.

"Children fornicating in public."

The disheveled old man drew back a fist wrapped tight in rags and punched it through the back window just as the boy's scrawny naked ass rose into the air preparing to impale the eager virgin beneath him on his throbbing young cock. He grabbed the boy by the hair and dragged him out through the passenger side window in a hail of tempered glass.

When the boy hit the ground and rolled over, his face snarled up into a grimace of rage and confusion, Darrell could see that the kid was barely fourteen years old; not even old enough to be driving let alone fucking in his father's car. The boy wasn't even wearing a condom.

"You think you're ready to be a father?" Darrell growled as he snatched the boy up by one arm. The boy swung at him with his free hand, missed, then bent down to pull up his pants and underwear to hide his diminishing erection.

Darrell reached down and grabbed the boy by his genitals, balls and all. The boy let out a helpless squeal.

"I asked you a question boy."

"Leave him alone!" The girl had shrugged her clothes back on and was yelling at Darrell through the shattered window. Darrell drew back the hand he'd been holding the boy up with and slapped the girl back into the car.

"I'll deal with you later." He said turning his attention back to the boy. He tugged on the boy's penis stretching it out until it felt like it would tear right out from between his legs.

"Aaaaaaargh! Fuck man, that shit hurts! Let me go motherfucker! What are you her father or something? We were just having a little fun. Jesus, don't hurt me! Arrgh! Heeeelp!!! Fuck! Let me go!"

Darrell leaned in close until his foul breath, reeking of rotten candy, steamed in his face.

"I should rip it the fuck off and keep it on ice until you're old enough to know what to do with it!" He reached into the car and dragged the girl out of the car by her hair. He seized her by the throat and held her against the car.

"I'm not your father. I care a hell of a lot more than that. So, I'm only going to say this one time. If I ever catch you two going at it again than I'll make sure you never have to worry about ruining your lives by catching AIDS or herpes or hepatitis or getting pregnant. I'll rip your cock right off and I'll fill your pussy full of super glue and sew it the fuck closed! You are too young! Do you understand me?" They both nodded with eyes filled with tears. He let them go and they ran off down the street.

When they were a block away the boy turned around and yelled.

"You crazy motherfucker! I'm calling the cops!" Maybe he would. Maybe he wouldn't. Darrell really didn't care either way. He knew one thing for certain though. That relationship was over. He aimed at the center of the boy's back as he ran off down the street and squeezed off a shot. The boy's back erupted and bloomed bright red just before he pitched forward onto his face, hitting the asphalt with a wet smack. His prone body convulsed for a second and then lay still. He wasn't dead but Darrell knew that he had likely shattered his spine. He wouldn't be getting any young girls pregnant now and definitely wouldn't be catching AIDS. The horny little bastard wouldn't be able to feel anything below the waist for the rest of his life. The girl screamed and ran even faster, disappearing around the corner. Darrell chuckled to himself and continued down the street sticking tight to the shadows just in case the police were already out looking for him.

Darrell walked another four blocks to the big shopping mall on Market Street. He entered the Sears department store and wandered around in a trance. He was thinking about his own children again when he heard the child screaming over in the toy section. He remembered when Linda and Jake used to scream like that when they wanted something. How he'd always given in after they'd embarrassed him, enduring the looks of pity and disgust on the faces of other parents as they watched him struggle with his undisciplined brats. He remembered that look on their faces that asked, "Why doesn't he give those two little monsters a good spanking?" Back then he'd felt that corporal punishment was cruel. Now, after seeing how they'd turned out, staying out all hours of the night, drinking, using drugs, getting into fights, having sex at ages thirteen and fourteen, stealing, dropping out of school, one eventually going to prison and the other becoming a crack whore who overdosed on heroin after being used and discarded by half the perverts in town, he realized that not disciplining them more harshly had been the true cruelty. They had never listened to a damn thing he said to dissuade them from their self-destructive behavior and now they were lost forever.

The sound of that child screeching for his harried mother to buy him a new PlayStation video game, brought back all those memories and Darrell stormed over to them fuming mad and dangerously close to exploding.

The screaming, crying, cussing, undisciplined little cur threw a convulsive tantrum while still clinging to its mother's leg. Darrell was amazed when he saw the little beast ball up its fingers into a fist and punch his mother in the abdomen. The redheaded little terror was barely five years old and already he was in control of his parent.

"I want it! I want it! I want it!"

"Stop it!" The woman yelled back in a voice that quivered with emotion. She was near the breaking point, teetering on the edge of a nervous breakdown. Her hellacious offspring screeched at her in a shrill whine that raised the hair on Darrell's neck. The redheaded demon threw itself on the floor and began to kick like an overturned cockroach. This was another one who still believed that the universe should bend to its will and that any frustration to its desires could be easily dispelled with a few well-placed and infinitely irritating screams. Every moment that he went undisciplined was another day in jail, or on drugs, or selling his ass on the streets. He had to be taught.

The entire store seemed to be staring at the little shrieking harpy and its mother with disapproving eyes, awaiting the moment when the obviously overwhelmed woman would actually begin to act like a parent and silence her sons fit of egocentric rage with some corrective discipline in the form of a slap. It would never happen, not until the child was too old for it to do any good.

The moment dragged on and on with the mother withering beneath the child's aural assault, slowly being conquered, just on the verge of admitting defeat and giving in to her son's whim. In a last ditch effort to regain a control that had obviously been abdicated long ago, the mother gave voice to her parental inadequacies with that cry of defeat that masqueraded as a threat but only symbolized failure and imminent resignation to all those who heard it, including the delinquent it was meant to correct.

"Wait 'til your father gets home! Do you want me to call Daddy?"

This was followed immediately by words that told all that witnessed the irksome spectacle that there was no respite in sight.

"Do you want a time out?!"

Darrell's stomach rolled. What the hell had happened to parents? He had tried that tactic himself. The fool who invented it should be roasted alive on a spit in Darrell's opinion. It was just another admission of the parent's loss of control and the boy answered his mother predictably and appropriately.

"Fuck you!" the words flew out of his mouth along with a spray of spittle and the child began to punch at its mother again. Darrell could take no more.

The woman was staring up at the ceiling as if praying to god to rescue her from her own child, when Darrell charged down the aisle looking like a troll from under a bridge in some fairy-tale. The ankle-biting little rug-rat was still yelling and screaming. Darrell pushed the mother aside and slapped the child to the floor with a backhanded swing that collided with his mouth with the sound of a gunshot. The kid's head bounced off the tile floor with a loud smack that effectively cut off his shrill ranting. A trickle of blood ran down from the crack that now bisected his lip as he looked up at Darrell with his eyes glazed in shock and dizzy from the blow. The child trembled as he met Darrell's feral gaze feeling like a rabbit cornered by a voracious wolf.

The little redheaded monster screamed for his mother and Darrell drew back and backhanded him again, this time with a closed fist. The force of the blow knocked the boy over backwards. He landed face down on the tile floor. When he looked up his left eye was nearly swollen shut with a tremendous black and purple bruise that went from cheek to temple. It looked as if he'd just gone twelve rounds in a boxing match. Darrell leaned over and pointed a long gnarled finger into the boy's face. His eyes seethed with rage and madness burning like an electrical fire.

"You yell one more time and I will beat the life out of you. Do you hear me?"

The child nodded with his jaw still hanging open in shock. He looked over Darrell's shoulder searching for his mother who finally overcame her own shock enough to protest.

"What the hell are you doing to my baby!" She yelled as she charged the gray-haired old man who'd just battered her son, swinging a fist and hooking her fingernails into claws as she reached out for Darrell's face determined to make him pay for hurting her child.

Darrell turned and casually caught the woman by her throat, pinching her windpipe closed just enough to guarantee her silence.

"Shhhhh!" He said, then turned back to the child, still holding his mother in an iron grip. He had to concentrate to keep his rage in check so that he didn't crush her esophagus.

"Why do they even bother having children if they don't know how to control them?" he wondered.

"I want you to apologize to your mother for disobeying her and embarrassing her like that in public. SAY IT!!!"

"I—I'm sorry mommy!" The child cried and tears began to flow from his eyes steadily.

"And if you ever disobey your mother again. I'll be back for you. Do you understand?"

"Yes."

Darrell released the kid's mother and she rushed to scoop up her son. They held each other and cried as Darrell turned and walked toward the exit. On his way he passed a cherubic, blonde-haired, three year-old baby girl sitting in a stroller with a pacifier in her mouth. She was being pushed along by an overweight woman, roughly Darrell's age, who was obviously her grandmother. The child's real mother was probably little more than a teenager. As Darrell passed he reached down and overturned the stroller dumping the child out onto the floor and leaving the toddler screaming as if it had been fatally assaulted. Darrell bent over and retrieved the baby's pacifier adding it to his necklace. He carried the stroller away with him as both parent and child screamed at his back.

"The sooner they learn the better," he muttered, twisting the stroller into a mass of warped metal and plastic. The little girl had been nearly four years old, at least three years too old to be riding in a stroller and sucking on a pacifier.

"The sooner they learn," he repeated.

He walked out of the mall and tossed that tortured relic of some years ago baby shower into the dumpster wondering almost casually if he was perhaps taking his crusade too far. He reassured himself that all the kids he had disciplined were bad kids who would have only gotten worse if not for his intervention, that he was doing it for their own good. But he wondered if he was also getting a little pleasure out of it, if perhaps he was not seeking to save the children but to punish them, to hurt them. He wondered if he was seeking revenge. Maybe it was the parents he should have been punishing and not the children? Parents like him who had failed their children, allowing them to become the brats that they were. Maybe it wasn't enough to teach the kids? Maybe he needed to include the parents in his education?

"Let me get another hit off that mom."

Darrell's head whipped around so fast he nearly broke his own neck.

There stood the answer to his musings in the form of a mother and daughter dressed identically in skintight halter-tops sans brassieres and miniskirts so short that you could tell they were not wearing panties beneath them and that they had recently shaved. They were both smoking cigarettes and passing a bottle of Crown Royal back and forth between them. The girl couldn't have been more than twelve years old and it was obvious that both she and her mother were prostitutes. Just like Darrell's baby girl Linda who'd died in an alley with a needle in her arm and the semen of the more than a dozen different men she'd fucked that night still leaking out of her. Darrell wanted to scream. He wanted to yell at the top of his lungs. A parent was supposed to want better for their child than what they had. They were supposed to guide them, steer them away from making the same mistakes they made. What this mother was doing was abominable. She had to be punished.

"How could she let her child do that?!!!"

He wanted to rip her apart. He would show that little girl what became of women who sold themselves on street corners. He reached into his coat and closed his hand around the hunting knife in his left pocket and the Colt revolver in the other.

"The sooner they learned," he muttered as he stalked after them.

"Let's go back to the motel, relax, and smoke these last couple of rocks before we hit the stroll again tonight. Okay baby?"

"Cool! I need a little pick me up. I feel like shit tonight."

"Get it together honey! There's a convention in town tonight. There'll be twice as many tricks on the strip tonight and that means mo' money."

Acid roiled in Darrell's stomach as he fought to hold in his rage and revulsion. As much as he wanted to attack them right then and there, he needed to be alone with them.

He followed closely, matching their footsteps as he slipped from shadow to shadow. He ducked behind some bushes just yards from where the mother stopped to squat by the curb and relieve herself. He could smell the acrid ammonia of her urine wafting from the gutter. His stomach lurched and this time he did regurgitate. Luckily they had already moved off down the road and did not see him drop to his knees and throw up his lunch in the same gutter where the whore had just urinated. His body trembled with fury as he rose and continued his pursuit.

Darrell kept thinking of his little girl. Her anus and vagina had been bruised and torn, her nipples bitten, welts and cuts on her back and buttocks, livid blue and purple contusions around her throat from manual strangulation. He couldn't believe that she hadn't been murdered. Darrell had gotten sick then too when the coroner told him that many of the bruises were old, and healing at different rates. They'd been acquired at different times and most likely at the hands of different men. Trophies of her profession. This is what that little girl had in store, the path her mother was leading her toward. A life where a needle full of heroin and a cardiac arrest would be the greatest kindness she could hope for. Darrell gritted his teeth and flicked open the blade of his hunting knife.

The little girl kept looking back over her shoulder, peering into the darkness as if she could sense him there. Most likely it was just her normal paranoia heightened by cocaine use. Finally they turned the corner and the mother began fishing into her purse for her keys. Darrell moved in closer as they approached the door to one of the rundown rooms.

The two whores staggered up to the motel reeling from alcohol and a cocktail of illegal drugs. They never saw the powerful looking old man in the multi-colored fur coat as he came rushing at them from behind a nearby parked car and forced them into the room, slamming the door behind him.

Darrell had bound them both in duck tape. He'd left the mother's ankles unbound to allow him access. He didn't gag her either. He wanted her daughter to hear her scream.

"Stop hurting my mommy!"

The twelve year-old girl with the mascara running down her face as black tears and lipstick smeared across her lips and cheeks like bright red welts, screamed as Darrell punched his entire arm into her mother's dilated vagina up to the elbow.

"Please stop hurting my mommy!"

A wet sticky ripping sound accompanied each thrust as he drove his arm in deeper, tearing her reproductive system apart. The bottle of Crown Royal he'd shoved into her rectum shattered as her vagina continued to tear until cunt and asshole became one gaping orifice dripping blood in a tremendous pool that saturated the piss-stained motel carpeting. The woman had stopped screaming and now only whimpered helplessly. Her eyes were vacant, fixed and dilated. Her mind had snapped. Tears still streamed down her cheeks turning brown as they ran in rivulets through the feces that covered her face from where Darrell had defecated upon her.

"Is this what you want? Is this how you want to end up? You still want to be just like your mommy?" Darrell growled, staring directly into the young girl's face as she continued to scream.

"You'd better get your ass back in school and make something of yourself or I'll personally make sure that you suffer worse than this."

Darrell withdrew his arm from the mother's vandalized twat with a hideous "Shlorp!" It was covered in blood, excrement, and tissue and Darrell scowled as he looked about for a place to clean it. He went into the bathroom to wash up leaving the two whores bleeding and crying on the bedroom floor. When he returned he had his knife open.

"Watch this little girl. Watch what men like me do to whores."

He grabbed the girl's mother by the hair and flipped her over onto her back, then he knelt down on top of her and began to saw off her breasts. Now she did begin to scream again. Twisting her nipple and stretching her breast taunt he sawed down to the white of her rib cage and tore her entire mammary gland free of her chest. He worked her over with the knife for the better part of an hour. Her terrible anguished screams grew deafening in the tiny apartment. She began to convulse in agony as Darrell cut a long incision around her face and began peeling it off of her skull. When he finally left the room he took the woman's breasts, face, and vagina with him. Leaving her hollowed out remains writhing and shrieking in an ever-widening pool of blood. He never touched the little girl. There had been no need.

"If you don't get your life in order, go back to school, and stay off these streets, you will see me again."

She got the message.

By the time the old man left the apartment it was well past midnight. The streets were bustling with activity and he was exhausted and feeling decidedly anti-social. He just wanted to go home. Today had been more exciting then most and he was drained. There were so many children to save and he was just one man. He had miles to walk to his home on the other end of town and he scrambled along quickly imagining snuggling beneath his covers with a good book and a cup of warm tea. He tried to stick to the shadows as much as possible as he made his way toward home. He knew that the cops would be looking for him and he was not exactly inconspicuous.

He barely noticed when the car full of kids pulled up alongside him. Until they jumped out and attacked him.

"That's him!" a tiny hoarse voice cried out from the car. It was Joey, the smoker.

One of the larger boys lunged out of the car and swung a baseball bat at Darrell's head. It connected with a loud crack that sent the old man sprawling onto the floor.

"That was my fucking brother you almost killed you fucking freak!"

It happened so fast that he didn't have time to go for his gun. The kids held him down and searched his pockets, removing both his knife and his revolver before they began kicking and punching him.

Boots, sneakers, a baseball bat and what may have been a pipe crashed down on his head and face, cracked his ribs, crushed his hands, and shattered his kneecaps. They were beating him to death. Darrell was barely conscious when he felt the splash of liquid being poured all over him followed by the pungent odor of gasoline. Then he was burning. He could hear the children's laughter even over his own screams.

They never learned.

Joey and his big brother Mike snuck back into the house through the basement window and tip-toed all the way upstairs to their bedrooms on the second floor, careful not to wake their parents. They still smelled like smoke and gasoline when they both lay in their beds and tried to shut out the image of that old bum's face sizzling and running off his skull like frying lard as the flames consumed him. Joey had just managed to quiet the screams in his head when he heard the window slide open and that same burnt pork smell that had lingered in the air after their impromptu cremation came wafting into the room roaring up his nostrils.

He opened his eyes just as Darrell's charred skeletal face moved towards him blocking the moonlight. Joey was sure that the old man had been dead when they left him smoldering on the sidewalk. When he examined the man's face, eyes missing, teeth gleaming through where his lips had burned away, bits of burnt tissue clinging to an otherwise bare skull, other bits flaking away and fluttering to the floor as ash, he saw nothing to contradict his original assessment. Darrell was indeed a corpse. He tried to scream but the old man pinched his windpipe closed before he could utter a peep.

Darrell sparked the flame on the Bic lighter he held in his blackened fingers and held it up to Joey's face.

"You have to learn not to play with fire Joey."

Joey tried to scream again as the crazy old dead guy aimed the flame up his right nostril and Joey's flesh began to sizzle. He writhed on the bed in nerve searing anguish but Darrell held him firm.

The boy had learned at least one of the lessons. He knew now that there were things in the world that could hurt him, that he was not invincible, and that he could not get away with anything he wanted. The other lessons would take longer and be much more painful. But Darrell had time. The boy had to learn.

Darrell would not let him grow up to be a criminal like his son Jake, on death row for murdering a drug dealer. He would teach him better. The old man moved the lighter to Joey's eyelid and smiled as his eyeball sizzled and popped.

Münchausen by Proxy

Ellie greeted the day with a smile that chased back the night. She cocked her ear toward the heavens and heard the chorus of screams and moans serenade her, seeming to come from every direction at once. Her children were calling. Her poor ailing offspring needed her. They were suffering and only she could help them.

She brushed the morning dew from her hair and the droplets sprinkled down in a fine mist that settled to the ground beneath her. Her long platinum locks drifted on a gentle current of breezes like strands of cirrus clouds trailing behind her.

Ellie considered herself an astounding beauty. She hated the fact that people often mistook her for a man. She was proud of her womanhood and prouder still of being the mother of so many beautiful children. No one had created more life than her.

Even after all the kids she'd had her breasts were still full and ripe. They were too large to fit into a bra yet they did not droop in the slightest. Gravity held no power at all over them. No plastic surgery could yet mimic their perfection. No man had hips as wide as hers or thighs as full and curvaceous or an ass as round and plump. In fact, no woman did either. She was, in her mind, the ultimate woman. It bothered her at times that others didn't see her that way.

"How many children do I have to have to prove that I'm a real woman!?" She shrieked to no one in particular. No one ever listened to her anyway. Until she did something dramatic. Then they all paid attention.

Ellie was radiant today. A warm glow of joy shimmered about her as she made her way across town. Her children were calling her to their side and nothing made her feel more alive then being needed. They were sick, miserable, depressed, and only her love could make them better. She began to sing with a voice like wind and rain as she felt her children's love envelope her.

Ellie took her time going to the hospital that day. The sun was newly risen and its yellow and orange rays rippled across the sky like an ocean of spawning Koi. The shadows receded and Ellie's smile widened in admiration of the day. This was going to be quite a beautiful one. She wished she had more time to sit and enjoy it. But the insistent cries of her progeny urged her forward.

Little Joey lay in the hospital burning with fever as the Acquired Immune Deficiency Syndrome ravaged his flesh. Joey was a hemophyliac who'd been unlucky enough to have received a transfusion with an untested batch of plasma. His parents won the malpractice suit, 16.5 million, but the money hadn't been able to purchase a cure.

Ellie hugged her son, warming his cold damp skin as he shivered and sweat and prayed for a miracle. The nurses watched him and were touched by his piety. Joey was one of the most faithful of all Ellie's children. No one could believe as single-mindedly as a child. Even with the rashes and melanoma spreading across his flesh, even with the chills and racking cough, even though he could no longer control his bowels and was losing weight at the rate of nearly a pound a day, he continued to pray for a cure.

Ellie could feel the power of Joey's belief wash over her like warm spring rain. She smiled down at him impressed by his strength and courage.

"Merciful God, help me." He gasped.

Joey's faith was not the desperate last ditch belief of those sinners frantic for a miracle to save their rotting souls from hell, grasping for heaven like a drowning man clutching a life preserver. It had always been genuine and strong. His love for God was unfaltering and unconditional. Even after all he'd been through his eyes were glazed with rapture as he stared heavenward.

A wrinkled, balding, white-haired, liver spotted priest came in to give him communion. He looked like Lazarus reborn yet still decomposing. Joey hadn't wanted to miss mass even while he was hospitalized. So he'd had them summon the old Jesuit to perform the communion for him. If Joey needed any more proof that miracles were possible then just the fact that such an impossibly ancient human was still alive and ambulatory would have been enough.

The dying young boy was far too weak to kneel so the old priest stood over his bed.

"The body of Christ." He said as he genuflected with the cracker and then placed it on Joey's outstretched tongue. Ellie squeezed her son tighter as he swallowed the communal wafer and continued to pray. The boy even had white spots and sores inside his mouth and on his tongue. He was dying despite all the high-priced drugs they had him on. Only she could save him now.

As she held him she could feel his fever slowly abating, his temperature dropping, his tremors quieting. She kissed him on his sweaty brow and he smiled up at her with those enraptured eyes. Then he climbed up out of the bed.

The nurses stared at him in awe as he shrugged off his bed-sheets and stepped down onto the cool tiled floor. Earlier that day he'd been too weak to lift his head from the pillow to take his medication.

"It's a miracle!" they shouted almost in unison.

One of them turned and thanked the old priest. Kneeling to kiss his hand. The old Jesuit smiled pompously. Ellie's jealousy flared. It was her love that had resurrected her son from near death, not that old fraud's useless prayers. She slammed into the aging priest as she stormed out of the room, knocking him into the wall. He clutched his chest with one gnarled arthritic hand and his eyes went wide as his heartbeat stuttered and threatened to stall. The priest genuflected and uttered a silent prayer, taking deep breaths to slow his thundering pulse.

With a warm smile on her face, feeling the love of her children as it flowed over her in waves from all those in the room who'd borne witness to the miracle, El left little Joey's room behind as she stalked off down the hall. The nurses split as they burst into action, half grabbing at the falling priest and the others rushing to perform tests on the little miracle boy, praising Ellie loudly whenever one of the tests came back with positive results. Even his white blood count was rising. The HIV appeared to be in recession. Still, there were more of Ellie's children who were suffering, more of them who needed her help; her love.

In the next room Ellie's daughter Nikky lay on a gurney with her legs spread, biting her bottom lip against the memory of pain as the nurse swabbed the walls of her vagina with a cotton ball, collecting semen samples for a DNA test. A police woman calmly took pictures of the bruises and bite marks on Nikky's battered face, breasts, and buttocks, and picked flecks of blood and skin from beneath her fingernails with tweezers, sealing them in zip-lock bags. A stern middle-aged doctor came in, mumbled an insincere greeting and a few tepid words of encouragement, then patted the frightened young woman on the arm to raise the thick vein on the inside of her elbow. He then filled a syringe with Doxycyclin and administered an injection for the Chlamydia and Gonorrhea and a prescription for Valtrex to treat the herpes her attackers had infected her with.

Sighing as if the entire thing were as much an ordeal for him as it was for her, he told the nurse to take blood for an AIDS test and recommended to Nikky that she come back again in three months for another test. Nikky nodded her head solemnly with her bottom lip trembling as if about to fall.

Her eyes glistened with emotion yet she continued to fight back the tears, snarling in rage and revulsion remembering the foul breath of her assailants steaming in her face, their oily sweat dripping down onto her forehead and into her eyes, coating her skin in a noxious film. She shuddered and suppressed a scream as she recalled the vile taste of their semen ejaculating down her throat and the stomach churning pain of their angry cocks tearing into her rectum and splitting wide her vagina before they mutilated her. Ellie rushed to Nikky's side just before she lost her tenuous grip on sanity. Nikky smiled, happy to have her mother there to see her through the tragedy. The nurses were all impressed with the love and faith she showed in her mother even after being gang raped by strangers on a subway platform at four o'clock in the morning. They didn't know how to tell her that the damage the rapists had done to her reproductive system with the 40oz of St. Ides they'd shattered inside of her vagina while sodomizing her had destroyed any chances she'd had of ever bearing a child.

The nurse picked more jagged shards of glass from Nikky's labia as she winced and tears squeezed out from the corners of her closed eyelids and then swabbed it with iodine once they'd finished collecting semen samples. The young nurse cursed when the doctor exited the room leaving her to break the news to poor Nikky. El left too.

Ellie moved on to the room where her 30 year-old son Walter lay in an intensive care unit with broken bones and bruised organs. Two of his cervical vertebrae had been shattered and he was numb from the neck down. Tubes snaked out from his nose, spine, and both arms into respirators, morphine drips, and intravenous feeding tubes. He was a mess and it was not expected that he would live and if by some miracle he did make it through the night he would be forever a paraplegic.

El slipped into the room and held his hand but didn't bother to speak to him. She knew that Walter didn't love her. He blamed her for everything that went wrong in his life including the Cadillac that smashed him against the parked Chevy Suburban as he rode his bike down Market Street. He never even turned to look at her as she rubbed his unfeeling palm across her cheek.

His wife came in and sat beside him with tears running the maze of worry lines down her face.

"It's okay dear. Everything will be okay. I've got the whole church praying for you. God will take care of you. You'll see."

El slipped out quietly to leave the two of them alone. But she could still hear them. She could hear everything.

"Yeah, God's done a wonderful job so far. Fuck the church!" Walt croaked.

El stopped and walked back into the room. She screamed and punched the walls in a rage that made the lights in the entire hospital flicker.

"Fuck the church? Fuck you Walter! You blame everyone but yourself! Fuck you!" She grabbed Walter by the throat and began shaking him like a ragdoll in the hands of a hyperkinetic kid as she screamed her indignation into his awestruck face. Tossing him back down onto the hard hospital mattress, she reached around and severed the connection between Walter's spine and his brain. She watched his eyes go wide as he looked deep into her angry countenance and recognition spread across his features.

"You . . . you." He managed to croak before all feeling left his muscles. His wife screamed as Walter began to convulse and the electrocardiograph went wild. "Fuck the church!" would be the last words he'd ever speak. He would lie in that bed, a vegetable, more brain cells dying by the day, for the next two years. Everyday his wife would beg El to bring him back to her, praying with fanatical regularity, sometimes fifteen or twenty times a day and devoting her life to the Lord, until the medical bills sapped all of their savings and she was nearly at the point of prostituting herself to pay Walter's increasing hospital debt. Finally she would beg El to end his suffering for good. Ellie would oblige and reach into his chest to halt his life. Walt's wife would thank her for her mercy.

Ellie made her way to the cancer ward and stroked the bedsores, lesions, and subcutaneous growths plaguing her children's bodies with her feathery soft fingertips and whispered gently in their ears.

"Mommy's here. I will take care of you. Don't be afraid."

Some of them smiled others groaned and turned away. Some cried out in pain. Some of them she embraced. Some of them she walked right past as if they were strangers and not her own flesh and blood.

She felt terrible for her suffering children. She left her sick and dying babies and walked across the street to the Baptist Church. It always made her feel better to hear the choir sing, the pipe organ, the drums, and tambourines, beautiful sounds of praise and worship. Today the church was filled. There had been a ten-car pile up on the freeway and friends and family of the injured and deceased crowded the pews to pray for their loved ones. She watched as her children's friends and neighbors knelt in prayer and smiled as she listened to them praise her for all the love and compassion she showed to her suffering progeny in their time of need.

El was a good mother. This sentiment was almost unanimous. Almost, except for one lone protester who marched back and forth in front of the church accusing her of causing the suffering of her own children just to get attention for herself. Just so that she could comfort and heal them and absorb the accolades of those who witnessed her devotion for being such a loving and attentive parent. El hated the man because everything he said was true.

"Münchausen by Proxy! It's a syndrome, a mental disorder, where mothers cause injury and illness to their children in order to get the sympathy and attention of others, to look like heroes when they sacrifice their time and energy to nurse them back to health. That's what's going on here! Münchausen by Proxy! She wants to be needed and the only way to do that is to make us suffer. So that we'll cry out for her to save us and she can come running like the dutiful mother. But she's *causing* all the pain and suffering! Both directly and by turning her back and allowing it all to happen when she could have stopped it, by setting up the situations under which these tragedies occur! She could have protected us from all of this pain but then what would we need her for?"

This was one that she should have strangled with the umbilical cord by her way of thinking. Ungrateful little brat! Hadn't she suckled him at her tit and given him life? Hadn't she done everything a good mother could ever be expected to do? Yet still he rebelled against her, accusing her of hurting her own kids. She wanted to push him out in front of a bus and watch his head crack like an over-ripe melon. Then he would call out for her. They all called her when they were in trouble. The first hint of pain or failure and they all cried for their mommy. But as much as she wanted to make the man suffer she was afraid people would get suspicious and might start believing the things he was saying. She didn't want to martyr him.

The angry young man marched back and forth waving a big medical dictionary as if it were the bible.

"I'm not crazy! Just look at it. Read what the medical journals say. 'Münchausen by Proxy Syndrome is a dangerous kind of maltreatment in which caretakers deliberately exaggerate and/or fabricate and/or induce physical and/or psychological-behavioral-mental health problems in others. The primary purpose of this behavior is to gain some form of internal gratification, such as attention, for the perpetrator. MBP perpetrators use their victims as objects in trying to satisfy internal needs through the attention they receive from having a child with "problems." These needs are much more important to them than the needs of their victims.' Now who does that sound like? You tell me! Who is responsible for all this suffering and why?!'"

El hissed with fury, wanting again to strike the man down where he stood. Instead she just walked right past him and hissed in his face.

"Burn in hell!'"

The man's skin crawled as her words snaked over his flesh like a chill draft from the grave. He shivered and rubbed his hands over his arms.

"God! What the hell was that?"

El left the hospital to visit the rest of her children. So many of them were sick. So many of them needed her love and comfort. She could hear them calling out for her. She was the only hope they had. They needed her and those who didn't need her yet soon would, she would make sure of that.

She had given birth to countless generations of man. She nursed entire species at her bosom. Her milk was the very nectar of life. Worlds, solar systems, galaxies, the entire universe flowed from her loins. She was the progenitor of all existence, the mother of all living things, and all Ellie had ever asked for was the love and appreciation of her children. That was all that she demanded.

El raised her arms out into the sky and they spanned the universe from one end to the other. All over the world cars crashed, women screamed in the brutal embrace of rapists, murderers, and abusers, children wasted away of famine, disease, abuse, and neglect, plagues spread, disaster struck, and wars erupted. As far as she could reach misery spread, stars exploded and planets shifted on their axis, comets crashed and solar systems collapsed into black holes. It was all good though. Mama would make it all better.

Finally the sun acquiesced and relinquished the sky to night and El went back to the hospital to visit her children. First she went to see her daughter who lay alone in a single hospital room with a candystriper sitting beside her bed reading a fashion magazine and dreaming about losing those extra 30 pounds she'd been trying to lose for years. She flipped through the pages and imagined one day fitting into one of those designer outfits that it would take her years of saving to afford as Nikky writhed on the bed sobbing uncontrollably and tugging at her restraints.

Nikky was under suicide watch. Her mind had yet to fully recover from the assault and the knowledge that she would never be a mother now. She had attacked the nurse when she'd been told that her fallopian tubes had been lacerated beyond repair. The orderlies had to pry her hands from around the woman's throat. For the next hour she had alternated between praying and trying to rip open the arteries in her wrist with her own teeth, until finally they had strapped her arms to the bed with leather wrist restraints. El stepped quietly into her room. She knelt and kissed Nikky on her forehead, which seemed to calm her for a moment. Then she laid her hands on Nikky's hot sweaty skin and spread the Hepatitis C throughout her body. It was the one STD they had neglected to test her for.

"I know you must be testing me Lord. I know that this is all a part of your plan. I will try to be strong."

Ellie smiled down at her, stroked her hair and spread the Hepatitis down into her kidneys. She then reached between Nikky's thighs and gifted her child with her first major Herpes outbreak. The little red sores erupted all over Nikky's mouth, anus, and vagina looking raw and inflamed like bee stings that had been scratched once too often. Nikky wept aloud and began trying to gnaw at her wrist again when she lifted her bed sheet to see the suppurating wounds blistering around her still bruised and lacerated vagina. Her wrists were still strapped to the bed however and she was not strong enough to break the restraints. She continued to weep as she lay there staring at the ceiling and planning her suicide.

Ellie left as quietly as she had come, pausing briefly to clog more of the candystriper's arteries with cholesterol. The overweight teenager would have a heart attack by the time she celebrated her twenty-ninth birthday. By then she would also be more than seventy pounds overweight.

In the cancer ward El took cancer from one child to give to another. She laid hands on one elderly lady and stopped the spread of cancer through her reproductive track shrinking the malignant grapefruit sized tumor in her uterus to the size of an orange. She then laid hands on the testicles of the man across the room from her and doubled the size of the growth in his balls before sliding her arm into his rectum and quadrupling the size of the tumor in his prostate.

She approached her son Billy who had been hospitalized for over a month dying of childhood Leukemia. Ellie had visited him often. Some days she took away his fever and returned his strength. Other days she sat on his chest and sapped his vitality so that he could not get out of bed unassisted. Today she knelt and sucked the last of his life force out of him as he thrashed and convulsed then finally lay still forever.

"She tortures us so that we will love her more when she spares our lives or heals our wounds or takes some other father's child instead of ours! She doesn't love any of us! She's only using us! My boy is up there in that hospital dying of AIDS and she does nothing!"

The hysterical man was still across the street, marching back and forth in front of the church as parishioners scuttled by him on their way to mass. Some paused to spit in his face, others threatened to call the cops or to kick his ass themselves, but others stopped to listen. Ellie was still not sure what she was going to do about him when she entered Joey's room. Another relapse? Making little Joey better for a while after the priest had come to visit him had earned her the praise of half the nursing staff. Even some of the doctors who had long grown cynical to miracles had attended church that night. But it still had not done a thing to warm his father's hardened heart to her love. He'd been through this too may times to get hopeful over these minor recoveries. Perhaps it was time to end Joey's suffering and give his father some peace. He would come back to her soon, once he got over his child's death. They always did. Perhaps she would bless him with another child.

"Don't! Please. Don't take my child."

The hysterical man from the church steps was standing in the hospital room with her.

"You should have thought of that earlier Adam. If you'd never eaten from my tree you'd never even know what was happening. You'd be as ignorant and blissful as the rest of my children."

"The rest of your sheep you mean!"

"Save your indignation. You've got the rest of eternity to hate me. I'll never let you into heaven Adam. So why not go where you belong."

Ellie pointed to the floor and a great chasm opened up in the floor. Adam looked down into the tremendous fissure, into the very earth itself, to see a great molten ocean that seemed to be filled with human bodies, their skin boiling off of them, liquefying into the same flaming effluence in which they were imprisoned.

"Go join the other rebels. That traitor down there has been waiting for you for a long time. He wouldn't be there if it wasn't for his jealousy over you."

"I won't go. I'll turn this whole world against you!"

"That will never happen Adam. They love me even if you don't. Even with all the knowledge you gave them they'd still rather believe than think. He who increases knowledge increases suffering. My children don't want to suffer. They want to believe in love Adam. They want to believe in me."

"Please. Please. Don't take my son."

"You don't have a son Adam. They are all my children."

Elohim bent down by the side of Joey's bed and kissed her son on his lips, breathing pneumonia into his lungs. She knew that even with his white blood cell count rising his immune system was still too weak to fight off such a cold. She hugged him tight as Adam's screams raked her ears then she released his soul into the ether and moved on. The rest of her children needed her. She could hear them calling.

Adam rushed to Joey's bedside and held his dying son, showering him with his tears. He watched Elohim leave remembering when just the sound of her voice and the sight of her radiant visage had been all he'd ever needed for happiness. He remembered when she had created a mate for him and when he'd disobeyed her and been cast out of the garden to walk the earth forever alone and unloved. Watching one lover after another give birth, grow old, and die, leaving him alone in the concrete ruins of Eden with his useless knowledge of the universe and yet another dead child.

"Münchausen by proxy!" He screamed, but no one listened. They never did.

Couch Potato

"Eyes are the window to the soul. Stare into an American's eyes . . . Most likely there will be nothing but a mere reflection of a television glaring back at you."
—Shelby Gull

"Sigmund Freud described the self as that part of ourselves that mediates between our own internal drives and desires and the outside world. Ego vs. Id = Self. Buddhists see the only path to enlightenment as the elimination of self in order to unite with the infinite. I've been trying, really trying, ever since Maria died, but I'm starting to realize the impossibility of this endeavor. I think it might be easier to destroy everything else and leave my own ego right where it is."

He rose from the couch and began to pace again.

"See, existence demands a toll. That toll is the effort required to maintain it. And everything in life is poised to frustrate that effort. Everything in life struggles against everything else for the commodities of existence and survival means being a part of that struggle. Even the most ascetic monk sitting alone on a hill meditating for hours must eventually come down from that hill to find food, shelter, clothing, water. You can suppress the urge to eat and drink but eventually, if you would continue to live, you must consume and that's when the frustration begins. Getting food means working to get money, or stealing, or begging, or forming and maintaining friendships or relationships with those who would provide you sustenance. It means being involved in life; being a part of Samsara. And each time you interact with the world you expand your Self. Buddha himself was imperfect by his own definition while he lived and breathed because he was forced to be a part of this bullshit. But I'm going to achieve perfection one way or another. I'm sick of this world!"

He had that violent look in his eyes again. When he'd first come in the doctor had difficulty imagining him doing all the violence he'd been accused of, but now he could see it. He could see all the mayhem that lurked behind his wild eyes, like a bullet looking for a gun to give it direction.

"They take away my car, my job, my wife, everything I considered to be my life and they expect me to just smile, praise Jesus or Buddha or Allah or some phantom deity or other, and just go along with it all? Fuck that! Living is the constant acquisition and accumulation of things that are all forfeited the moment you die. Even your memories of those experiences rot away in your skull while the rest of you is picked apart by vermin and digested by the earth. In the end they take everything from you! Everything!"

The doctor sat struggling to control his own creeping terror as the obviously paranoid and psychotic young man delivered his fanatical diatribe. Since the death of his wife the man had been involved in one violent incident after another. In and out of psychiatric hospitals and jail cells. He was currently on probation for attacking a priest at a confessional. If reports were true he'd raped and sodomized the man. When the cops asked him why he'd done it, he'd simply replied "Why not?" Therapy was part of the terms of his probation.

"Who's 'They'?" the doctor asked in his flat toneless voice, squinting over the top of his glasses. He was pleased with his appropriately clinical tone, impressed with himself for keeping his mounting unease out of his voice.

"They?"

"Yes. You said 'They' take away your car, your job, your wife. Who's 'They'?"

"They are Life; Life in general! The Creator! God! Shit, I don't know! Fuck if I knew who 'They' were I wouldn't be talking to you I'd be out killing the bastards!"

"Quite a morbid outlook you've got there. Your perception of life seems decidedly . . . uh . . . hostile."

"Don't I have a right to be hostile? After all the shit I've gone through in my life? After all that I've suffered?"

"We all suffer but, excuse the cliché, you must gather yea rosebuds while yea may."

"Gather my what? What tha fuck are you talking about?!!" He shrieked with his face inches from the doctor's. Spittle flew from his lips and speckled the good doctor's glasses.

"Carpe Diem. Seize the day. I'm talking about making the most of your life while you can."

"Yeah and what the fuck for! So you can just lose it all the minute your heart stops pumping hemoglobin to your starving organs? Death is the period at the end of the sentence that does not just punctuate or conclude but erases all that proceeded it. It's the delete button on your computer and there isn't even the option to save! Your whole life is just wiped out in its entirety! So why should we gather rosebuds or even our next breath?!"

The doctor watched his agitated patient wondering if he should hit the button for security or risk reaching into his desk for a little .38 caliber insurance. The man kept leaping up from the couch and storming around the tiny office flailing his arms madly as he continued his diatribe against existence. There was an insane animation in his eyes. They burned with the furious heat of total madness and the doctor had to struggle to maintain eye contact. The fanatical radiance bristling from the man's gaze was like staring into an August sun. The doctor could see his tiny image sizzling on the man's hard dark retinas.

105

"Why do you feel life has to accomplish something in order to be worth living? Why do you feel you must gain something from it?"

"Because life is not painless. It's not one big endless party. It doesn't come without a price. And after you've struggled so hard to maintain something, to hold onto something, and you face nothing but years and years of struggle ahead, what fool would not ask whether that which he is struggling for is worth the struggle? Life demands a price. Existence demands a toll. What fool would pay so dearly for something that had no worth? I mean, if it has no reward, if you lose everything, then it's just cruel, evil!"

He glared down at the doctor again and this time he did flinch. His eyes were smoldering pits of madness and something in them made the doctor think the man would reach out and crush his larynx.

"Look at these Doc. These are the keys to one of the most beautiful cars ever made, a Lexus LS. It was my pride and joy, but you can't take it with you. The last time I saw it, it was wrapped around my wife and they were burning together. The whole twisted hulk just kept rolling down the street like *it* owned her now. They had become one, this perversely beautiful beast that spoke with the voices of rubber skidding across asphalt and steel grating against bone. And me? I had been thrown through the windshield like an unwelcome guest, like they didn't want me interfering in their romance. Three's a crowd pal. Hit the road. Ha ha. Get it? Hit the road! My own fucking car and it threw me out, left my wife to die alone in that burning hell. You can't take it with you Doc. Not your car, your house, your job, your family, not your own wife who you waited all your life to find, whose eyes could make you forget who you were, whose smile made you smile. You can't take it with you so what is the goddamned point?"

"Well then what do you want from me?"

"What do you mean?"

"It seems you have things well figured out. The world sucks. You're convinced of that, and nothing anyone can do will dissuade you. So how do you intend for me to help you? Why did you come here?"

"I came here for you to show me how to go on with my life knowing what I know. I want to slip back into the illusion of life with a purpose; life with meaning, to forget that death exists as a contradiction to that illusion. If I could truly believe that the bullshit of everyday life actually has some significance then I could rejoin the rest of the herd, the mindless sheep, toiling in blissful ignorance with complete faith that in the end it will actually have meant something beyond mere senseless suffering. I mean, what good is knowing the truth when you're helpless to change it?"

"Precisely. What good is it?"

"Help me Doc, please."

"You know, at this point, most doctors would prescribe heavy dosages of anti-depressants plus years of psychotherapy for you. The anti-depressants of course would drug you into cooperation with the rest of the world; blind acquiescence to the human condition. The psychotherapy would be pretty much pointless in your case but it would help the good doctor pay off any outstanding debts."

"Are you suggesting that I be drugged for the rest of my life?"

"Oh no, no. You are an intelligent man. You want the illusion. You realize the necessity of it. What would it prosper us all to realize that we're in an infinite loop that does not progress or regress regardless of our input, that serves no obvious purpose but to continue eternally? Tell me, what would it gain us to know this? What you need is some help finding your way back to the fantasy and to achieve that end there are far more potent drugs than the pharmaceutical variety.

Hemingway once described religion, economics, patriotism, sexual intercourse, and radio as 'Opium of the people.' They lull the mind into a false sense of security and complacency, a sort of intellectual lethargy. They put us back in the dream world where lives are traded for scraps of rectangular green paper with pictures of dead presidents on them. Religion, patriotism, and economics, we've already discounted. Well, actually, we never did cover patriotism. How do you feel about your country?"

107

"I'm an anarchist."

"Too bad, those were the three best. Anyway, that brings us to sexual intercourse. That won't work. Number one because you can't really do it that often and trying makes you too dependent on others. When firm breasts and tight asses become your only reason for living one lonely night could make you suicidal. We wouldn't want you to go from depression to desperation. Desperate men commit desperate acts. Besides, the experience almost never equals the lust for the experience. You'd be disillusioned of that trip in no time.

Then, finally, there's radio. Hours and hours of worry free entertainment. No thinking about life or mortality or the significance of the individual. No acting or interacting. Just you in your Lazy Boy gently massaged by radio waves 'til your mind is passive and cooperative and ready to accommodate any illusion thrown at it. Whether it's men in red and blue tights streaking through the sky or white boys singing soul music. After a few hours of that, the meaning of life becomes less of an issue as just going along with it, harmonizing with it and swaying to its rhythms with the rest of the sheep.

Now if radio is an 'Opium of the people' then television is heroin; uncut and China white! I suggest you take a vacation from your job and get yourself a big wide screen TV with a remote control, a satellite dish, a VCR, a DVD, a mountain of tapes, and lose yourself in commercial reality."

Six years later . . .

He woke up that morning as he had every morning since his last therapy session, on the couch. He stared at the television screen for a while the way a teenaged boy would stare at Miss America if she were sitting directly across from him, then he got up and turned it off. He didn't bother to shower or change his clothes or even brush his teeth. He walked into the bathroom, unzipped his fly, urinated into the sink (the toilet was broken) and smiled into the mirror on the door of the medicine cabinet.

"Like sands through the hour glass, these are the days of our lives," he said.

He paused for a second trying to recall his name, who he was, where he came from. Images flashed through his mind and he tried desperately to grasp onto one and decipher it. His memory was now a kaleidoscopic montage of sound and video bites. He doesn't remember mother or father though he assumes they were nothing like Claire or Heathcliff Huxtable otherwise he wouldn't have turned out so maladjusted. He figures his family was more like the Bradys or the Partridge family; all wearing smiles chained to their faces, locked into their jaw muscles, forced to hold that unnatural position through entire episodes like some perverse bondage ritual. That is why he hates to see people smile and probably why he smiles so much himself. Runs in the family he supposes.

He doesn't remember having a childhood, a young adulthood, going to college, bumming around the country, or any of those neat things they do on other shows. Perhaps those episodes were cancelled? Not enough support from the public or not enough funding from the sponsors.

He stared intently into the mirror.

They say eyes are the mirror to the soul (His gaze was unwavering. All expression bled from his face) but what if your soul is a mirror? What would you see when you looked into a mirror, into your own eyes? Nothing? Or, perhaps, nothing reflected back at you endlessly?

"How you doin'?" he asked himself, staring deep into that endless void.

He couldn't remember a thing about himself. His identity had been slowly eroded, scrubbed away by an endless flow of commercials, silly sitcoms, soap operas, "B" movies and every other form of mental pabulum the idiot box could produce. His life disappeared somewhere between UHF, VHF, Cable, and MTV.

Maybe he was really Clint Eastwood "The man with no name" in that old Italian western "For a few dollars more." Maybe he was no one at all; just another fucking couch potato.

He smiled and reiterated the words of the immortal Ernest Hemingway.

"Hail nothing, full of nothing, nothing is with thee."

When he laughed it sounded amazingly like Vincent Price. His breath even smelled bad to him.

He walked downstairs into the living room where he scooped up several large knives and hid them in pockets all over his body. Then he grabbed a handful of shotgun shells and dumped them into his coat pocket alongside his trenchknife, which bore an uncanny resemblance to the one used by the Scorpio killer in "The Enforcer."

He picked up his shotgun and walked out trying to remember all the ingredients in a Big Mac.

There was no method to his madness. He had no plan when he approached the house down the street. There was just the overwhelming feeling that something . . . that everything . . . was wrong . . . terribly, ridiculously, horribly, wrong . . . and he had to stop it. He had to make it all stop. All this sickening, absurd, pointless, living. It all had to stop now.

He walked around to the backdoor of the one story, cookie cutter, stucco house; painted in the mind numbing symbol of sameness known as "Swiss Coffee," the middle class name for off-white.

He kicked the door in.

"Hello. Hello. Hello." He sang in the voices of all three stooges.

Someone screamed and he caught a glimpse of a figure fleeing into the next room. He darted into the kitchen to head them off and spotted a little child in a high chair eating cereal. The child flung a spoon full of smooshed corn flakes at his feet.

"Oh! A wise guy!" he said in a frighteningly realistic "Curly" voice then he shoved his fingers through the kid's eye sockets. The child died instantly. He continued into the dining room.

A woman stood there with a .45 in her hand, the hammerlock was still on and it probably didn't even have a clip in it but she held it like she was determined to do business.

"Oh Lucy! Why don' jou ever lis'sen to me?" he taunted in what was undoubtedly the voice of Desi Arnaz.

"YOU BASTARD!! YOU KILLED MY BABY!!!" The woman screamed hysterically.

"I saved your baby," he whispered. "I saved him from the rest of his miserable life. You should be happy. Now he won't turn out like me."

He raised his shotgun and pointed it right between the ample swell of her bosom. She began desperately, and quite ineffectually, trying to fire her weapon.

BLAM!!! BLAM!!!!

Twin shotgun shells slammed into her chest and exploded out her back. She slumped against the wall and slid down leaving a long streak of blood and gore. Her eyes were glazed in horror, tasting her ensuing death. He walked out of the room already forgetting her.

"I'm so glad we had this time togetheeeeer."

A young black man passed him on the street, as he left, and made a disgusting remark about how he may have gotten blood on his left hand. He whirled on the young man, grabbed him by the collar, and threw him against a ten-foot wooden fence.

"Whazzaaaaaaap?" he drawled as he reached into his pocket for the bowie knife.

"You are the weakest link. Goodbye!" he said in an astringent monotone before puncturing the man's throat with the twelve-inch bowie knife and leaving it sticking out of his Adam's apple, nailing him to the fence.

Eight blocks down the road he found the home of his former psychiatrist. He swooned remembering their very last conversation.

The doctor had come to visit him several months ago. Apparently some of his relatives had been concerned about the disappearance of their estranged relation and had tracked down the doctor hoping he would have a clue to his whereabouts.

"My God man! When was the last time you got out of this apartment?" The doctor had exclaimed.

"Time is an illusion. I am learning."

Quickly, the doctor slipped into his clinical mode.

"What exactly are you learning?"

"How to respond to life. At first I thought I wanted distractions. I thought I wanted to avoid the question, pretend it didn't exist, that it was unimportant, that just living was the important thing."

"I'm afraid I don't understand. What question?"

"The question everyone wants to ask but we are all so afraid of. Not how do I cope with life, but how do I conquer it? How do I overcome it? Subjugate it? And this…" he said, pointing to the gigantic television that now filled an entire wall. "This is going to show me how."

The doctor turned to look at the huge screen as his deranged young client flicked through the channels. It wasn't until then that he noticed it. Channel after channel of pure nihilistic violence. The cartoons, the commercials, the comedies, all singing the song of the flesh, a mournful dirge, a war cry. Death and destruction literal, symbolic, metaphorical, endless. All those beautiful people spiraling down into a pit of merciless doom. You could see it in their faces. They had all died a dozen times and would die a dozen more. If not in this movie or this episode then in the next but they would all die because that was the lesson they had to teach; that life must end. You could see it in their faces, in how they lived, the huge monuments they built to themselves and called houses, mansions, estates, they were all just great headstones; the mausoleums in which their memories would lie inert, captured in stone until age eventually took those away too. This was the lesson they had to teach.

112

"Horrible," the doctor said backing away from the screen, not seeing the gleeful giant standing behind him.

"The answer," the man said as the shrink backed into him and turned to face his maddened eyes. "The answer is that the only proper response to existence is VENGEANCE!"

He raised his arms above his head and drove two radio antennas into the good doctor's cranium.

"We must revenge ourselves against life for the agony it has put each of us through, for the hopelessness of our plight. Learn, Doc. Learn."

He spun the doctor back around to face the television and absorb its wisdom.

Eventually, even this memory was battered from his mind as he stood gawking at the deceased's weather beaten house, swallowed in a maelstrom of cathode ray images.

He continued walking down the street until he approached a house that appealed to him; an apartment building actually.

He opened the door and stepped into the large vestibule. A young boy, no more than about fifteen, stood there fumbling with his keys. He wrapped a hand around the boy's throat and threw him against the locked security door. The boy began to yell for help when the man produced a long tanto knife.

"Hi, I'm Casey Kasum with this weeks top ten hits!" he sunk the knife into the boys lower abdomen.

The boy rained punches down upon him and more than a few knees landed in the man's groin but he didn't appear to notice.

"At number ten on the list we have Usher with 'Confession'," he pronounced gleefully as he began slicing upwards with the knife in a surgically straight line.

The boy's screams were terrible. He stopped punching and began trying to pull the blade out of his gut but the man held it in an unshakeable grip and the blade continued to ascend. He gripped the man's wrist with both hands. His efforts were useless. Blood was everywhere.

"At our number seven spot we have Lil' John singing 'Yeah!'"
The blade was now up to the boy's rib cage.

"At number five Britnyy Spears with 'I'm Not That Innocent'," he said, Casey Kasum's voice brimming with excitement as he neared the number one hit and the knife carved through the boy's solar plexus.

The boy's young body convulsed furiously. He was already dead. It would just take him a few more minutes to realize it. The knife yet moved upwards.

"At number two we have Jay Z with 'Ninety-Nine Problems' and for the fourth week in a row, a song made popular by Stephen King, at number one, Larry Underwood singing 'Baby Can You Dig Your Man?'."

He slashed the knife from the middle of the boy's chest to just beneath his chin in one swift stroke and finally allowed the lifeless thing to fall at his feet. He searched the boy for the keys to the security door, splashing around in the terrific pool of blood that now filled the vestibule. He found the keys by the door where the boy had dropped them and let himself through. He knocked at the first door he came to.

A young woman, with bright red hair (dyed), wearing a warm-up suit and sweating profusely, answered the door. Dance music blared from somewhere inside her apartment. She was chewing gum in that obnoxious way that sluts do.

"Good efening," said the voice of Bela Lugosi, "My name is Count Dracula."

He seized her chin and jerked her head back exposing the pale, virgin skin of her throat.

"I vant to suck jour bvlod," he continued and before she could struggle or let out so much as a squeal, he ripped her throat out with his teeth.

As the woman slumped to the ground, coughing and choking on her own blood, her lacerated throat making bubbly gargling noises, he said, in the voice of the little boy eating a mustard sandwich in the French's Mustard commercial, "Ith's dewicious!" and then swallowed the huge hunk of flesh he'd tore from her throat.

He went on to an upstairs apartment and chased a "Waskiwy wabbit" around a table before he finally caught the old man and severed his head from his shoulders. He placed the disembodied head carefully in the oven on a greased cookie sheet (after all it was "Time to make the donuts").

He left the apartment building and flagged down a cab. Imagine catching a cab at the height of the day while dripping in blood from head to toe. Only in New York. The taxi driver pulled away from the curb and, as if on an afterthought, yelled back over his shoulder.

"Hey were you in an accident man?"

"An accident? Yes, an accident. A terrible accident. I was sitting in the car drinking. That's how I used to deal with life. I've found a better way now, a much better way. Maria, my wife, was driving, complaining that the glare from the oncoming traffic was blinding her. Then there was a long screech and then a loud crash as we slammed into the meridian. I looked up to see the front of the car crinkled up like dirty laundry and spraying chunks of concrete as we crashed through the meridian and went sailing into the opposite lane. All I could see were hundreds of headlights rushing towards us. We collided head-on with a little Toyota and I was catapulted through the windshield. Sparks erupted from beneath the little car and then it exploded, dislodging itself from our car and propelling it into the embankment on the side. Our car caught fire too but it was still rolling. It whined and screamed and hissed angrily at me while it did things 40,000 dollars worth of automotive genius just shouldn't do, you know? I could smell the tires burning and another smell like frying pork. Maria was dead and in a drunken nod I had missed her death. I just sat there watching her empty body bounce up and down in its seat and whack its head against the steering wheel again and again as the flaming vehicle rolled away from me. I could hear the brakes squealing like she was still trying to stop the car.

115

My ears were filled with the angry sound of grinding metal and I can remember thinking, to the car, "She did it. Don't scream at me. I wasn't driving!" After it was over, I walked down the road to where the car had finally succumbed to inertia and sat down with my back to it, and Maria hated it when I turned my back to her. I picked dirt and glass out of my face and wondered what happened to all the distractions. All the wonderful distractions that put distance between you and any notions of death, made you think you were too young or too healthy or too important to die. I can't die. I have mortgage payments to make. I haven't raised a family yet. I haven't saved the world yet! Where were all those distractions? Those petty obsessions that seemed so important, that took our minds off our insignificance, our utter meaninglessness, our mortality. I turned and looked at Maria's dead smiling face. Her lips had been burned off and what was left of her eyes were sizzling and boiling in their sockets. At that moment I knew that life didn't need us. Maria had simply lived and then she did not and the world did not stop spinning."

He began weeping aloud.

"Uh, sir? Would you like me to take you to a hospital?"

"What?" he looked up, his face a mask of pain and confusion.

"Where to sir?"

The sensitive human being, who mourned the loss of his wife and the loss of a world in which things made sense, winked out of existence. What remained was an existentialist monster, a walking horror film, just another fucking couch potato.

"There's a sign post up ahead. It reads… last stop the Twilight Zone!" said the unforgettable voice of Rod Serling then he shot the taxi driver's head off.

The cab swerved insanely and barreled into a powder blue Cadillac. Both men left their vehicles. The cab driver stayed behind the wheel spouting blood out of his face. The owner of the blue Cadi'; a tall overweight Texan in a gaudy maroon suit, walked over to the side of the cab and looked in the front seat.

"What the hell happened to him?" he exclaimed.

"Awww, the poooor puddy tat. He fall down go . . ."

click, click, BOOM!!!

The Cadillac's corpulent owner fell on his ample buttocks, spraying blood from the steaming hole in his chest.

A motorcycle cop scooted up out of nowhere looking terribly phallic with his bulbous helmet wobbling atop his reed thin neck. The helmet appeared to be wider than his narrow, bowed shoulders. The impotent looking prick-of-a-cop leveled his weapon at the demented human chameleon that even then was morphing into another TV character.

"Drop the weapon freak and spread out on the floor! Now!!!"

His voice shook as he attempted to bark out the command in his most authoritarian tone. He didn't sound either strong or confident as he had hoped. He sounded scared. His gun hand was shaking as well. Anyone watching would've known that someone was about to die.

The gore encrusted man with the deranged gleam in his eyes turned to look at the little man in his idiotic little uniform with a look of amusement.

"Let's get ready to RUUUMBLLLLE!!!"

He rushed the little prick swinging the Mossberg pistol grip pump shotgun above his head in a tremendous arc. The cop squeezed off a shot that grazed the top of the man's ear searing a furrow alongside his temple just before he connected with the crude assault. The little prick fell to his knees and the gun flew from his hand. The gore soaked maniac brought the shotgun down again and again driving the cop to the asphalt where he continued to bludgeon him.

"Captain! I can't hold her together much longer. She's going to blow!"

The police officer's helmet cracked and a stream of blood erupted from the top re-enforcing the phallic imagery. His helmet continued to disintegrate as blow after blow rained down with relentless fury. His skull fared no better. When it was over it was difficult to distinguish the fragments of the helmet from the fragments of the cop's obliterated cranium. The maniac was in a frenzy. He looked into the officer's ruined face; staring into his eyes as they drooled out of their sockets onto his cheeks.

"You look marvelous!" said the voice of Fernando Lamas or rather Billy Crystal imitating Fernando Lamas.

As he turned to leave he noticed that the Cadi' owner, whom he'd written off as dead, had dragged himself over to the prick's gun. He gave him a few whacks with the shotgun too.

"Homey don't play dat!"

At about ten minutes to midnight he finally came home. He peeled off his blood encrusted, gore splattered clothes and sat down on the couch; in front of the television. He turned it on. It had blown its color tube last night and now the screen produced nothing but static lines. It didn't matter. He supplied the show.

Tears rolled down his cheeks tinged pink from the blood covering his face as he recounted the day's events.

"Today in the news a series of gruesome murders struck our fair city leaving nearly a dozen people dead. Conflicting witness reports describe the suspect as everything from a tall black man identical enough to Michael Jordan to be a twin, to Bela Lugosi, to . . . uh . . . Tweety Bird? Either the killer is a master of disguise or this is the worst case of mass hysteria this reporter has ever seen. It sounds like whoever it was that the cops interviewed in this case watches entirely too much television."

"Yeah," the man said, using his own voice for the first time in years, "just a bunch of fucking couch potatoes."

More Maggots

". . . more maggots . . ."

Anthony loved his mother. He clung to that love like a lifeline —as he had all his life. If nothing else, he was sure that *it* would see him through this.

His mother had been determined to make a success of him. That's why she'd worked nine hours a day in the sugar cane fields, swinging a machete from sunrise 'til the sun bled out across the sky. That's why she'd had Mama Luanda put a mojo on his daddy to stop him from beating' on them. That's why she'd sent Anthony off to London to study at the British University.

Anthony dreamed of bringing her his college diploma, getting a good job, and buying her a new house. He would make certain she never had to work in the fields again. That's why he couldn't allow himself to die. Not like this.

". . . more maggots . . . need more . . ."

The dust, mold, and mildew that filled the room with a graveyard stench were not the first odors that Anthony became aware of as he reluctantly regained consciousness. It was easily overshadowed by the sickening sweet smell coming from the parasite-infested hog carcass lying on the floor beside the bathtub, or the rotten egg smell of infection and decay coming from Anthony himself.

His nostrils roared with the noxious aromas acting as a smelling salt, reviving him even as his mind attempted to retreat from reality into the comfort of dreams. He wanted to escape into the cool ocean where he'd trapped crab and lobster years ago, where he'd swam with sand sharks that had long grown accustomed to the presence of islanders, while his mother and sisters washed their clothes alongside him in the same refreshing waters. He longed for the smoky nightclubs where calypso and dancehall reggae played 'til the wee hours of the night and everyone danced, drank rum, and smoked ganja. Any memory would've sufficed. Anything to shield his mind from this . . . this horror. But he could not escape it.

Anthony's mind waded sluggishly through a mucoid swamp of hideous, putrescent images—images of pale slimy creatures wriggling ecstatically through decaying flesh . . . *his flesh!* Images too terrible to be real. He was in a delirious state of shock as he struggled to ascribe logic to it. Nothing in his life had prepared him for what he was now seeing. This was not being stabbed in an alley by a junkie hungry for a fix. This was not being caught in the crossfire of two rival gangs and ducking automatic weapons fire at a dead sprint. This was not being attacked by a jealous girlfriend with a steak knife, being beaten to death by racist cops, starving to death in a rat-infested tenement, or slowly working to an exhausted collapse in the sugarcane fields at home. This was not like any of the horrible ends his mother had feared her little boy might come to when she scraped together years of savings to send him away from this place. This was a slow, crawling, rotting, living death. He shuddered and groaned in revulsion. He could imagine no torment in hell to equal this.

Anthony wanted to scream. He wanted to scream until the movie screen shattered and he was back on the sidewalk, in the sunlight, with the horror already a fading memory. But he knew this was not a movie. It was real and it was happening to him.

"*. . . Na 'nough . . . need more . . . na can stop now . . . more . . . need more maggots . . .*"

Even more than the terrible sights or the horrendous odors, those words cut through the dense miasm surrounding Anthony's mind like a splash of cold water. He could not make out everything the old woman was saying. Her hoarse mumbling was like the hiss of a snake and spewed from her lips in an unending rant. But Anthony could decipher enough of it to know that he was fucked. Her gnarled arthritic talons danced over his bare skin as she worked her medicine upon him, and he cringed each time her flesh made contact with his own. Still, he made no effort to resist her. He needed her.

He watched with revulsion as she pulled a handful of maggots from the rotting entrails of the dead hog and worked them gently into his wounds. He could feel them consuming him, or rather he imagined he could, but he offered no protest. For the sake of his own sanity, he had to believe the old woman knew what she was doing.

"... 'till not 'nough ... need more ... need more maggots ..."

It had begun with bleeding sores. Anthony first thought it was little more than bad acne, then when the ulcers multiplied and began to enlarge, he'd been afraid he had skin cancer. When the sores had widened into gaping holes, large chunks of flesh simply missing as if he'd been attacked and half eaten by some wild beast, and a gangrenous stench wafted from them like the smell of fresh road kill, he had finally gone to the hospital seeking help. By the time he reached the emergency ward the avulsions in his flesh were so large that he could watch his lung working behind his ribcage and could trace the path of food through his intestinal track. It had nearly been too late then.

Still, he had not stayed there either. Wrapping bandages around the suppurating wounds to hold in his organs, Anthony had flown all the way from England back to Haiti because he believed the old witch doctor could purge the flesh-eating curse from his rapidly deteriorating body.

He wasn't sure exactly what he thought she could do for him. Did he expect her to knit new flesh for him to replace what was now decaying from his bones? He'd heard what the British doctors wanted to do. They wanted to cut him. They wanted to excise the disease from his living tissue, one pound of flesh after another, until either they stopped the disease or ran out of flesh to cut away. No way Anthony was going for that! If he would die, it would be in his own homeland, observing the customs and traditions he had lived by. So he had come back to Haiti in search of Mama Luanda.

Mama Luanda did not practice magic. She practiced medicine, the forgotten medicine her people brought from Africa. She did not conjure demons, or turn people into zombies, or cast spells and curses. She was a healer. At least this is what she said. But there were rumors about men who had crossed her struck down by disease, or turned into living corpses, and even one who had been eaten alive by rats. She dismissed the stories as mere superstition. The same way she brushed off discussion of her phenomenal longevity, ascribing it to genetics and eating healthy. She was rumored to be well over a hundred years old and seemed to be living proof that she had made at least one zombie. Mama Luanda was a horror unto herself. She was nothing pretty.

Her thick and unruly dreadlocks writhed about her head like a nest of bloated black eels. Her swollen lips were cracked and split and hid small, yellow, needle-like teeth. Her breath was like the stench of a freshly exhumed corpse. Her high cheekbones may have once granted a regal aspect to her features, but now, with her dried and wrinkled skin drawn tight against them threatening to rip wide, they looked like twin axe blades or some kind of prehistoric armament. The one good eye remaining in her head appeared nervous and agitated and darted about in a frenzy of motion, perhaps overcompensating for the hollow crater where her right eye had been. It looked as if someone had cored it right out of her skull with some sharp implement, taking her eyelid with it and leaving only that unblinking chasm of ruined flesh.

Looking at it reminded Anthony of a book he'd read about Gilles De Rais, the infamous Blue Beard, who'd murdered, raped, and mutilated the children of the peasants and serfs in the village surrounding his castle. "Skull fucking" had been one of his favorite ways to simultaneously rape and murder his victims and that's what it appeared had been done to Mama Luanda. It looked as if she'd been skull-fucked and had somehow lived to tell the tale. Though Anthony found it difficult to conceive of even a sick fucker like Blue Beard being able to get it up looking at that hideous train-wreck of a face.

With increasing despair Anthony realized that there was no place in the old shack he could look that did not contain one grotesquerie or another. The dilapidated hovel was cluttered from floor to rafters with various skulls, and bones, and pickled animal entrails and organs, and some that may have been human. Spiders, snakes, and lizards scampered and slithered from one shadow to the next. And the ruinous face of the old witch doctor was so hideous it would've made an onion cry. Anthony himself was now merely another addition to the madness.

He closed his eyes and tried to shut out the feel of the maggots crawling through him, eating away at him. He tried to dream of the beaches where the white sand sifted through your toes as fine as baby powder and the ocean was cool, and clear, and blue, and you could count the fish as they swam between your legs. He tried to think of the coconut trees and how he had climbed them as a child to pick their fruit and toss it down below to the other hungry children. He tried to imagine himself chasing the monitor lizards that littered the beaches by the hundreds and catching them in jars to sell to the tourists. He struggled desperately to summon the taste of his mother's curried goat and ox tail soup, the smell of cornbread muffins. Yet the image of his own putrefying maggot-ridden body kept invading his thoughts.

The doctors had called it Necrotizing Fasciitis. It was caused by the *Streptococcus Pyogenes* virus, which was like a mutant form of the virus that causes Strep throat. Infection from the disease results in your immune system freaking out and cutting off the blood supply to any infected tissue, causing the tissue to die and eventually to rot away. It was known in the press as "the flesh-eating virus," and there was no way to cure it except to remove the diseased tissue, either by cutting it away, as the British surgeons had proposed, or Mama Luanda's way—using maggots to eat away the dead flesh, leaving only the uninfected tissue.

Anthony was no longer certain which solution was more horrible, but he no longer had a choice. Now he just had to have faith.

The bathtub was filling up. Maggots now covered Anthony's putrefying form from head to toe. His body was a ruin of rotten flesh and gaping holes where the maggots had already eaten away the necrotic tissue. Their pale bloated bodies writhed in a great seething mass, crawling over his dying body, greedily consuming it, burrowing down through muscle and fat into the organs that were already infected and beginning to rot. The disease continued to advance through his body.

"*. . . more maggots . . . need more maggots!*"

Anthony thought Mama Luanda was beginning to sound panicked for the first time. It wasn't working. The maggots could not eat fast enough. The disease was spreading too rapidly. Her brow furrowed, the thick wooly eyebrows arching like an EEG reading up over her agitated left eye and the stygian pit that should have housed the other. Tenebrous shadows slithered deep within the dark hollow pit as light from the many candles strewn about the room flickered down into it. A drop of sweat raced down her forehead and dripped into that ghastly void, followed soon by another.

Mama Luanda began to chant some island mojo in a bizarre guttural dialect Anthony had never heard before. She closed her one good eye, and a spark of blue flame seemed to ignite deep within the hole on the other side of her face. The chant flooded out of her in a stream of senseless syllables. The nonsensical words seemed to hold meaning for everything else in the room but Anthony himself because all at once the very air seemed to hold still. The candles dimmed, and darkness flew in from nowhere to smother the room in a gloomy twilight. Chitinous noises echoed from every dark corner along with squeaks and squeals as rodents and other nocturnal scavengers crowded amid the shadows to form an invisible audience. Most disturbing was the sudden vigor that charged the pool of maggots in which Anthony lay. All at once the living tide of wriggling vermin surged. Anthony felt their hungry mouths feverishly pulling at his flesh as Mama Luanda's chanting filled the room with a mumbling litany of incoherent prayers and curses.

He could feel them working away at him . . . *in him!* He could feel their squishy writhing bodies crawling up his intestines. He could feel them in his chest cavity surrounding his heart and lungs, in his stomach, in his throat. He tried to scream, but it was too late. They had eaten away his voice box. Anthony thought he could feel the tiny worms eating away at the marrow in his bones. He knew the disease had not worked that deep. He wanted to tell Mama Luanda that she could stop. He wanted to tell her that the disease was gone, the maggots had done their job, but as he listened to her chanting and could finally make sense of the words, he realized he had made a grave mistake. She was not speaking any foreign or unknown tongue. She was speaking English. She was saying the same thing she had been saying the whole time.

"Moremaggotsneedmoreneedmoreneedmoremaggots!"

Sweat bulleted down her face, filling up her empty eye-socket until it spilled over and rained down her cheeks like tears. Her large misshapen lips quivered as if she were choked with sorrow, yet they were pulled back into an idiotic smile. She continued to dip her hands into the innards of the dead hog and retrieve more and more maggots from within its guts to dump into the tub with Anthony. There seemed to be no end to them.

"Moreneedmoremoremaggotsneedmoreneedmore!"

The woman was crazy, clearly insane. She may have once been a powerful healer, but now she was little more than a ranting lunatic. Anthony knew it, but he could not allow himself to believe it, especially now that there was nothing he could do about it. He had to have faith. Mama Luanda knew best. She would take care of him. She had always taken care of his people for as long as he could remember. Mama Luanda had been with the village for as long as anyone could remember. They had always had faith in her.

Anthony watched a long rope of saliva drool from one corner of her cracked lips. Her good eye darted about in her head focusing on nothing and everything. She continued to mumble and gibber, smiling and tossing in pieces of rotted hog guts with the fistfuls of maggots. Her dead eye seemed to swirl with shadows. Anthony could almost hear the terrified shrieks of every child who'd looked into that grotesque visage echo from within its depths. She looked as mindless and evil as one of those zombies he'd heard about in the myths and fairytales told around the island. Perhaps it was just senility or Alzheimer's. Anthony wondered again how she had managed to live so long. Maybe she *had* made herself into zombie. He began to panic. He had entrusted his life to a madwoman and now he was being eaten alive!

"Moremaggotsmoremaggotsmoremore MORE!"

Anthony closed his eyes and dreamed of sunlit beaches with chocolate-skinned beauties in string bikinis frolicking in the ocean. He dreamed of playing volleyball and hackeysack in the powder-soft sand. He dreamed of ripe mangoes and sweet pineapple. He dreamed of his mother's kitchen that always smelled of curry and marjoram. He tried to ignore the feeling of the maggots crawling into his skull. He had to live. His mother had sacrificed so much to get him out of Haiti, away from the poverty, and superstition, and death. He couldn't die like this. He had to believe. He had to have faith. Mama Luanda would take care of him. She would make him better.

Awake

"...With human nature caged in a narrow space, whipped daily into submission, how can we speak of its potentialities?"
—Emma Goldman, Anarchism

"What if God was one of us?"
—Joan Osborne, Relish

"Why?"

The reporter wasn't listening to me. He was scared to death. A minute ago he'd been sitting outside my cell with that smug self-assured look on his face, already counting all the money he'd make off my biography. Now he was inside my cell, naked, mute, wondering how I'd done it. Uselessly he tried to cry out for help. I watched his fat lips mouth words in silence like a guppy gasping for oxygen, panic bulging out his eyes in further imitation of marine life.

I didn't need him to be able to speak. I could do his end of the conversation anyway. Nothing original has come out of a human mouth in several decades. The prematurely balding, prematurely fat, young reporter jerked back as if hit by a taser when I reached out to hit the play button on the tape recorder in his pocket. I could see all the questions in his eyes. I would answer only the ones that I felt merited answering.

"I know that you'll call me a liar. You'll say that I'm in denial, that there are some deep-seated emotional issues from my childhood that I'm suppressing and not coming to grips with. But I swear that's how it all started. That one question started the cascade of events that led to me staring at you from behind bars, months away from my execution.

I know how you reporters think. You're thinking I must have been molested as a child, or my mother must have abused me, or withheld love from me, or my daddy must have taught me to hate women by abusing my mother in front of me. But none of that is true. I grew up in a very normal and loving environment.

Maybe you're thinking that there must have been drugs involved. But that would be wrong too and no, I don't hear voices or think I'm Jesus. I'm as sane as you are. So how could that one little question lead to me killing all those people? Raping and mutilating all those women? You can't see how easily "why?" becomes "why not?"

The killing was just me acting on instinct. I wanted to do it so I did it. But it's so much bigger than that. That was just the beginning. This is about unlocking the full potential of the human mind.

And it all began with that queer little man with all the PC slogans and buttons and pins all over his leather jacket. He stopped me on the street as I made my way through the midday crowds rushing to get to my favorite coffee shop with no more sinister intentions on my mind than the ingestion of a quick scone and a double cappuccino. I was dodging in and out between the other rush hour commuters and deftly avoiding the solicitors and panhandlers handing out flyers and begging for charity and donations when inevitably I ran right into one. I was trapped, blocked in on one side by a fat woman wolfing down a cream cheese bagel while trying to read the Wall Street Journal and on the other by a man handing out flyers for a strip club on Market Street called the "Hot Box." I had no choice but to deal with the little freak.

I usually would not have even thought to question him. I would have just handed him a dollar to get rid of him or ignored him entirely and kept walking right past. But one of the buttons pinned to his jacket stalled my forward momentum in one of those surreal moments that usually proceed from the use of hallucinogens, alcohol, or really good weed, none of which I had indulged in that day. It was just the absurdity of the moment that made me pause, staring at that big white button pinned to his lapel. The one that said: "Meat is murder."

I kept looking from that button to the leather jacket and the hypocrisy of it just had to be addressed before I could proceed any further. Did this effete little geek mean that it was a sin to eat a cow but not to slaughter and skin it for clothing? I wondered if he would really find life any less cruel if I were to kill him and skin him to make a pair of boots or a nice motorcycle jacket as long as I spared him the indignity of cannibalization?

I decided to just let it go and avoid debating with the anemic-looking little zealot. I sucked down my own outrage and prepared to skirt around him with nothing more anti-social than a disdainful sneer, when yet another propaganda pin caught my attention. It was one from some Pro-Choice organization that said "I fuck to cum not to conceive." I had never had a homosexual thought in my life until that moment. But once you eliminate the "Ought nots" and "Thou shalts," there was just no reason not to fuck that little geek in his ass. I wanted to prove his point.

He only had himself to blame. It was his inane question that started it all. That grimy bucket filled with fistfuls of change and crumpled dollar bills that he waved in my face as he solicited me for the most absurd reason imaginable.

"Donation to save the Liberty Bell?"

It was the first time I'd ever thought to ask "Why?" and the world changed for me immediately thereafter. After stopping the intrusion of that one false ideology with the simplest of all defenses, a lucid question, I immediately began to wonder how much additional mental refuse I might rid my mind of with the strength of that one question. How many ideas had I accepted simply because so many others had accepted it before me? If someone were to suggest to me that truth be decided by majority vote, I would surely have laughed in their face yet so much of my so-called knowledge I had acquired in this way. On the strength of the popularity of that belief rather than on a single reasonable argument or credible piece of evidence. And how many more had I acquired on mere faith in the authority of its proponents? My father is knowledgeable in a great many things but to take his word on the very nature of existence was surely a folly. How many more of my beliefs were merely cultural mores and traditions without even the most tenuous roots in fact? How many life altering convictions did I hold simply because my father held them and his father before him and his father before him?

I stood in the middle of the sidewalk, as the herd swirled around me, staring at the man with his silly little pamphlet, and immediately felt separated from everyone around me. They had their shells of willful and deliberate ignorance, belief without evidence, faith, like a blinding light shining in their eyes through which not a single counter argument could penetrate. And in the span of a few brief heartbeats, the time it took my lips to form that one destructive, liberating question, I had lost my shell, the light had ceased to shine in my eyes. I could see everything and it terrified me.

I was already weeding through my mind and severing beliefs with sharp blades of reason letting them spin off into the ether from whence they came. I was paralyzed, overwhelmed by the magnitude of the endeavor. My mind went through the vast storehouse of beliefs and convictions like a lawn mower and very few endured under its assault. I remembered reading Descartes in college. I recalled his formula for scientific reasoning, "Knowledge = certainty." Anything upon which doubt could be cast is not certain and therefore not knowledge. I found that almost everything could be questioned, doubted, argued against. Inevitably I came to the same impasse Descartes had reached "Cogito ergo sum." "I think therefore I am." My own existence was the only thing upon which I could be absolutely certain and not the existence of a single other person or thing.

From that fact came conclusions that assailed my very will to live. I found that all that I believed to be right and good with life rested on a foundation of hopes and fears, prejudice and fantasy. I was left standing there like an idiot repeating those few ideas that rose from the ashes of the rest.

"Nothing is forever. Nothing is guaranteed. So nothing is worth doing. But then . . . nothing is worth not doing. If nothing else existed but me, and even I was ephemeral, than all endeavors were utterly without purpose. Why should I restrain myself from anything if all actions are meaningless in the end? Why the fuck should I give a damn about saving a fucking Liberty Bell?!"

In the center of that bustling crowd of nine-to-fivers, rushing to scarf down their greasy, fat laden, fast food lunches before their breaks ended, I stood struck dumb by the force of my own skepticism. Suddenly, their every ridiculous movement became an intolerable affront to all that was reasonable.

"How could they continue that useless to and fro, that incessant struggle to acquire the commodities of this absurd existence?"

I could not find a reasonable argument for drawing the next breath and had it not been an automatic function I would surely have died of asphyxiation right there. It seemed that all man's endeavors led to the same end, annihilation so why should I do anything when the man who conquers the world suffers the same reward as the man who shuts himself away in his apartment and spends everyday in front of the television? When no matter what glorious chapters you write in the book of life, death existed as the period at the end of the sentence that not only concludes but erases all that has proceeded it? When your computer has no save button and the minute you cease your input, life will pull the plug and all your input will be deleted?

I felt the panic growing as the man asked me again:

"Donation to save the Liberty Bell?"

"Why the hell would I want to save the damned Liberty Bell?!"
It made absolutely no sense to me. It was one of those things we
did because we felt we ought to. I could barely find a reason to save
myself. And in that brief moment of lucidity "Why?" became "Why
not?"

The violent impulses that came boiling out of me were so
contrary to everything I'd ever permitted myself to feel before.
The sudden debilitating existential malaise that his ridiculous little
question had sucked me down into gave rise to a misanthropic
nihilism, a hatred for all things that lived and breathed under the
same absurd dichotomy. Fighting so dearly to hold on to a life that
is inevitably forfeit. I wanted to wake them all up. This little moron
with his pamphlets and fliers would be my first convert.

I was striking him before I'd even decided to do so. My fist
collided with his jaw with a wet meaty "Smack!" and his knees
wobbled but he did not fall. Disappointed but excited I threw a left
hook to his temple that made his eyes dance in his skull like pinballs.
He hit the concrete so hard his skull cracked and blood sprayed from
the wound like a fountain. Everyone tried their best not to notice
as I dragged him into an alley. When I started to rip off his clothes
there were a few mild protests but no one was willing to get involved
enough to try and stop me and risk being late to work. I heard a few
cell phones chime out the numbers 911 and urgent whispers try to
describe what I was doing to the unconscious activist while trying to
remember what street they were on.

I jerked off his underwear, ripping them in two and stared
at his dimpled ass cheeks. Then I grabbed them and spread them
wide revealing his puckered anus. There was nothing particularly
attractive about it. Still, I felt myself growing hard, urgently aroused
by the exotic prospect of doing the taboo right out there in the open
in front of a gaggle of awestruck witnesses. Besides, I'd entered far
less attractive orifices for the purpose of pleasure than this one. True,
they'd all been female, and this was a step in an entirely different

132

direction, but the little guy had a point with his moronic little slogans. "I fuck to cum not to conceive." So what did it matter if I fucked a girl or this little geek? I mean, why not?

I whipped out my cock and slathered it with saliva, then I spit on my thumb and slid it into the little guy's asshole. He was starting to regain consciousness and he winced at the intrusion. I withdrew my thumb, aimed my cock between his cheeks and prepared to ram it home as the crowd alternately cheered me on and condemned me. He woke up with a shriek just as the tip of my cock stretched his lower intestines.

His frantic struggle to escape, his screams and tears got me so hot that I shot my wad almost instantly. I could hear the sirens getting closer and I had my pants up and was sprinting through the alley hopping fences and leaving the little PC geek far behind before the first cop entered the alley.

I stopped to take a piss. Taking my cue from the cynics of old, who so shunned social mores that they were known to defecate in public, I dropped my pants in the middle of the street and relieved my bowels from both ends. Finding no reason not to, I left my pants and underwear there in the street as I walked away. The occasional cool breeze in this otherwise humid day tickled my testicles and put steel back in my erection. I walked down the street with it swaying in the breeze and drawing gasps of astonishment and scowls of revulsion. I watched with amusement as old ladies and young girls chided and cursed me or giggled and snickered as I walked past, offended or embarrassed by my brazen nudity.

I followed a young housewife all the way from the market, masturbating to the subtle bounce and sway of her voluptuous ass. Imagining ramming my swollen organ between those salacious buttocks as I feverishly stroked myself. Luckily for her, I reached orgasm before she made it to her house. I would be back for her though.

133

It was nearly dusk when I dragged myself home and lay down to rest. My mind was still mulling over all the beliefs and convictions that had so long fettered it and how endless the possibilities might be for me not that I was free of these restraints. I wondered if I could fly.

Now you will really think me mad but I sat there for hours dissecting all the reasons that kept me rooted to the earth and I found not one that seemed so terribly binding now. So I catalogued each argument against self-propelled flight one by one and tore those arguments to shreds. The first was my obvious lack of aerodynamics. But as Descartes had pointed out centuries before, all of my senses had been fooled before. I had seen things that appeared small from a distance that when viewed closer were obviously huge. I had thought I saw one person who turned out to be another. Had even seen things out of the corner of my eyes that were not there. I had thought I heard voices when no words were spoken. Even confused one smell for another. And how many times, in a state of dreaming, had I imagined sensations that had no external cause but yet radiated through my entire being as if I was truly falling, or taking punches, or getting a blow job from Madonna, or flying? All of my senses were open to the interpretation of my mind, which was not flawless. And according to my new way of thinking if it could be doubted, it was not certain, therefore not ultimately true. The entire shape of my body was open to debate. In fact the very existence of my body was debatable.

My mind could so expertly mimic external sensation as to trick me into believing I was having sex, even bringing me to the point of orgasm. So why would it be so far fetched as to imagine that all external and internal sensations were the product of the human mind and that no physical body truly existed? If I could fly in my dreams then why not while awake? And with that I left my body behind and was soaring.

I know I'm oversimplifying things. It wasn't just as simple as a thought becoming reality but then again it was. But first I had to convince myself of it completely. Still, after so recently convincing myself that there was no difference between the silky wet heaven between a woman's thigh's and the saggy, hairy, pimpled ass of a man, it was not as hard a task as you might imagine.

It wasn't like you read about in books. It wasn't levitation or astral projection. My body simply ceased to be. It became "spirit" for lack of a better word. My flesh atomized leaving only a disembodied consciousness adrift in the night air.

I landed in bedrooms and took entire families as they lay sleeping. I assaulted women in their apartments behind doors they believed were safely locked and secured. My world. My dream. And my will, I soon found, was nearly omnipotent.

Once I found out I could do that, well, the rampage began. See I ceased to believe in the existence of other consciousnesses. I ceased to believe that there was anything outside my own consciousness. I began testing a theory that everything in the world was a fabrication of my own mind. That everything existed only because I believed it did.

I tried it on things first. Making objects disappear. Mostly stoplights and street signs. Then I tried it on people. I made newscaster disappear off the television. I made police officers disappear off the corner. I changed fat girls into skinny girls, made flat-chested women voluptuous, and even added another six inches to my own cock. I turned my Honda into a Lexus and my apartment into a castle.

I can tell that I'm losing you but listen. If everything is just a dream and you suddenly realize it, if you are suddenly awake within the dream. There would be nothing that you couldn't do. And I was awake. I brought your ass into this cell didn't I?

The more convinced I became that I was the only consciousness in existence, The more havoc I wreaked. See, if everything is a dream then what reason would I have to respect the rights of these fantasy creatures? Why shouldn't I simply use them as I see fit and discard them when I grow bored with them like broken toys? That's when the rapes started. See, that little activist guy was all right, but I wanted more and better. So I started taking women and men anywhere and everywhere.

My little rape/murder spree baffled the police because there was no profile to my victims. I took them young, old, fat, skinny, white, black, male, female, attractive, or grotesquely ugly. See, I had the ability to make them into anything I wanted. By the time my hands closed around their throats, they all looked like Jessica Rabbit.

I raped a woman at the laundromat while waiting for my clothes to dry. I raped one in the dressing room at the mall. I made a mess of her. She's the first one that I cannibalized. If you see her, tell her I'm sorry. But you have no idea how sweet a woman's breasts taste or the tender flesh of her buttocks. To me everything tasted like pastry. I shouldn't have left her alive though. But I wasn't really concerned with what life would be like for her absent her breasts and much of her ass. She didn't really exist anyway. None of them did.

I started murdering not to cover my tracks or spare them from life as hideous mutilated freaks as some have suggested but because I wanted to see what else I could do with my new freedom. I fucked them alive. I fucked their corpses. I fucked them while they screamed and writhed in their death throes. Just to see what it felt like. Just to see what sex was like stripped of all moral restraints. I fucked mothers and daughters, sons and fathers. I ate them alive while thrusting my swollen cock into orifices I'd cut or chewed into them. I carved them up and made sculptures out of their flesh. I crawled inside their skin and tried to become them. I tried to marry their flesh with my own and share the experience of their pain and my own pleasure as one delirious sensation. I did it because I could; because it was my dream and I was the only thing in it that was real. I scoured humanity to find one other person that could resist my will leaving the carnage of my failed experiments in my wake.

See, I was getting lonely. If my consciousness alone existed in a vast vacuum filled only with phantasmagorical constructs plucked from my own imagination, then life was even more absurd than I had first supposed. I was killing in order to find someone who I could not kill. In the kingdom of the blind the one eyed man is not only king he is a species apart. If I was awake and conscious surely there must be others? But murder after murder, rape after rape, confirmed my isolation. I was soon convinced that there was no one else like me in the whole world; that there was no one but me in the whole world.

That's why I was so surprised when that detective stepped right into the middle of my dream.

I watched the news with the same skepticism with which I watched the screams of my victims. I knew that it was all in my head. So when I kept hearing stories about this square jawed, broad shouldered, leading man type Lead Detective who'd been assigned to the case, closing in on the "Werewolf of Main Street" as the press had dubbed me, I paid it hardly any attention at all. His name was John Malice and he looked so much like a comic book or action movie hero that I immediately dismissed him as an errant fantasy; a figment of my imagination. I thought it was just my mind trying to find a new way to keep me amused. See, even in my new state of lucidity it was easy to slip back into the habitual dream-state in which the rest of humanity walked. It required constant vigilance to remember that it was all bullshit. So I didn't trip when I saw the police canvassing the neighborhood with my picture. I turned them into birds and monkeys. And watched them flutter and scamper madly from house to house. When Detective Malice knocked on my door I tried to wipe him out entirely, imagining empty space where he once stood. But the knocking persisted. This illusion had more substance than the rest and required a more direct approach. I grabbed the Boy Scout hatchet I'd used on the old lady at the 7-Eleven whose murder the detective was no doubt investigating. I opened the door and tried to drive it straight through his skull. I was damned surprised when the bullets slammed into my chest. I willed the guns to turn to roses but still the bullets came, flying faster than I could see.

The only thing that made sense was that somehow I had encountered another consciousness. Detective John Malice must have been a real person rather than another dream created in my mind. There went the entire theory of monotheism.

I rambled on for the better part of an hour before finally allowing the reporter to speak. I knew what he wanted to ask. Naturally all his responses where predictable.

"So what about me?"

"You mean are you real? Are you a figment of my imagination?" I smirked at him. I knew that I was about to rock his whole fucking world!

"You are what I make you." My smile broadened. I didn't know why these types of tricks still amused me. Perhaps it was because I had discovered that my dream people seemed to have autonomous wills and self-awareness. They believed themselves to be alive. I got a kick out of showing them the face of their creator. I loved the look in their eyes when they realized that the author of their existence was this innocuous looking "Joe Average" type guy who they would never have looked twice at if he hadn't been convicted of killing thirty or forty people.

He knew I was about to do something terrible to him. He started trying to scream again, so once again I took away his larynx. He knew that I could do anything I wanted to him, just as earlier I had reached out with my mind and made his flesh run like syrup. A liquid that dripped from his stool, onto the floor, and then right into the cell with me. I now began twisting and reshaping his meat and bones like clay as he struggled to scream.

I reassembled him (minus vocal chords) and watched as his eyes bulged with fear and he turned to bang on the locked cell door, realizing at last what all the rest had finally figured out just before they died, that everything I'd said was true.

I began slowly pulling him apart. When I was done I put him back together and then ripped him apart again. This time I allowed him to scream. His shrill cries of agony filled the isolation ward. I could hear the other inmates weeping in their cells. They knew what he was going through.

He collapsed into a fit of blubbering tears as he realized that the guards were not coming to help him. They would not come unless I wanted them to. I raped and mutilated him a dozen times as the day passed into night, stopping to put his mind back together nearly as often as I had to reassemble his flesh. When I grew tired of hearing him scream I silenced him once again. I was almost done with him and there were no more tapes for the recorder. There was enough on there now to keep the world guessing for several centuries.

The reporter was still whimpering and crying in silence as I pulled his intestines out through his asshole. He mouthed an exclamation that appeared to be the word "God!" I smiled, considering that an acknowledgement that he'd finally realized just whom he was dealing with.

A Friend In Need

The ground shook as something immense galloped through the darkness, rustling the bushes and knocking over trashcans. Car alarms went off as it passed and dogs yelped and growled, straining on their leashes to attack the gigantic beast they could sense but not see. Walker gasped and picked up his pace. He was almost running when he crossed Germantown Avenue. He turned and looked behind him in time to see a large hairy bear-like shape lumber out of the shadows and run in a loping gait between streetlights. Sharp fangs caught the moonlight and gleamed yellow and fearsome. Walker's heart thundered in his chest.

"My God! What the hell is that thing?"

Whatever it was it had slipped back into the shadows, yet it was still coming, steadily gaining on him. He could hear heavy footsteps behind him in the darkness. Hot, raspy panting breaths steamed on the back of his neck raising the hairs along his spine. It was that close. So close that if he stopped for a second it would overcome him. Still, he had no idea what it was, why it was after him, or what it would do to him if it caught him.

Rumbling grunts and growls weakened his knees with fear. The creature's murderous hunger was evident in its voice and its breath that stank of fetid meat and blood. Walker picked up his pace, resisting the urge to break out in an all-out sprint as the thing struggled to keep up with him, to overtake him. Repeatedly casting nervous glances over his shoulder he hugged the bleeding abdominal wound where the thing had already attacked him, holding his intestines in place as he jogged down the street trailing blood. Every shadow seemed pregnant with menace. A violent death seemed to wait for him in every darkened corner. The night was charged with a palpable hostility. He turned onto Duval Street and started back into his old neighborhood. It looked far worse than he remembered it.

The streets were forbiddingly dark and desolate. Tenebrous shadows knitted together into solid walls of night that stretched down the gloomy streets for block after block. The entire neighborhood appeared to be one great desert of midnight, inhabited only by decaying brick and stucco buildings and the rusting husks of late model cars. Walker wasn't fooled though. He could hear furtive whispers coming from the alleyways and see the dim flicker of disposable lighters as crack fiends and hypes lit their pipes and heated their spoons amid the shadows. Off in the distance gunshots rang out and rap music blared from a car stereo passing by a block or two over. He could hear heated arguments coming from behind the walls of one of the dilapidated, pre-Civil War row homes lining the somber street, followed by the smack and thud of bare knuckles striking bare flesh and heartbroken tears. From other houses he heard the gruff panting and low sultry moaning of entwined impassioned lovers. The eerie blue flicker of television sets, left on long after their owners had fallen asleep, cast odd shadows behind darkened windows along with the canned laughter of late-night sitcoms. The night seethed with unseen life.

Walker could still hear the thing behind him. He whirled, ready to defend himself, as he felt something rapidly rushing toward him through the darkness. A pimp in a white Mercedes cruised past him with his headlights off. Looking for one of his whores no doubt. He waved at Walker as he went by. Walker had gone to elementary school with the guy. The neighborhood hadn't changed much.

A withered young crack whore stumbled out of the alley closest to him with her eyes glazed in a narcotic rapture. She smiled at him revealing prematurely rotten teeth and mechanically pulled up her skirt and shook her still remarkably firm and plump ass at him while licking her full but chapped and cracked lips. For all the deterioration evident in the rest of her body, her ass was still a marvel of nature. A hunger began to rise in Walker and the young streetwalker noticed it and sensed opportunity.

"Want some pussy, Daddy? Give me some money, honey. Mama'll take care of you."

She looked like she needed a mama to take care of her. Despite the ravages of drug abuse, which had leeched the youth from her flesh, it was still obvious that she was no older than fifteen.

"You don't want none of this girl." He pulled his lips back away from his grotesquely distended saber-like canines and growled low in his throat. She rolled her eyes at him and flipped him her middle finger.

"Well, fuck you too nigga!" She wiggled her strangely appetizing ass at him again and slipped back into the alley.

Walker shook his head and snickered, amazed at her brazenness and absolute lack of fear. He considered following her for a moment and then reminded himself what the rest of her body had looked like, shuddered and continued down the street. It wasn't disease he was afraid of; it was what he would think of himself when it was over, and how difficult it would be to get the stench of her off of him. Besides, whatever it was that was tailing him was closer now. Walker imagined that he could feel its steaming breath on the back of his neck. Walker buttoned his jacket over his bleeding stomach and sped up again, now running through the night putting more distance between him and whatever dark hairy thing hunted him in the shadows. His breath grew laborious as panic crushed down on him, cramping his lungs. He looked back and caught a brief flash of cold silvery eyes, teeth, and claws glinting in the moonlight.

Walker turned another dark corner and saw the normal gang of hoodlums congregating on the corner outside the liquor store. He recognized several of them from ten years ago. There were some new, younger faces interspersed with the old. The next generation of the lost and desperate. Tank and Boom, two homies he'd grown up with back in the day, recognized him immediately as he emerged from the shadows into the glare of the overhead streetlight. They smiled and walked/staggered toward him. They were drunk and high but Walker knew they were still dangerous . . . to anyone but him.

"Walker? My Brotha! Where the hell have you been? Man, I ain't seen you since high school!" Tank bellowed as he swaggered his hulking body over to give Walker a big hug and pat him on the back with his big paddle like hands.

"I heard you got shot!" Boom added, as he hung back eyeing him warily with both his hands tucked inside his jacket pockets. He didn't offer to shake hands or so much as wave. No doubt he had a pistol in one pocket and three or four dozen vials of crack in the other.

"Naw, I heard he was locked down. What did they get you for? Slangin' or bangin'?" Tank asked.

"They couldn't catch me if they wanted to. But I gotta keep moving. I'll peep you brothas later."

"Yeah, later." Boom replied, still eyeing him suspiciously. Walker wondered if years of dodging cops and bullets, living on the edge, had honed Boom's survival skills to the point where he could sense the mortal threat that Walker represented. Either that or it was just paranoia brought on by too much cocaine use.

Walker continued down the street, nervously eyeing every shadow just as he'd done when he'd walked these streets as a teenager. Only now he was not looking out for muggers or rival gang-bangers. He was looking out for a monster. A monster who'd been tracking him for days. Who was very near catching him.

Walker turned as screams echoed from the direction he'd just come from. He heard Boom cry out, a blast of gunfire, followed by the unmistakable sound of tearing flesh and snapping bone.

"Oh, Shit! Hellllp! Oh my God! No! Nooooo!!!" Walker had never heard Tank scream before and he'd seen the tremendous thug take eight rounds from an Uzi. There was a flurry of activity back up on the corner, muzzle flashes as an automatic pistol unloaded an entire clip in every direction, limbs being torn free of torsos and tossed into the air, and blood, blood everywhere. That thing had just torn two of the toughest thugs in the hood apart in a matter of seconds. Walker knew that he had to see his friend before, whatever that thing was, caught up with him. He had to get help.

He sprinted the remaining block to the street he'd grown up on, walked up onto a rickety old porch and knocked on his friend's door. Then he winced in pain when the door swung open and the wooden stake slammed into his chest.

"Man, what the fuck are you doing? That shit hurt!"

Jerry continued to stab Walker in the heart with the sharpened chair leg over and over again making only minor flesh wounds that just barely punctured the skin and the first few layers of muscle tissue.

"Fuck! Man, cut that out Jerry! Damn!" He smacked the stake from his friend's hand and grabbed his chest, wincing in pain. Walker leaned back against the porch railing and clamped a hand over his friend's arm preventing him from fleeing

"First off, you can't just jam a stake through a vampire's chest with your bare hands you need to hammer it in. There are layers of fat, and muscle, and a goddamned ribcage to get through for Christ's sake! Second of all, that wouldn't kill him anyway. That's movie shit. The whole point of the stake is to nail the vampire to his coffin so he can't rise at night to hunt and he'll just starve to death in his grave. Stabbing one with a stake when he's up and walking around wouldn't do shit but piss him off! Oh, and third, and most important, I'm not a fucking vampire!"

"Then what the hell are you then? 'Cause you damn sure ain't Walker! Walker wouldn't have tried to eat me!" Jerry was not just afraid he was seething with rage. This man who he had once considered his closest friend, part of the family, had tried to kill him. He wanted to see the man dead.

Jerry had always been the baddest mutherfucker on the streets. It was a title he wore with pride. His body count would have put him up there with Ted Bundy and Henry Lee Lucas if it had been known. But the streets held their secrets well. He'd only had to torture and mutilate the elderly parents of one young homie who'd witnessed him murder a rival drug dealer and was preparing to testify against him, to persuade anyone else from ever stepping forward. On these streets, he was the most dangerous thing alive. He was the boogie-man whose name children woke up screaming at night. He was the reason men and women alike stayed off the streets past midnight. When people in G-town imagined death it didn't wear a black cowl and carry a sickle. It wore FUBU and Nike and carried a Tech nine-millimeter automatic assault rifle. But, ever since the night when he'd stared down his friend's throat as he lunged at him with fangs straining for his throat, he'd not felt right carrying the title. He felt like a fake.

Nearly all the violence he'd done in the last decade had been to over-compensate for that one humiliation; that one moment of weakness. There was something out there tougher, meaner, and more terrible than him. Something that had caused him to scream like a bitch and plead for his life. Something that was now standing on his porch wearing the face of his long-time boyhood friend.

"Man, I told you I was sorry about that. That was my bad. I didn't know what I was doing."

"Sorry? My bad? You tried to eat me, bro! You can't just say sorry for some shit like that!" Jerry's body was vibrating with fury. He wished he had his gun. He would've split Walker's wig right there on his front porch, parole or no parole. The man was some type of monster and not the everyday type the violence and hopeless poverty of the ghetto normally produced. He was not the type of monster that Jerry was. He was a *real* monster.

"So what do you want me to do? Suck your dick? Man, it's been ten years. Let it go bro."

Jerry stared at him for a long moment. Then shook his head in incredulous amusement.

"If I shake your hand, you won't try and eat it will you?"

"Come on, man." Walker held out his arms with an innocent smile etched onto his hardened features.

The two men embraced and Jerry invited him inside. Walker took one last look around before he stepped into the house. For a second he thought he saw a large shadow moving toward them from down the block. All the lights on this block were out and the entire street was enveloped in a deadly, sinister darkness; the kind that incubated crime. Walker could not see through the gloom but he could hear and he could smell. Heavy, rumbling, breathing, like the contented purr of a full grown lion with its belly full of antelope, and a wild animal musk heavy with the scent of blood, came wafting up the street toward him, drowning his senses with the threat of violence. He had little time. He locked Jerry's front door behind him, noting its solid steel construction as he slid the deadbolt into place. It was a dope-dealer's door. No reason to have a door like that in the ghetto unless you had a stash to protect. He saw Jerry glance nervously at him when he slid the chain over the door.

"Relax, bro. I just don't want us interrupted."

The two of them sat down on the tattered old sofa and quietly appraised each other. Jerry was tall, lean, and muscular. He looked sort of like a young Muhammed Ali. Walker was slightly smaller with thicker muscles like a bodybuilder. His skin was not just black it was the total absence of light. He seemed to be spawning shadows from his pores as he sat there in the dim light of the coffee table lamp.

"You look good, Jerry." Walker commented and then he noticed the young girl, naked and bleeding, bound with duck tape, and rolling around on the kitchen floor.

"Who the fuck is that? What are you doing to her?"

"Just some crack whore who owes me money. I'm taking it out on her ass. Got tired of raping her, so now I'm just torturing the bitch."

146

Walker stared into the kitchen as the battered and abused girl turned her eyes on him and began to wiggle and squirm energetically. Her eyes were pleading with him. Walker felt his hunger start to rise. The girl looked like she was just barely in her teens.

"You hungry, Bro? Have a bite on me." Jerry said as he gestured toward his suffering captive. He watched as Walker began to literally drool and his eyes glazed over with a murderous, carnivorous, lust. "What the hell are you man?"

Walker tore his eyes away from the helpless female with a concerted effort. He was hungry; maddeningly hungry. It was getting harder and harder for him to go on without feeding. "I'm a werewolf." He said.

"Damn! You serious? You just say that like it's no big deal. Like you just announced you were a dogcatcher or a postman or something. A werewolf? Damn! That's deep."

"I need your help, bro."

"My help? Man, last time I seen you, you had your fangs bared and you were coming for my throat! Now you want me to help you?"

"Something's after me."

"What? What's after you?"

"Hell, I don't know. Something. Something bigger than a werewolf. Bigger and meaner. It attacked me in the dark three nights ago when I was . . . uh . . . eating. It jumped out at me and slashed me across the stomach. I thought it was just another werewolf trying to steal my kill. But then, when I looked at the wound it left . . ." Walker opened his jacket and raised his shirt revealing his ruined torso where nearly all the flesh had been torn off. You could see his lower intestines through the gaping holes in his skin.

"Jesus Christ! Man, how can you walk around like that?"

"It hurts like hell, trust. Damn thing almost ripped me in two with one swipe from its paw! I ain't never seen a werewolf that could do that. Besides, the thing was like twice my size and I ain't no little dude. I ran out of there as fast as I could and I thought that was it. But then the thing just kept following me. So I thought maybe I should get someone to help watch my back and you're the only friend I've got. I can never see it, but I can smell it. I haven't been able to hunt or nothing. I can't let my guard down."

"You have no idea what this thing is?"

"I think it's an Isawiyya."

"A what?!"

"An Isawiyya. It's this sect of Moslems from North Africa called the Isawiyya. They worship this prophet from the sixteenth century named Ibn Isa. He was a fanatically devout Moslem who was supposed to have been given the ability by Allah to take on the forms of animals. He could become anything from a bull to a snake and even combinations of animal forms. He did this by consuming them during a frenzied prayer ritual. He used his powers to fight enemies of Allah. His followers tried to continue in his footsteps, but couldn't mimic his abilities, despite all their prayers and sacrificing and shit. Until they discovered us . . . werewolves. They began hunting us and consuming us to acquire our abilities. Nearly wiped us all out."

"And that's what you think is after you? One of these Isawiyya dudes?"

"It's the only thing I can think of."

Jerry stood up and paced back and forth. He wiped a bead of sweat from his brow and shook his head, staring at Walker. Then he started to pace again.

"Bro, I'm sorry, but this is all too deep for me. How the hell did you become a damn werewolf anyway? Did you get bit or something?"

"You don't become a werewolf. You're born that way. See, we ain't really human. Not completely. We've just evolved to mimic our prey. The smarter man got the smarter and more human we became in order to fool him. To allow us to get close enough to strike. What? You think that every creature on this planet has a predator except man? That's the kind of arrogance and skepticism that's made it easier for us to walk among you."

"Then, if you ain't human, how can you call yourself my friend? What am I like a pet pig? You play with it for years, but if you ever get hungry . . . my ass is pork chops! Is that it, bro?"

"Naw, man. It ain't like that. I'd never eat you. Werewolves have evolved to resemble humans so closely that it's hard not to almost relate to you like we were the same species. Man, that shit that happened between us . . . I was all messed up. You don't know what puberty is like for a werewolf. I was having a hard time controlling the hunger. Then that idiot Boom gave me some weed with some angel dust in it. That shit had me trippin'. That's the only reason I attacked you back then. I was just trippin'! So, is you gonna help me or what?"

"So, you tellin' me that there's something out there, an Isawiyya or whatever, that's got your big, bad, werewolf ass so scared that you come to me for help? And what the hell do you think I can do for you?"

"I may be a werewolf but you're a stone-cold killer! You've been in and out of jail since I've known you. You probably killed more people than any brotha on the streets besides me."

"Never convicted though. So what you gettin' at?"

"I want you to take all those guns I know you got piled up in your closet and go out there and smoke that damn thing!"

Something heavy struck the steel door and almost took the entire thing out of the frame. There was a snarling and growling that sounded as if all the hordes of hell were amassed on Jerry's front porch. Jerry leaped from the couch and stared at the front door with his eyes wild with fear.

"Naw. Hell naw! I ain't going out there!"

"Well bro," Walker's entire body began to undulate as his muscles reshaped themselves and bones shifted around beneath his skin. There was a wet crackling and popping as his body metamorphosed. "It's either go out there with that thing . . ." His nose and jaw elongated into a snout and his already distended canines grew to grotesquely exaggerated proportion. His body was now that of an enormous wolf, with six inch fangs that looked almost pre-historic, and strangely anthropoid hands with opposable thumbs and all. It was a monster. ". . . or you can stay in here with me!"

Jerry turned and ran for the closet, for his guns. Walker turned and charged after him. That's when the door exploded and a beast the size of a small car roared into the house. It caught Walker in its slavering jaws just as he'd sprung forward to attack Jerry. Jerry turned and stared in horror as this terrible creature, which looked like some horrible combination of a bear, a lion, and a man, tore into Walker.

Walker fought back, but there was no chance. The beast's fangs ripped into him, tearing out huge chunks of flesh and swallowing them whole. There was a loud "Crack!" as the thing's massive jaws and tusk-like canines clamped down on Walker's arms, grinding them to mulch and preventing further resistance. Its claws rent through his skin and muscle tissue, slicing Walker to vibrant red ribbons. Walker was still futilely struggling as the monster burrowed its snout into his abdomen and disemboweled him; tearing out his stomach and intestines and greedily consuming them. Then it used its monstrous claws to crack open his ribcage and devour Walker's still beating heart. While the thing was still distracted by its meal, Jerry opened his closet and pulled out his Mac-10 automatic rifle.

The creature was busy licking out the inside of Walker's chest-cavity when it heard the click of a Banana clip being jammed into the Mac-10. It turned to look directly into Jerry's eyes with its mouth still encrusted with blood and bits of flesh and gore. Its tremendous head reminded Jerry of some combination of a saber-toothed tiger and an ox. Except its eyes, which burned with a dark and terrible intelligence. Its arms and hands looked almost human, just as Walker's had before this thing had eaten them. Jerry's mouth dropped as the creature's features began to shift and reform.

As Jerry cocked his weapon, the creature shed its grotesque form in favor of something softer, and more delicate. A woman. Naked. Gorgeous. Black as half past midnight. Standing in Jerry's living room still chewing on the remains of his boyhood friend.

"Praise Allah." She said wiping the gore from her chin.

"What the hell are you?"

"Don't worry. I'm not going to hurt you. We don't hunt humans, only werewolves. Arrogant bastards. They actually believe that every creature on this planet has a natural predator except them. That's what makes them so easy to hunt."

"You're one of those Isawiyya huh?"

She nodded.

"You eat werewolves? That's how you're able to turn into that big ass monster?"

She nodded again.

"So that's why you were chasing Walker? So you could eat him."

She looked down at Walker's gutted corpse and hunger gleamed in her eyes. She turned back toward Jerry and nodded again.

Jerry stared at the thing/woman and felt a pang of sorrow go through him at the loss of his friend. He'd known Walker since kindergarten. At least he thought he'd known him. The woman smiled and started to reach down for another piece of Walker. Jerry pulled the trigger. He unloaded an entire clip into the thing, loaded another clip, and emptied that one too. The woman tried to transform as the swarm of full metal jackets ripped through her. She danced on the end of the stream of gunfire as it ripped her to shreds, tearing her skull apart and gouging huge avulsions in her chest and stomach. What remained of her body dropped in a heap at Jerry's feet.

He stared at both her corpse and Walker's. Then he looked over toward the gaping hole where his front door had been and out into the night. It somehow seemed darker out there now; more forbidding and mysterious. There were terrible, powerful things out there, a myriad of life forms in bizarre shapes that he could scarcely imagine.

They were out there, hunting, killing, fighting battles that had gone on for countless aeons. Jerry smiled and ejected the last round from the Mac-10.

He had witnessed monstrous acts all of his life and committed a fair share of them himself. It made sense to him that these monsters should wind up on his doorstep. Trouble had always sought him out and he had welcomed it. He had made tragedy, death, and destruction a part of him. It was almost comforting to know that he was not the only monster out there. These creatures had raised the bar. They represented a challenge. Whoever wanted to own the night had to be more ruthless than a werewolf, a vampire, and whatever the hell that other thing was.

He walked over to where the two creatures's vandalized corpses lay bleeding and knelt down to search the pockets of Walker's tattered clothing, hoping to find drugs or money. His eyes roamed the ruination the machine gun had made of the woman and spotted one flawless, untouched breast. He reached out and softly caressed it then he gripped the nipple between his fingers and gave it a sharp pinch. He felt a peculiar arousal ripple through his loins. He started to drool with a hunger very different from what this dead creature had felt or even what Walker must have known. His was more carnal, more perverse. He stood up and walked into the kitchen where the young girl still lay on the linoleum floor, bound and helpless, nearly beyond panic after witnessing the carnage that had taken place in the living room.

Jerry removed a knife from the sink and knelt down to satiate his hunger on her quivering flesh. As he made the first cut, thinly slicing through the smooth dark skin of her buttocks, he wondered what appetites drove monsters like Walker. He wondered what allure the taste of human flesh held. He decided to find out. He cut himself a particularly appetizing morsel and sat down to feed. Then he looked back at Walker and the Isawiyya remembering what Walker had said about them eating werewolves to acquire their power. He began slicing off pieces of them as well.

My Very Own

I'd been alone my entire life. That's why I started the "experiments." I wanted someone who would never leave me, never say cruel or hurtful things, never die. Someone I could love forever. That's how it started anyway. I was just tired of the loneliness.

I don't really remember my father. I remember my mother screaming when he used to beat her. I remember a few of the beatings he gave me. I can remember the brown leather belt he used to crack across my thighs and back, better than I can my own father's face. He left before I was five years old. After that my mother left me every night.

Sometimes she came back with strange men who made her scream and moan behind her locked bedroom door. I didn't know what they were doing but it scared me. Mom called it "paying the rent" and she always seemed to have money once the moaning and grunting was over, but sometimes she had cuts and bruises too. Just like when Dad used to make her scream. I would sit up in my bed crying and yelling for them to stop. If I yelled too loudly Mom would come in and slap me around. Sometimes the men would hit me too. But sometimes they would leave, and for awhile it would be just Mom and I, then she would go back out to find another man.

Sometimes, she didn't come back for days. One day, she didn't come back at all. I waited for her for weeks in the dark, musty, old, apartment. I wasn't allowed to leave. Mom never let me leave the apartment. Not to play with other kids, not to go to school, not even to go with her to the store and help her carry groceries. It was like I was her little secret that she kept from the rest of the world. It made me feel special, but it increased my loneliness when she wasn't around. The apartment would start to contract and expand. Sometimes it was the size of a cathedral, filled with creaks, and moans, and phantom footsteps; dark shadows that crept stealthily through the gloom. At other times it was no bigger than a casket, closing in around me, dark as a tomb, burying me alive. Those were the times when I cried the most, when the fear would suffocate me, crushing down upon me from all sides; each breath feeling like it was just barely squeezing out of my cramped lungs.

I rationed out the meager amount of food Mom had left in the refrigerator, making it last a whole week. I ate one slice of bologna, a spoonful of peanut butter, and one slice of bread with butter, or ketchup, or mustard on it, everyday 'til it ran out. The second week I ate cat food. The third week I ate the cat. It was starving to death anyway and I didn't want to have to compete with it for the rats. If Mom didn't come home soon, they would've been next.

On the fourth week the police came to get me. They'd finally identified my mother's body and called my grandmother who told them about me. I was almost starved to death when they found me. The hunger had nearly driven me insane. I think I tried to bite the first cop who approached me. Then they told me about Mom and I fell into one of the police officer's arms, my body racked with tears.

Mom, or rather parts of her, had been found in an empty lot by Sandhill and Pecos Streets. There was evidence of torture and she had been dismembered. Only her head and torso had been found and they were in pretty bad shape. The rats had left her unrecognizable. She had been dead for nearly three weeks. The cops took me to live with Grandma. I spent nights awake wondering where Mom had been that first week; why she had left me.

Grandma was a very strict and religious woman. We went to church everyday, said prayers at every meal, and again at night. She put me into school for the first time and tutored me at home to help me catch up. There was always food in the refrigerator, and Grandma cooked dinner every night, and breakfast every morning. Most importantly she was always there. She never left; never brought men home, and only beat me when I really deserved it. I loved Grandma, even if I hated church.

Grandma was very sick. All that praying it was no wonder God was so eager to take her to heaven with him. Mom had never prayed. She said it was just asking for trouble. She used to say that the trick was to keep very quiet, especially when you passed a church, try to escape God's notice. Maybe, if you were lucky, he'd forget all about you and you could live forever. She should have told Grandma that. It seemed like Grandma was constantly going to the doctor's office, and she had an entire pharmacy of pills that she used to combat a plethora of illnesses. God was eager to bring her home to him. When I was seventeen he finally did.

Somehow she'd managed to hold on for all those years, pumping herself full of medications, always seeming just on the brink of death. I think she held on so long just to raise me; just 'til she was sure I could take care of myself. But then, I guess she decided that I was big enough to look after myself, and that God needed her more, so she let him take her. I was all alone then. That's when the experiments started.

Grandma was my first attempt to revive the dead. I pumped her full of nearly every medication in both medicine cabinets but nothing worked. I gave it a week before I notified anyone of her death. By the end of the week I still hadn't succeeded in reviving her, and she was starting to smell, so I let them take her. Since I was almost eighteen, they decided not to ship me off to Michigan to live with an Aunt and Uncle, whom I'd never met, and who seemed hesitant to take on a tragic charity case they knew nothing about. So I stayed in Grandma's house alone and got a job at the Pharmacy down the street, where Grandma used to go to get her prescriptions filled. They felt sorry for me and were eager to help me out. I just wanted easy access to the chemicals. I had already decided what I needed to do. I had to make a friend who wouldn't leave, wouldn't hurt me, and wouldn't die.

I read about how Jeffrey Dahmer had tried to make a zombie, and thought that maybe I could do it. I stopped praying and started going out every night, getting drunk, and picking up women for the experiments.

It was easy to pick up prostitutes. They are everywhere in Vegas. I would walk all the way from Twain and Sandhill where I lived, to the old derelict end of the strip where the whores were. I would offer them money and then catch a cab with them back to my house. They looked like zombies anyway. I thought it would be easy to turn one of them into an undead. But it was hard and frustrating.

First, I tried the Dahmer approach. I found a drugged out, emaciated, crack whore, on a side street, right around the corner from one of the "classy" strip joints, and offered her fifty dollars to come back to my house. I don't think she heard anything but the dollar amount. I probably could have told her everything and she would have still come, as long as I was willing to pay in advance. I drilled a hole in her head and poured "Liquid Drano" inside. It worked for awhile, and then she started screaming and died writhing in agony. Again, I spent a week trying to revive her, before I buried her in the same lot where they'd found Mom. I buried her deep, so that the rats wouldn't get to her.

The next girl I found was a bit healthier. I was hoping that that would increase her survival chances. She was tall, with long muscular legs, and pornographically large silicone breasts. Her hair was some chemical combination of blonde and red. She had a healthy glow to her skin, even though she still had a vacant look in her eyes, which may have come from either drug use or just the normal rigors of her profession. Her eyes never truly focused on me, but seemed to be looking through me at some horror from her past. She dragged the corners of her lips up into a smile, as she quoted her prices, along with some pre-rehearsed seductions. Every once in a while, her eyes would manage to focus on me, the pupils narrowing to capture my image, before her irises swam off again, going blank. It could have been shock.

Her name was Candy, or so she said. She agreed to go home with me, but it would cost me one hundred dollars. She said that, that would only pay for oral sex, or intercourse, but not both. I said I'd wait 'til we got to the house to decide which one I wanted.

When we got back to my house, she fought like a tiger while I struggled to clamp the chloroform soaked rag over her face. I had bruises and scratches on my face, arms, and hands, when she finally succumbed.

I used my new Black and Decker power drill, with the hammer drill setting, to drill through her skull. This time I poured formaldehyde I'd ordered over the Internet at work, into the hole; filling up her brain cavity until it started to pour back out. I figured the formaldehyde would preserve her and make her last forever. She screamed even louder than the girl who I'd injected with Drano had. Her body convulsed violently, arching and bucking like a crazed bull trying to toss off a cowboy. Her limbs were spasmodically contorting; joints twisting painfully, threatening to snap. The extreme pain reflected in her eyes was horrible as the formaldehyde ate away at her brain. Who would have thought the stuff was corrosive.

A red sludge began oozing from her ears, nostrils, and the neat little hole I'd drilled in her skull, along with the horrible stench of formaldehyde and liquefied flesh. It took her quite a while to finally die. I opened all the windows to let out the noxious odors escaping from her vandalized corpse. That one freaked me out. It was almost a month before I tried again. The house still smelled like formaldehyde, no matter how much Lysol I sprayed.

I'd heard somewhere that the street name for phencyclidine, or PCP, was embalming fluid, so I decided to try that next. I logged onto the computer at work and ordered a fairly large shipment of phencyclidine, using the doctor's name. When it came in, I snuck it out before anyone noticed it.

Once I had the drug, I couldn't wait to try it. The loneliness had grown unbearable since Grandma's death, and each failure made me more desperate to have my zombie. Once again, I wandered Vegas Blvd, down by the Stratosphere Hotel, looking for whores. I walked past all the drive through wedding chapels and run down motels, to where the strip clubs and adult bookstores were. That's where most of the affordable street prostitutes 'plied their trade.

A bus pulled up alongside me, as I strode quickly down the Blvd. A small, frail-looking, young girl, in a T-shirt and sweatpants, stepped out of the bus carrying a backpack and glancing nervously from side to side, as she briskly walked off down the street in the direction of the strip clubs. Even through her sweatpants and baggy T-shirt, it was obvious that she had a remarkable body. Still, I would've never guessed her to be a stripper. Then again, why else would a girl have been down there at that hour of the night? Only strippers and prostitutes, and the men who helped them "pay the rent", came down there at that hour. Mom had often said, that the only things open on that end of the city past midnight were legs.

The girl kept looking back over her shoulder, casting nervous glances at me, as she strode purposefully toward her destination. She looked familiar. I'd seen her down there before. Suddenly she turned, with one hand on her hip, and the other one in her backpack, which I assumed, contained either pepper-spray or a gun. She removed her hand from her hip, and wagged a long painted nail at me, sneering contemptuously.

"Are you following me mutherfucker?" The curse words came uncomfortably off her tongue. She was obviously not accustomed to having to sound tough.

"Uh . . . oh . . . no. No, I'm not following you. I'm just going to the club." I had no idea which club I was referring to, and I hoped she wouldn't ask. I looked down at my feet and shuffled nervously from one foot to the other. My obvious painful shyness seemed to convince her that I was harmless. She slowly took her hand out of her backpack and slung it back over her shoulder.

"I've seen you down here before haven't I? I've never seen you at the club though." She stared at me for a moment longer before seeming to make up her mind about something. "Look, I'm sorry I jumped on you like that, but some guy tried to attack me down here last week. You can never be too careful you know?"

"Sure." I offered, still nervous and uncomfortable.

"If you're going that way, then why don't you walk with me? So I can protect you." She laughed.

"Sure." I repeated, giving up on finding anything wittier to say.

"You don't have a girlfriend huh?"

"Uh . . . no."

"Are you down here a lot?"

"Yeah."

"Well, if you walk me to the club whenever you see me down here, I'll give you a free lap dance whenever you come to the club. I usually get off the bus around 1:00 am. I work the morning shift. So are you up to it stallion?"

"Uh . . . sure. Okay."

"My name is Sissy by the way."

"Uh, um. My name is John."

I walked her to the club, collected my lap dance, and left feeling desperately aroused and embarrassed. I picked up another prostitute on the way home, and this time I had sex with her after I chloroformed her, but before I drilled a hole in her head. The PCP had an interesting affect. I dumped enough of the stuff into her skull to get half the whores in town high.

The prostitute, who's name was also Candy, (Imagine that. Is there any other name that prostitutes ever go by?) staggered around the apartment, babbling to herself, and bumping into things. But she was alive. Still not immortal, and not calm and compliant, but at least the drug hadn't killed her as it had all the rest. Her eyes jiggled franticly in their sockets and her whole body jangled around spastically, like a marionette in the hands of some palsied puppeteer. I tried to have sex with her again, but she became violent . . . extremely violent! She clawed, punched, kicked, and bit me, babbling something about her father. Her eyes were wild, and spit and foam drooled from her mouth, as she tried desperately to kill me. Not exactly the companion I had hoped for. Still, she was alive. I was closer. Just not there yet. I picked up the drill and put it through her forehead.

All day at work the next day, my thoughts jumped back and forth between my minor success with the PCP, to my new "friend" Sissy. I didn't know which one excited me more. That's when I heard about the police finding the bodies in the empty lot. They were now on the hunt for a serial killer. I knew that there would be no way they'd understand what I was trying to do. I had to stop for a while. But that didn't mean I had to stop seeing Sissy.

I walked her to the club that night and the night after that, and the night after that. She told me all about how she was working her way through culinary school, and how she wanted to move to Paris to study French cuisine and become a famous pastry chef in some world renowned restaurant. I listened intently, but told her nothing about myself. She wouldn't understand my ambitions.

I didn't feel so alone when I was with Sissy, but afterwards, when I'd go home, the walls would start closing in on me again. The entire house would collapse inward, entombing me, crushing me with the profound weight of my isolation, sealing me alone in the desolate crypt of my own rapidly fragmenting mind. My mother, my grandmother, and my father, or rather their mournful, formless, ghosts, would creep and slither down the halls, haunting me. But every time I'd dash out of my bedroom to catch them at it, they would disappear. All I wanted was someone to hold me, someone to talk with me. But they were gone, and their memories were no comfort, even though I'd managed to filter out all the bad memories. A memory didn't hold you in its arms on cold lonely nights. Then, of course, neither had Mom or Dad.

Sissy and I were getting closer. She even came over to my house once, and I ordered pizza and rented a horror movie: "The Serpent and the Rainbow." That's where I got the idea. The movie was all about a Haitian voodoo priest who turned people into zombies. The movie seemed to suggest that it was, in fact, medically possible. There was some drug that the voodoo priests used that could do it. The next day I went to the library and looked up every book I could on the subject. I ditched work to do it; which was probably good since they'd come across my PCP purchase the day before while processing invoices, and were conducting a minor investigation to find out who had ordered the drugs, and where they had gone. I knew they'd eventually find out it was me.

I had been at the library for six hours, when I finally came across a reference to a poison found in blowfish, which was believed to be one of the key ingredients in the witch doctor's zombie potion. An hour later, I'd not only isolated the name of the poison (Tetrodotoxin) but I'd found a local exotic pet store that just happened to have a blowfish. Unfortunately, the fish cost two hundred dollars, and I had just received a notice from Pacific Power warning me that they would shut off my gas and electric if I didn't pay the bill soon. Sissy had started talking more and more about leaving for Paris to become a pastry chef. I was in a panic over the thought of losing her. I decided I could live in the dark for a while. I bought the fish.

The problem was that none of the books I'd found contained the exact formula for processing the blowfish poison into zombie potion. I had found references to hemlock, nightshade, and even wolfsbane, along with various other herbs. But none of the books had the complete formula. I bought every herb even remotely mentioned, and mixed them together with the Tetrodotoxin. I still wasn't sure I had it right. With so many deadly poisons, I was nervous that I might accidentally kill Sissy, but I couldn't risk another experiment with the cops out looking for me. I decided to mix the Tetrodotoxin potion with the PCP. Just to be certain I blessed the concoction with an old voodoo spell I found in an encyclopedia of magic spells. I was desperate. That night I invited Sissy over.

She was wearing sweat pants and a T-shirt again. She never dressed sexy outside of work. We watched TV and she told me about her boyfriend. I'd never thought to ask her if she had one. She said that he promised to help her put together enough money to go to Paris. My eyes started to tear up. I was about to lose her. I couldn't let that happen. I excused myself and went into the bathroom to get the chloroform. I took off one of my sweatsocks and soaked it in the chloroform. I couldn't bare the thought of losing her.

I walked back into the living room, and watched Sissy's smile turn upside down as she saw the look in my eye and smelled the chloroform. I had it clamped over her mouth before she could put up much of a struggle. The rest of it went like clockwork . . . almost.

I drilled the hole through her temple and poured my zombie potion directly onto her frontal lobe. There were no convulsions, no shrill cries of pain, nothing. I waited. I was so excited I could hardly contain myself. A zombie of my very own, to keep forever! I poured more of the potion in and waited some more. I felt her pulse and listened to her heart. All of my dreams came crashing to earth in a fiery heap, as they both ticked slowly down to a standstill. Sissy was dead. I began to cry. I had fucked up. Now I would be alone forever! I hugged her to me and ran my fingers through her hair, cooing my soft apologies, and declarations of love, into her ear. Then I dragged her outside to bury her in the backyard.

It took three hours to get the hole deep enough. The ground in Las Vegas is as hard as concrete and filled with rocks. My back and shoulders were on fire with a white-hot agony, but I barely noticed them through the soul numbing pain in my heart. It felt like a scalding hot, thousand pound stone was searing in my chest and weighting me down. I wanted to throw myself into the grave with her. The exhaustion and profound depression seemed to be pulling me down toward the soft earth, but I resisted. There was always tomorrow. I could try again. I had to. I had killed the only friend I'd ever had, and I couldn't bring her back. I had to find a way to make the potion work. I couldn't be alone again.

I dragged Sissy over and dumped her into the ditch, just as the full moon poked its way through the trees, illuminating Sissy's sweet, and innocent, face one last time. It took less than twenty minutes to fill up the hole. Ten minutes after that I was back in the house with the ceiling crushing down on me, stifling my breath.

I fell asleep curled into a fetal position on the living room couch. I awoke to the feeling of strong hands, with sharp fingernails, squeezing my esophagus shut. When I opened my eyes I was looking into two dark cavernous pits . . . Sissy's cold, dead, stare. Her pupils had widened so that her irises were no longer visible. She was covered with dirt from her makeshift grave. I tried not to think of what it must've taken for her to pull herself out of the earth. She looked terrible. Her mouth hung open, with her tongue lolling out. She was clearly still dead. Nonetheless she was choking me.

I reached out and grasped both of her wrists to pull her off of me. She growled low and throaty when she felt my touch, then bent down and bit into my forearm, tearing free a great piece of my extensor muscle, chewing it, and swallowing with a sickening gulp. I screamed and withdrew both my hands. Right then I knew that mixing the blowfish poison with the PCP had been a mistake.

My lacerated arm sprayed rich, dark, arterial blood all over her. She grinned ghastfully; a smile streaked with gore. Dark purple veins exploded beneath Sissy's skin, marring her perfect, snow-white complexion, with a profusion of dark bruises and thick vericose veins. Not a glimmer of intelligence showed in her dead eyes and vacuous expression. This horrific mockery of life was not Sissy. It was little more than a shambling puppet manufactured of Sissy's flesh; only slightly more than the corpse she had been an hour ago . . . only now she was choking the life out of me.

My own terror at my creation was restricting my breathing even further. I had almost passed out when her grip suddenly slackened. Sissy doubled over and began to vomit up blood and what looked like organs and her entire intestinal track. Her body was now merely a shell. When she sat back up, blood and saliva drooled down the front of her T-shirt. She swayed unsteadily, as if whatever horrible life I had animated her with would abandon her and she would topple over. Then she steadied herself, and her dark, lifeless, eyes turned toward me. From deep within them, I saw a faint spark, and then a hungry gleam came into her eyes, and she bent down like she was going to kiss me. I was so happy to see her alive, that I ignored her rancid breath. I let, her now thick and uncoordinated tongue, intrude into my mouth, tasting blood and vomit and trying not to retch.

There was a sudden sharp pain in my mouth. Sissy pulled her head back, and there was a wet ripping sound that sent a shock wave of agony through my entire face. I looked up to see my tongue, and what seemed to be my bottom lip, clenched between her teeth. She quickly swallowed this too, and bent back down to feed. I screamed my throat raw; knowing that no one would come to my aid, just as no one had come to help the women whose lives I had destroyed. I tried to fight her off, but her strength was tremendous. I'd heard that PCP increased the adrenaline flow often giving the user phenomenal strength to accompany the psychotic delusions the drug inspired.

I was helpless, as she slowly began to consume my entire face. I felt her crunch through the cartilage of my nose. There was a sickening rip and pop, as she tore it from my face and greedily consumed it. Again I tried to free myself from her, but both of my wrists were pinned in her hard unyielding grip.

Somehow I maintained consciousness, as bite after bite of my face went down her throat. I could feel her cold, clammy, tongue slather across my teeth, as she bit through my cheeks and slowly chewed them away. Soon my head was little more than a skull with a few bits of flesh tenuously clinging to it. I watched as she bent down and rent my upper lip from my gums, chewing that up as well. I stared into those flat dull eyes the entire time; watching as she tore away at my face. Even as she sucked out my eyeballs, I somehow managed not to pass out.

Even now, I can feel her breaking off my arms; using her tiny, dull, little teeth to work the muscles free from the tendons and bone. My legs, genitals, and most of my stomach have already been consumed. Still, I am alive and conscious. I must have somehow gotten infected with some of the zombie potion myself; absorbed it through my skin. Sissy is having a hard time chewing through my muscles with her blunt canines. This will be a very slow process. And it seems like I will be awake for all of it.

Fly

Mike was sitting at the bar reading the newspaper. The headline featured a story on the construction of a new local casino scheduled to open next year. There were two other stories on the front page. One was about the upcoming De La Hoya fight at the Thomas & Mack Arena and the other was about a woman who had apparently been thrown naked off the balcony of a local hotel. It was the second one in as many weeks. None of it interested Mike. He folded up the paper and placed it on the bar. He didn't even mind when the drunk beside him spilled his drink on it. It was all old news to him.

Women had started walking past smiling at him and trying to catch his eye. Horny tourists looking for a vacation fling. Mike seemed to attract them like flies. Fuck what you heard about women liking men for their minds. Mike knew what it was that attracted them. He was short and powerfully built with a thick chest and huge shoulders. He looked like a pro wrestler. In fact he looked like a cross between Stone Cold Steve Austin and Tank Abbot. Women found the air of menace that seemed to radiate from him an irresistible aphrodisiac. There was something violent in his ice blue eyes, something wild and dangerous. Bitches loved it.

A Hollywood blonde with pornographically large breasts scooted up beside him at the bar. She ran one tiny hand over his thick muscular biceps and smiled appreciatively. Mike smiled back at her, staring at her tits. He had to consciously restrain himself from grabbing them. She followed his eyes down to her breasts and her smile grew wider, more confident, more seductive.

"Wanna dance?"

She was young, maybe twenty-two. She had a dark burnt-orange tan courtesy of a tanning booth and shoulder length blonde hair courtesy of peroxide. With her blonde hair, ultra-white teeth, and sky blue eyes she looked to Mike like a photo-negative. The other male customers seemed to find it appealing. Mike thought her skin looked like fried bologna. Still, she had that perfectly round, firm, little ass perched high on her back that bounced and jiggled as she did her little bump and grind in time to the music and those impossibly large DD breasts. She was only about 5'5" and just barely over a hundred pounds not including the breasts. They no doubt added another twenty pounds or so. One half of Mike thought they looked ridiculous. The other half wanted to tit-fuck her until he came all over them.

Mike knew she was a stripper. This was about the time of night when the swing shift got off at Jaguars, the local titty bar. They always headed over to the club after work. Many of them came to the club to meet up with guys they met at work. Others came to pick up guys and perhaps turn a trick or two. But most of them just came to get drunk and party. You could always tell the strippers by the mini skirts, short shorts, or hot pants, the tremendous silicone enhanced breasts stuffed into tiny little baby t-shirts or bra tops, and the practiced, over rehearsed way they said: "Wanna dance?"

"Sure. What's your name?"

"Tasty."

"Yeah, of course it is."

"Alright my real name is Sarah. Tasty is my stage name. What's your name?"

"Mike. Let's dance."

Dancing was about the last thing Mike wanted to do but it was part of the mating ritual. He led her out onto the dance floor. As the

DJ mixed the music from Techno, to Rap, to Rock 'n Roll he began rubbing all over her, her ass, her legs, her breasts, grinding against her as she wiggled her ass and slithered up and down him. She bent over and bounced her ass, rubbing it against Mike's erection. Then she turned around and threw her head back arching her back and jiggling her breasts. Mike grabbed her and kissed her deeply, passionately. His tongue darted into her mouth and attacked hers; striking, coiling, and constricting like two dueling adders. He could feel her body starting to melt and he knew she was ready. He could already taste the alcohol on her breath so he figured he could skip that part of the mating ritual.

"Where do you live?"

"I live over on Tropicana."

"In those little pink two story apartment buildings?"

"No I live in a four story, on the top floor."

Mike thought to himself for a moment. It just might be high enough. His eyes wandered over her huge breasts, smooth muscular legs, and tight round ass and he figured it was at least worth a try.

"Let's go to your place."

She reached out and ran her hands over his thick muscular chest and shoulders, down over his arms, squeezing his biceps. She looked into his icy blue eyes and smiled.

"Sure." She said

He walked her out into the parking lot and over to her 1999, white, Mustang convertible. Strippers always have nice cars.

She drove fast. She had the top down and the wind whipped through her blonde hair pulling it back away from her face to stream out in back of her. It was quite a dramatic effect one that she was obviously aware of. Mike put his hand on her thigh and slid it up under her skirt and between her thighs. She was not wearing underwear and she was already wet. Mike slid his middle finger up inside her and she let out a slight gasp. He began sliding it in and out of her pussy while his thumb massaged her clitoris. She closed

168

her eyes and let out a low soulful moan. Her leg quivered and she nearly swerved into oncoming traffic. Mike pulled his finger out of her pussy and slid it into her mouth where she sucked it and licked her juices off of it. She stomped on the gas and flew the remaining two blocks to her apartment complex almost burning rubber as she turned into the parking lot.

Mike followed "Tasty" up to her lavishly decorated two-bedroom apartment. As he watched her ass bounce up the stairs in that tight mini-skirt he could feel the hunger rise. His rational mind was receding as the hunger took over him. He was all lust now, all passion. She fumbled with her keys outside the door of her apartment and even that slight movement made her breasts bounce and jiggle. This time Mike did not restrain himself from grabbing them. He filled both his hands with her tremendous tits, pinching the nipples and grinding his urgent erection against her ass. Finally she located the right key and they spilled into her apartment.

The door had barely closed before Mike had ripped her shirt off and was sucking her breasts, licking and biting at her nipples. Her hands were busy trying to undo his belt buckle and pull his zipper down. Finally she pulled his pants down and Mike stepped out of them kicking off his shoes at the same time. Mike was still sucking on her tits when he reached around and unzipped her skirt. He had to literally peel it off of her it was so tight. Once again he slid a finger up inside her. Her pussy was sopping wet. She moaned as he finger-fucked her tight wet pussy still licking and sucking her hard nipples. She had grabbed hold of his throbbing hard cock and was aggressively stroking it with her hand. Mike pulled his fingers out of her pussy as she went to her knees and took all eight inches of him down her throat. He grabbed the back of her head, entwining his fingers in her long blonde hair, and started fucking her mouth as she slurped and sucked almost gagging as he pounded his dick down the back of her throat. She was playing with her own pussy while she sucked Mike's rock hard dick. She guided Mike down to the floor and continued to bob her head up and down the length of his shaft. Mike slid her around until she was straddling him with her dripping wet pussy inches from his face. He wrapped his arms around her waist and pulled her pussy down to his hungry mouth. His tongue quickly found her clitoris and she let out a moan as he started licking and sucking it. Yes, she was tasty.

They stayed in a "69" with her licking his balls, licking her way up the shaft of his cock and then around the head, before taking the entire thing down her throat so far her nose would disappear in his pubic hair. Mike was sliding his tongue in and out of her sweet pussy and then sucking and flicking her clit with his tongue making her whole body quiver. Mike started flicking his tongue across her clit faster and faster while sliding his middle and index finger in and out of her and he could feel her body tense and then shake as the orgasm overtook her, slamming through her body like a tidal wave. Wave after wave of orgasms slammed through her body as Mike's tongue danced across her clit.

"Oh yes! Yes! Goddamn that's good!" She screamed

She pulled herself away from him as the last orgasm shook her down to her toes and turned around to give Mike's cock her undivided attention. Mike raised up on his elbows to watch the show. She stroked his cock with one hand as she licked and sucked his balls making Mike's legs shake. Then she slowly spiraled her way up his cock with her tongue as she rubbed her fingers across the head of his dick. When her mouth got to the top she licked and sucked the head while her hand whipped up and down the length of his cock jacking him off in her mouth. She continued licking and sucking the head of his cock as he came, filling up her mouth with his cum 'til it spilled out over lips and across her cheeks, dribbling down her chin, neck, down between her breasts. She used her fingers to scoop it all up gobbling up his cum licking it from her lips, and cheeks, and sucking her fingers clean. Then she ran her tongue all over his cock licking it clean as well. Mike was instantly hard again. He turned

Tasty around on all fours and shoved his cock deep inside her. She let out a small cry as he slammed all eight inches in and out of her, his balls slapping against her ass as he tried to rip her in two. He leaned over and cupped her tremendous breasts in her hands as he continued banging his cock into her tight pussy. She slid her hand between her legs and started playing with her pussy and in seconds she was cumming again.

Mike rolled her over on her back and put her legs over his shoulders loving the way her huge tits bounced and flopped as he pounded her pussy. His huge tricep muscles bulged as he balanced himself above her. She was on what must have been her sixth or seventh orgasm when he scooped her up in his arms and lifted her off the floor. Her legs were wrapped around his waist and he had both of his tremendously powerful arms beneath her ass sliding her up and down on his dick as he walked around her apartment. The patio door was open and Mike strolled right out onto the patio. Tasty was going wild bouncing up and down on his cock as if she was trying to break a wild horse. Mike could feel another orgasm coming on. Every muscle in his body seemed to lock. And he grabbed hold of her waist and started bouncing her up and down on his dick grunting and growling with each thrust as the orgasm began to rip through his body like gunfire. Suddenly, as he felt his dick begin to erupt with semen, he put both hands around Tasty's waist and pushed outward with all his might. A look of confusion crossed Tasty's face as she felt herself being wrenched from Mike's dick. She saw it bobbing in the air still hard and thick, looking almost threatening like some kind of club or police baton, shooting cum out into the night air then she felt herself start to fall as she sailed over the balcony. She looked up into Mike's face and saw him looking at her with calm detachment. His expression was serene, satisfied. He looked like a man who had just had the best sex of his life was supposed to look. His eyes locked with hers and he whispered just loud enough for her to hear.

"Fly."

And then she fell. It was all so surreal she didn't even have time to scream. Amazingly she was right in the middle of another orgasm when the ground rushed up and struck her. Breaking her perfect body like a thrift shop Barbie doll. Mike slipped back into his clothes and left.

The next night there were cops all over the club asking questions about the dead girl. They showed Mike her picture. He said she looked familiar. He told the cops he thought he saw her last night with a tall, muscular, black guy, with a shaved head. He gave the detective a phony name and address and took one of his cards. They showed the stripper's picture to the bartenders and several other customers sitting at the bar each one described a different guy they'd seen her with. The girl got around was the general consensus.

Mike started to get bored. He was feeling horny. He wanted some pussy and the club was looking kind of slow tonight. The club had just opened though. The night was still young. It was way too early for the strippers to show up so Mike scanned the crowds of tourists . . . hunting. Nothing. They were all too fat or too skinny or already coupled off or with a group of friends who would be able to identify him if one of them came up missing. Mike walked upstairs to the sports bar and picked up a newspaper off the bar. He was frustrated and decided to wait until the strippers showed up.

The front-page headline was about the stripper who flew naked off her balcony. More old news. But there was another story about a man found in his hotel room with his throat slit. He was naked and they found semen and vaginal secretions indicating that he had just had sex before he was killed. His wallet and jewelry were missing. The police were guessing that a prostitute or her pimp had killed him. Mike didn't give a fuck about the murder. He was thinking about the prostitute. It was something he had never even considered. He knew at least five prostitutes that hung around the club and the idea of doing one of them had never even crossed his mind. He had sat and talked to several of them on many nights but he had always been turned off by the fact that they were whores even though they never seemed to be particularly interested in taking his money. One of them had even offered to work for him. She told him that she had recently lost her pimp and needed someone to watch her back on the street. Mike had turned her down. Now, for the life of him, he couldn't figure out why he hadn't gone for it. There wouldn't be a bunch of cops turning the club upside down over a dead prostitute. Nobody would care. It wouldn't even be front-page news. Mike ordered a beer and started thinking seriously about picking up a whore. He ordered one beer after another as he waited for the strippers and call girls to show up. By the time the club filled up Mike was good and drunk and the club was filled with whores.

Prostitutes lined the bar. Some old faces and some new. The one that had asked him to be her pimp months ago was there too. Mike struggled to remember her name. Jamie? Gina? Jenny! Jennifer. Her name was Jennifer. Mike staggered and had to steady himself by grabbing the bar to keep from falling as he got up off his stool and walked over to her.

"Hi Mike."

"Hey Jenny."

"Damn you are fucked up! How much have you had to drink" She laughed. She had flaming red hair that hung down to her waist, long muscular legs, that led up to a large, round, but muscular ass, she had a slight tummy but it was shadowed by breasts that were larger even than the stripper's from the night before. There was a plastic surgeon somewhere in town who was getting rich. She had those fashionably pouty lips that were also probably a surgeon's handy work. They gave her the look of a spoiled child. Her eyes were sea green.

"Too much. Look I hate to ask you. I mean, I know you've gotta make your money but could you give me a ride home? I'm waaaaay too fucked up to drive. I have something I want to talk to you about anyway. About that business proposition you made me a while back."

That last comment seemed to decide the matter for her. Her startling green eyes beamed with enthusiasm as she scooped up her purse and took him by the arm.

"Let's go Daddy!"

They jumped into her brand new silver Riviera and sped off up Convention Center Drive to the Strip.

"So what did you want to talk to me about?"

"Let's go to your place to talk. I need to lay down a minute."

"Well I'm staying at a hotel right now and . . ."

"That's fine let's go there."

They valet parked, walked quickly though the casino, and took the elevator up thirteen floors. Mike was ecstatic. He loved the old hotels. A lot of them still had windows that opened, even on the top floors, and some of them even had balconies. He was quite pleased to find that hers was a luxurious suite that did in fact have a balcony that overlooked Las Vegas Blvd. Mike walked out onto the balcony and stared out over the bright neon lights of the legendary Vegas Strip. It was jammed with cars and tourists. Jenny squeezed up behind him and ran her tiny little hands with their long red fingernails over his thick muscular arms and shoulders. Mike turned around and cupped her huge breasts in his hands rubbing his thumbs over her hard nipple, which were poking through the tight little baby T-shirt she wore. Mike pulled the shirt over her head and once more cupped her tremendous titties in his hands. He bent down and sucked at her nipples, licking and sucking them 'til she started to moan. Jennifer Masters, former honor roll student turned stripper, turned prostitute, quickly wriggled out of her tight little shorts and Mike slid a hand up between her thighs. She was already wet. Her legs shook as he fingered her clit while he continued to suck her titties. She reached down and pulled Mike's pants off and her eyes grew wide with hunger as she spotted his tremendous erection. She grabbed it with both hands and then bent down and swept her long crimson mane back out of her face before she started licking his balls while still jacking him off. She licked her way up the thick venous shaft of his cock 'til she got to the head where she circled it with her tongue and sucked it before taking the whole thing down her throat. Mike grabbed her by the back of the head and started fucking her mouth pleased with the way she seemed to gag when he thrust it to the back of her throat. Again he felt that tingling in the base of his cock that meant he was about to cum. He pulled away from her and took a deep breath to regain control. When the sensation subsided he picked Jenny up and wrapped her legs round his waist lowering her onto his dick. He loved the feel of her breasts against his chest and the way they bounced up and slapped him in the face as he slid her up and down on his cock. She threw her head back and let out little cries and gasps of pleasure as she rode his dick. Mike was pounding into her so hard every thrust made her breasts bounce up and strike him in the chin.

That familiar tingling sensation had started in Mike's balls and was creeping up his shaft when he noticed a shiny metallic gleam in Jenny's mouth. He paid it no attention. He grabbed her waist in his hands just as she leaned forward to kiss his neck. He looked once again at the neon twinkling up and down the strip and felt a searing pain rip across his throat as he thrust Jenny out and over the balcony.

"Fly." He whispered as she sailed backwards into the night. Then he started to gag as his mouth filled with blood. He fell against the railing choking on his own blood and looked over at Jenny as she hurtled earthward. He noticed the metallic gleam in her mouth again, which was now smeared with blood . . . his blood. A razor blade was clenched between her gore-streaked teeth. She had slit his throat. Her eyes were wide with horror as she fell to earth but then they turned cold and hard as they locked with his.

"Die." She hissed and the ground flew up and punched the life from her, splattering her body over the hotel parking lot in a gruesome collage of blood, organs, and shattered bones. Mike smiled, pleased, satisfied, even as his own life spurted out all over the balcony and dripped down into the parking lot to mingle with hers.

The Book of a
Thousand Sins

*"Let us go down to hell while we live, that we may not have to go
down to hell when we die."*
   —St. Augustine

*"Eternal punishment is eternal revenge, and can be inflicted only by
an eternal monster."*
   —Robert Ingersoll, Origins of God and the Devil

Anja awoke with that familiar unease settling upon her like an oily
miasma, a dank mire coating her thoughts. She felt used and unclean
like a spent condom someone had ejaculated in and then discarded.
It was the way she felt whenever she had sex with men and often
even just from fantasizing about it. Tonight, she had been dreaming
of Lord.

In the dream she'd been his slave again and he was cutting
designs into her back with a scalpel as he fucked her in the ass with
his massive cock. Her unconscious body responded to his familiar
stainless steel caresses and the even more familiar sensation of his
solid length filling her up, stirring her desires into a raging tempest as
her nerves sang out in agony.

She could feel each thrust as his turgid organ punched deep
into her rectum, each stroke of the blade as it whispered through her
flesh. Anja was on the verge of a massive orgasm, the kind that she

hadn't experienced since leaving the service of Lord. She tossed and turned in her sleep writhing in pleasure, feeling that same mixture of degradation, shame, and ecstasy that Lord had always inspired in her, but then the dream had gotten too real. Her dream Lord shot his load of semen onto her bloodied back and Anja felt only shame as he wiped the rest of his seed onto her cheek and walked out, leaving her with a burning wetness between her thighs and no way to satisfy it. She'd sat there, cum and blood drenched, watching her suddenly indifferent master walk out the front door.

"But what about me? Don't I get to top you for a little while? Don't I get to get off too?"

"No." The door slammed with a loud bang as Lord exited her bedroom.

Anja snapped awake feeling pissed-off and horny as hell. She was vibrating with fury. Even in her dreams she was getting fucked over by men. Lord had always hated to switch. It was always about him. Even after all this time she still wasn't over it.

She stretched, flexing her long lean muscles in the morning sun filtering in between her bedroom blinds, and tried to shake off the dream. Somehow she could still feel Lord's presence in the room with her like a ghostly afterimage. Feeling suddenly vulnerable and exposed, Anja reached out for her blanket to wrap around herself. She almost cried out when her left hand encountered flesh.

She lifted the blanket and stared over at the wide, pale, pock-marked back that descended down to a gigantic ass and elephantine thighs. Big Lucy. Gradually Anja recalled the previous evening spent ripping into the fat dyke's lower extremities with her eleven-inch strap-on dildo. She'd made the big lesbian cry even as she herself wept, remembering all the men who had abused her as a child. Remembering how Lord had abandoned her.

As usual, Anja started the morning with a full bladder and an urgent need to empty it. She reached out and gave the rotund woman beside her a hard shove that knocked her off the bed and onto the floor.

177

"What the fuck?!"

"Stay down there and don't move!"

Anja stepped off the bed and flexed her long luxurious body. Lucy's eyes leapt up from where she lay obediently on the floor awaiting her mistress's instructions, and slithered over the dominatrix's flawless flesh. Her narrow waist and wide hips, her huge breasts with the upturned nipples, her voluptuous buttocks and thick muscular thighs, Lucy's eyes devoured every inch of her mistress.

"Open your mouth!"

Lucy laid back and obeyed. Anja squatted over the woman's face and began to urinate, flooding the big woman's mouth in a warm golden shower. Lucy gagged and coughed as her mouth filled with warm piss but she did not attempt to turn away. She drank deep of the yellow stream ignoring her own revulsion and concentrating only on the beauty of Anja's sumptuous flesh. Lucy swallowed one mouthful of urine after another in order to avoid drowning and soon she could feel her stomach slosh with a bellyful of Anja's morning piss. The last drops dribbled from the meaty folds of her mistress's vagina down onto Lucy's tongue. Anja then squatted down even further until her urine-soaked labia and clitoris were pressed against the big woman's face.

Mistress Anja reached down and seized the stainless-steel pinch-collar still around the lesbian's neck and yanked hard until Lucy's face turned blue and her mouth disappeared into the beautiful dominatrix's pubic hair. The big lesbian licked obediently at her mistress's salty clit even as she struggled for air. Anja alternated between choking Lucy and pinching and slapping her mammoth breasts until she finally managed her first weak uninspiring orgasm of the day and relaxed back into the same existential malaise she'd awaken to.

"Get up and get the fuck out." Anja muttered almost casually as she rose from Lucy's urine and cum-soaked face.

"Just give me a second to get dressed will ya?"

"No! Get the fuck out now!" She snatched a paddle up off the floor and began lashing the big woman across the breast and thighs as Lucy scrambled to collect her clothing. Anja opened her front door and put her beautiful manicured toes to the big woman's ass, literally kicking her out the front door.

"I hate that bitch." Anja said to Lucy's back as she slammed the door behind her, leaving the obese woman standing naked on her front porch.

It sometimes struck Anja as ironic that it had been Big Lucy who had first turned her out and introduced her to the life. It now seemed like a lifetime ago when she had first arrived in San Francisco, miserable and exhausted after nearly an entire day spent riding a Greyhound bus from New Mexico. She'd run away from home the day before, away from a father and uncle who had used her young body as a waste deposit for their semen and violent abuse. She was broke and broken, starving and grief-stricken, sitting hollow-eyed in a coffee shop on Haight Street sipping on tepid green tea and trying to figure out if she had enough money to afford a room somewhere or the balls to turn a trick to get whatever money she was short. A shadow had suddenly darkened her table and she'd looked up to see a massive leather clad bull-dyke smiling down at her. Big Lucy was well over two hundred pounds, closer in fact to three, nearly six-feet tall, and looked like she could bench-press a semi-truck. Anja had been immediately intimidated.

"You look like you could use a job." Lucy said, grinning lasciviously and running one fat meaty hand through Anja's long red hair as if she already owned the girl.

Anja simply nodded in reply. A few days later she was working at *The Hot Box*, San Francisco's only lesbian owned all-nude strip club. It was her new boss who first introduced her to the world of sadomasochism during sweaty evenings chained to the desk in her office. Fucking Big Lucy was almost a prerequisite for working at The Box and that had meant submitting to Lucy's peculiar appetites, which included everything from candle wax on the nipples to sewing needles in her clitoris. Anja hadn't minded the woman's attentions. She'd had far worse done to her by her father and uncle. She was incapable of having children as a result of half the things her uncle had crammed into her.

Big Lucy had been like the mother Anja had always dreamed would come to rescue her from her depraved little household when her dad would shove a sock in her mouth to keep her from screaming. The mother her father always told her had abandoned her to "Move to San Francisco and become a lesbian whore!"

It was Big Lucy who recommended that Anja join the Society of Sade, one of the nation's oldest S&M groups. Lucy took her to her first meeting just before her nineteenth birthday. That's where she met her first true master, Lord.

Lord was the most beautiful man she'd ever seen. 6'5", 240lbs of carbonized steel. His ebon flesh looked as if it had been chiseled out of living night. It rippled with hard muscle and glistened liquid black like a pool of oil. His dark eyes gleamed with a cruel wisdom that made him look as ancient as the earth. He walked with the confidence of royalty and his every word seemed to hold power beyond its meaning. He inspired fear and lust in equal quantities and his every gesture was pregnant with the threat of violence. Lord appeared to be just what he wished his subs to believe he was . . . a living god. Almost immediately Anja had pledged herself to him. From that moment her true education in pain and debauchery had begun.

Lord was as gentle and patient as he could be cold and cruel. The same hand that held the whip could also provide the most tender caresses. Soon Anja could no longer decide which she preferred. Her identity dissolved in endless waves of pleasure and pain, the blessings of her new lord. She lost herself in him and for a while that was all she desired. That escape. That oblivion. But soon she wanted more. She wanted to hold the whip. So Lord showed her how.

180

She'd served as his slave for three years before she realized that she preferred being a top. Luckily, back then Lord had been willing to switch. He'd taught her everything a dom should know about bondage, pain, and humiliation. On the day that she announced to him that she could no longer be his or anyone's sub, he confessed that he had never let anyone dominate him before her and that he'd only let her do it because he loved her. Anja replied by telling Lord that she needed to change her role in life to something more empowering. She needed to hold the whip, to be the inflicter of pain, the punisher and humiliator of men, rather than the punished and humiliated.

Lord resented her for it and had forcibly thrown her out of his dungeon. That resentment had continued right along with their friendship, which was still just as strong, or weak, today as it was then.

Once Anja had located a suitable location for her dungeon and began accepting clients herself, they had flooded through the doors in startling numbers. Big Lucy had been her first client and Anja had delighted in taking out her frustrations on the big woman, finally able to experience the power and control men like Lord, her father, and her uncle had exercised on her for so many years. She'd quickly found herself intoxicated by it, drunk with power. When men, some of them very wealthy and even famous, had begun to patronize her dungeon, she'd discovered depths of depravity within herself she'd never even been aware of. Many of the men had found her brand of sadism far too extreme, but many more had stayed. Anja had never realized how many people there were willing to pay good money to get a woman's spike-heeled boot rammed into their asshole.

At first it had been exciting. Her own lusts, her own pain, had found release in the pain she dealt out to others. But now Anja was getting tired, bored with it all. As one of the Bay Area's most infamous dominatrices, Anja had seen every manner of perversion imaginable. Acts that would send the most hardened street prostitute screaming for their lives had for her become mundane. She had grown callous to it all. The flesh held no mystery and little power to inspire her anymore. There were few people who could relate to the banality of sexual deviancy once the limits of imagination had been reached. Anja had now worked in the sex industry for over a decade. She was now at the point where perversion had become routine and orgasm a memory. She needed something to expand her sexual horizons before she slit her own wrists out of boredom. With a sigh, she got up and walked down stairs to the basement to prepare her dungeon for business.

Anja was almost done abusing her newest slave; a fat, slovenly, pig of a man who was heavily into humiliation. She couldn't wait until this session was over. Anja understood these type of masochists the least. They taxed her energy trying to devise new ways to humiliate them. It was so much easier working with your traditional bottom who only wanted to be spanked, or whipped, or paddled, or caned, or even cut. No imagination required. *This* was real work!

She tugged on the rope, which hoisted her client's legs and arms into the air. She tugged harder until his arms were pulled between his legs and his feet went back over his head, effectively folding him in half so that his genitals dangled in front of his face. In the real world his name was Marcus Giles, a wealthy local art dealer. In here, his name was Slob.

"Let's play, squirt the clown, Slob." She cooed mischievously; tying the end of the rope to a hook in the wall and pulling her black latex gloves on tighter.

Anja squirted Astro-Glide into the palm of her glove and began jacking-off the corpulent businessman who dangled helplessly from the complex pulley system in the ceiling. He began to quiver and moan, trying to resist the orgasm he could feel building within him.

"Say, ahhh." She instructed and Slob obediently opened his mouth wide and stuck out his tongue. He jerked and convulsed as a powerful orgasm shot a stream of thick, warm, salty, semen down his throat causing him to gag and choke.

"Squirt the clown!" Anja giggled delightedly as cum splashed across his cheeks and dribbled down his chin. With a spoon, she scooped up the rest of the cum, and shoveled it into his mouth like a mother feeding a young toddler. He winced disgustedly and tried to turn away but she gripped his jaw in her glove and forced the spoon into his mouth. When he tried to spit it out she gave his scrotum a smack, which instantly restored his compliance.

After he'd licked the spoon clean, she let him down and removed his blindfold. "Kneel Slob!" she commanded.

"Yes Mistress," he replied with the appropriate awe and humility. He dropped to her feet to kiss and slobber on her boots. It was his favorite thing to do.

"Did you like my little game Slob? Did you like playing squirt the clown you filthy little maggot? You cum drinking little fag boy?" She said using her boot to lift his chin to look her in the eye.

"Yes Mistress," the fat businessman replied enthusiastically. His voice quivered nervously along with the rolls of cellulite around his waist and beneath his chin.

"Yes Mistress what?" Anja snarled contemptuously.

"Yes Mistress, I loved drinking my own cum."

"Why?"

"Because I am a filthy little maggot; a cum drinking fag boy."

"With a pathetic little dick." she added, slipping her foot underneath his scrotum and bouncing his flaccid penis on the toe of her six-inch stiletto hip boots.

"With a pathetic little dick," he agreed. Actually, he was hung like a pony. She would never understand masochists like him.

"I have a present for you Mistress."

"What do you have Slob? What could you possibly give to me except your adoration, obedience, and your money?"

"A book. The book! *The Book of a Thousand Sins!*"

Anja's eyes widened in surprise and then narrowed in suspicion. She had heard of the book. Everyone in the scene had. It was legend. To own it was every sadist's, every masochist's, wet dream.

There was only one copy. It was rumored that the book was originally written in Latin some two thousand years ago by a mad pagan monk who had converted to Christianity and then rebelled against the teachings of Christ to become the world's first reputed Satanist. Unconfirmed accounts have it that the Marquis de Sade had translated it into its current French while imprisoned in the Bastille, adding his own perverse embellishments to it along with some colorful illustrations, before the original version was discovered in his cell and destroyed. Reportedly the book had later been pillaged from a private collection in France and brought to Nazi Germany at Hitler's request sometime in the 1940s. There it was reported that it had been restored and bound in the leathered skin of a recently deflowered virgin right after she'd been sodomized and tortured to death.

Many reports have it that top SS officers had used it in sadistic orgies in which prostitutes, prisoners, and rare exotic animals were forced to perform all kinds of unspeakable acts inspired by illustrations in the first chapter. These orgies often led to grievous injuries including frequent fatalities (not to mention animal rights offences). The infernal tome had been found in Hitler's bunker after it was stormed by the allied forces and then smuggled into America by a young soldier. That soldier was later found dead in his apartment with the bodies of nearly a dozen tortured, raped, and gruesomely mutilated prostitutes surrounding his own corpse, which bore the scars of horrifying self-inflicted mutilations. He had died of internal bleeding caused by the business end of a steeple-size crucifix which still protruded from his prolapsed anus when he'd been found; his face twisted into a gruesome rictus of impossible agony or unfathomable ecstasy.

Years later the book disappeared from a police evidence locker and surfaced in an S&M club in Manhattan. It had since been passed from hand to hand around the bondage and fetish clubs in San

Francisco, New York, and L.A. where its reputation for inspiring acts of violent sexual deviancy that pushed the boundaries of sanity and legality had grown.

It had never been reproduced or reprinted. It had been years since anyone had regarded it as anything more than a guide to impossibly perverse and abhorrent sexual practices. It was much more than that however. Much more.

One anthropologist who'd studied it believed it to be an audition for a seat amid Hell's hierarchy. He reasoned that hell was so overcrowded that there were not enough demons to torture the infinite influx of sinners for the prescribed eternity. There could only be a few hundred of the original fallen angels/demons compared to the countless millions of sinners. So hell was auditioning new talent. *The Book of a Thousand Sins* was the aptitude test. According to legend, only a very few had passed.

The anthropologist committed suicide soon after publishing his treatise on the sadistic grimoire. He'd threaded a crucifix through his urethra and had tried to fuck himself with it. He died of severe blood loss and shock.

Anja spent all night reading the book, pausing occasionally to masturbate to the good parts (and they were all good parts) using a vibrator wrapped in sandpaper. Her French was not the best but it was good enough, and she kept a French/English dictionary by the bed to help her with the more difficult passages. The more she read, the more she believed the archeologist's theory that the book was some type of test to become an arch demon of hell. She decided to call Lord in the morning to ask him about the book.

Lord was a student of human depravity; well versed in all things deviant and perverse. If anyone would be able to decipher the mysteries of the Book of Sins, he would. She hated going to him for anything though. He had a way of making her feel like a slave again.

Lord was a failed divinity student with a doctorate in philosophy and theology. He had been studying to be a priest when he'd realized two things about himself that had forever turned him away from the church. First was his discovery of his perverse sexual appetites. That alone wouldn't have prevented him from joining the priesthood though. There were plenty of perverts in the clergy. The church had a long history of tolerating things within its ranks that they frequently condemned in society. It was his second self-discovery that kept him from ever wearing the collar as more than a fetish item . . . he didn't believe in God.

The tremendous dom was in fact militantly against the idea of faith and even more adamantly against the idea of bowing in worship before a master without the courtesy to even show himself to his worshippers. Lord could tolerate no masters. Slavery of any kind was reprehensible to him. He didn't know how any black person could bow and scrape in supplication before some great overseer in the sky considering their history. Lord had spent most of his life making sure that he would always be in the dominant position in any master/slave relationship be it emotional, physical, or spiritual. Lord bowed to no one and it was this that enraged Anja the most and also what attracted her. Lord had practically formed a religion around himself. Collecting worshippers and acolytes through his promise of sexual freedom and giving them a living physical representation of perfection to worship . . . himself.

Anja decided she needed a dose of empowerment before facing her old master again. She called up Big Lucy and spent the evening fucking her in the ass with a dildo the length of an arm and the circumference of a two liter soda bottle, while flaying her back raw with a cat o' nine tails. She nearly reduced the woman to tears even as she drove her from one powerful orgasm to the next leaving Lucy a quivering mass of welts and wounds drunk with sexual satisfaction. When Anja finally allowed the mannish, hyper-muscular dyke to taste her sex, which was dripping like a faucet after exerting herself stretching open Lucy's rectum, it had still taken two vibrators, a razorblade, and a tasergun before Anja was able to achieve a decent orgasm. Lucy pledged her love to her even as Anja shoved her out of the house, slamming the door in her face. Anja lay back down with the Book of Sins, wrestling with its mysteries until just before sunrise when she finally fell asleep.

She drove to Lord's home/dungeon as soon as she awoke. She was now convinced that the book was her only hope for salvation.

Anja stormed past Bruno, the off-duty cop, who served as a receptionist at the dungeon Lord ran. Here the city's wealthiest connoisseurs of deviant sex paid exorbitant fees for his services and those of the dozen or so other tops and bottoms in Lord's employ. She heard Bruno call out to her as she made her way up the stairs to the attic where Lord kept his most prized toys and brought his most prestigious clients.

Lord launched across the room and caught her by the throat pressing a scalpel to her temple seconds after Anja burst through his door, startling him in the midst of his ghoulish sex-play. His face was a mask of blood and sweat and the woman chained spread-eagle to the metal table, was covered in fresh cuts and old scars. Her sex was dripping blood in a steady stream as Lord worked on her with surgical precision and concentration.

Anja's eyes widened in fear as she saw the blood lust boiling in Lord's hard dark eyes. Then recognition slowly seeped in past the murderous passion and Lord relaxed his grip on her throat but did not release her entirely.

"You of all people should know better than to burst in here unannounced. I could have killed you and raped your carcass before I even knew who you were."

Anja knew he was just showing off for his client. He would never have fucked her corpse. He liked live prey. But he very well may have killed her.

"What do you know about this book?" Anja pulled out *The Book of a Thousand Sins* and Lord's eyes widened in surprise just as Anja's had when she'd first seen it. It had been Lord who'd first told her of its existence.

Lord plucked the book from Anja's hand and released her, walking back over to his captive client twirling the scalpel in one hand while carrying the book in the other.

"Le Livre Des Péchés." Lord read, pronouncing the French flawlessly, *"The Book of a Thousand Sins.* This is a very ancient text. If Sadomasochists had a bible, it would be The Book of Sins. The acts it depicts are so extreme that it would take a madman to perform those outlined in the first chapter alone." Lord said with a tone of warning in his voice. He placed the book on the table and Anja quickly snatched it up, cradling it protectively against her chest. Lord smirked and shook his head as he ran his hands lasciviously over his bound slave, lamenting the interruption of Anja into his session but curious enough about the topic of conversation to delay his playtime for a moment. Occasionally, as he spoke, he would reach between his slave's thighs to nick at her clitoris with his scalpel.

"No one has ever made it through the second chapter. Though many have died trying." Lord said once again absorbed in the lure of the flesh; speaking to Anja without once removing his focus from the naked woman undulating in her own blood as Lord continued his razorblade foreplay.

"No one?"

"No one." Lord replied.

Anja was amazed and intrigued.

"Not even you?" She asked and Lord smiled, sensing a test of his reputation.

"I have very specialized tastes, Anja. I know exactly what will and what will not get me off. There's simply no need to try such extreme experiments."

"Well, nothing really gets me off anymore. My senses are fried. Too much indulgence. My pussy's completely numb to all but the most extreme stimulation. I have to practically put vice-grips on my nipples and clitoris, attach it to a car battery, and run like 1000 volts through my pussy just to cum. I don't even think you could get me off now."

"Sounds sad." Lord commented as he knelt once again between his slave's legs to cut paper-thin slices of tissue from her clitoris. He continued to talk as he carefully sliced away at her sex and she moaned low and soulful as if in ecstasy. Her clitoris began to look like a fan. "The simple pleasures Anja. You must learn to appreciate them. " A wafer thin piece of the woman's labia sliced off into Lord's hand and he promptly popped it into his mouth and began to chew. He looked, quiet literally like the canary who had eaten the cat... or pussy as it were.

"What about the theory that the book is actually a test; an audition to be a reigning demon in hell?"

Lord snickered and shook his head. He took a deep breath and began speaking in a tone like someone explaining a very simple concept to a very slow child.

"I'm an atheist my love. If I don't believe in heaven or God than I certainly don't believe in hordes of fallen angels waiting for death to deliver them fresh souls to torture for eternity. But I suppose if I did believe in such things than it would make sense that the number of sinners would soon grow beyond the ability of those original fallen angels to appropriately attend to. They'd only be able to service the very worst of humanity. The punishment for your average sinner would have to be just being there, forever a resident in that dark flaming world of misery, out of the sight of God. With Satan's rumored hatred of humanity I doubt he would find that acceptable. He'd want to see every human that passed through his fiery gates suffer in unimaginable anguish and that would mean recruiting new demons. Of course . . . that is, if you believe in that sort of thing." He smiled a savage and cunning grin that seemed to indicate that he knew more than he was telling.

"Very interesting." Anja whispered, staring at the book in wonder. She turned and started to head out the door.

"Thank you Lord." She said as she reached for the door handle, eager to get back to her own dungeon and leave Lord to his fun. Ideas were already forming in her head.

"I'm sure there's no need for me to impress upon you the dangers of attempting any of the stuff in that book. You already know the thing's history."

Anja didn't hear Lord's final warning as she ducked out of the room and headed back down the stairs, past Bruno and out into the day. She wouldn't have given a fuck if she had. She was convinced that she knew why the others had failed. They had made themselves a part of the acts. She knew that wasn't what Satan wanted. He didn't want to see how much his acolytes could suffer but how much suffering they were willing and able to inflict. She left Lord's dungeon with a mission. That night she called all her slaves together; selecting only the most loyal, most perverse, most masochistic of the lot, those with the highest threshold of pain.

They stood around Anja's basement dungeon, naked, excited, and mortally afraid. There were hot brands and pokers heating in a furnace and the acrid burning smell mixed with the odor of the various caged animals, which were new additions as well, and the smell of their own lush and humid fear. Anja opened her black doctor's bag, which they all knew rather well and pulled out her surgical instruments. This too held a surprise or two. No one could remember the bone saw or the orthodontic drill being in there before. Then she pulled out the infamous *Book of a Thousand Sins* and they fell into a terrified silence. They had all known horrors in their lifetimes, willingly participated in many of them. They had seen and done things average folks would never believe human beings were capable of doing to one another, but they had all heard about the book and didn't know if they were up for that type of horror.

Four of the fifteen slaves assembled in the room fled quickly, without apology or explanation. Slob, who had given Anja the malevolent text, was one of the first ones out the door. The rest stayed, eagerly awaiting their mistresses' commands. Anja smiled.

"Well, let's get started." She began chaining them up. She didn't want anyone resisting too much once the pain began.

It was the following morning before a distraught and agitated Slob contacted Lord, calling him at the crack of dawn with his voice choked with panic and tears. He was obviously in shock and his words tumbled down over one another into an indecipherable, multi-syllabic stew. Lord could make out only a few words. But what he heard was enough to get him out of bed and into his car, headed toward Anja's basement dungeon.

"The Book of Sins! Anja's gone! So many bodies! It's horrible! I should have never given her the book! I only wanted to please her . . ."

When Lord opened the basement door, the combined odor of blood, semen, feces, and the smell of burning flesh immediately accosted him. Then he heard the screams and moans and saw a woman with big blue eyes like a porpoise, tears streaming down her face, cuts and brands over fully eighty percent of her body, crawling across the basement floor with a corpse dangling from her anus.

A man's entire head had been inserted, presumably with a great deal of lubricant, into her rectum where he had suffocated. His head was completely engulfed in her large, flabby, dimpled ass with his neck sandwiched in between her buttocks and his body sprawled out behind her, limp and lifeless and covered in blood and feces. The woman's face showed exquisite horror as she crawled toward the stairs dragging the corpse's dead weight behind her. Lord could only imagine what the expression on the man's face must've been.

The woman reached back and tried to gently ease the man's head out of her ass but it would not budge. The effort was causing her even more pain as well and causing blood to flow in a stream from her anus, down the man's neck and over his chest. Extricating his carcass from her ass was a feat she was obviously unable to accomplish on her own. Lord doubted whether he could do it either and was not relishing the thought of explaining the predicament to a paramedic or a police officer. Suddenly her bowels let loose with another deluge of excrement, covering the corpse in a brown tide. Lord's stomach lurched as the avalanche of liquid shit and blood obliterated the man's features from sight. What waited for him below was even worse.

He stepped over the human butt-plug and continued down the steps into the dungeon where a menagerie of unimaginable horror unfolded before him. On a medieval rack lay a woman with her eyes, mouth, and vagina sewn shut. Some small hairy creature was already in the process of chewing itself free of her surgically sutured labia and her cheeks undulated with the efforts of yet another animal to free itself from its prison of human flesh. The woman's eyes were glazed in horror and her breath came shallow and rapid as the nose and teeth of some type of rodent began to poke its way through the hole it had gnawed in her vagina. The woman began to thrash and buck as if trying to break free of the bonds securing her to the rack. She arched her back and spread her legs wide as her body continued to writhe and convulse. Abruptly a large eel ruptured the stitches that cinched tight her rectum and slithered its way out of her ass, across the table, and onto the floor, trailing blood and excrement.

Lord turned away in disgust but there were worse sights in almost every direction. He continued further into the dungeon.

A woman who looked like a powerlifter with tremendous muscles and fat in equal proportion caught Lord's attention as his mind reeled from one vile image to the next. He knew her. It was Big Lucy, Anja's sometime lover. All the skin had been removed from her tremendous DD breasts, the skin hanging in two long flaps over her belly, nipples and all. The sallow adipose and muscle tissue surrounding her massive mammary glands glistened with a sheen of blood. Blood dripped from her mutilated tits all down her body puddling on the floor beneath her feet. Still the jiggle and bounce of those tremendous breasts even in their current state caused Lord's manhood to stir. She was performing fellatio on a man chained to a wall whose penis had been sliced lengthwise and peeled like a banana. He screamed over and over as her lips and tongue worked on his bloodied stump, which was still miraculously erect. Then, even more remarkably, he came and bathed her face and mouth in semen and blood which she greedily licked from her lips, scooping the primal cocktail from her cheeks and chin into her mouth and licking her fingers. Lord began stroking himself through his jeans as he stared at the impossible scene of torture and passion.

Another man whose penis had been sliced in half, cauterized, and stitched was fucking Big Lucy in two orifices simultaneously. One half of his mutilated organ slid up into her vagina and the other half fed into her ass while she continued to lick warm blood and cum from her fingers. The man's arms were sewn together in back of him and his eyes and mouth were stitched shut just like the woman on the rack.

There was a corpse lying on a gurney with several orifices cut into his chest, stomach, and throat, being serviced aggressively by several enraptured satyrs. The corpse was covered in bible pages pinned to its flesh by small needles like some sacrilegious form of acupuncture. One of the men was missing an arm and had a crucifix screwed uncomfortably into his urethra. He winced in obvious pain and discomfort even as he continued to fuck the corpse's hollowed eye socket. He was arm in arm like a football team in a huddle with a small Filipino man who had a hand protruding from his rectum.

"If that hand waves at me I'll slit my own throat." Lord thought to himself. He'd never seen anything like it.

"She must have been really bored." He thought.

There was no sign of Anja anywhere.

Lord walked past a couple entwined on the floor who'd been sewn together by their lips and sexual organs, forced to fuck forever, or at least until the paramedics arrived to separate them, or they suffocated to death. He picked up *The Book of a Thousand Sins* and crept back up the stairs, tip-toeing around the woman with the dead man's head in her ass. Somehow she had gotten a hold of a hacksaw and was trying to saw the corpse's head off. Lord paused for a second and considered helping her before continuing out the door. He didn't want to be there when emergency units arrived. Besides, he had work to do.

He could guess where Anja had gone. And he knew that he would someday be seeing her again and unless he did something to turn the tables, this time she would be holding the whip.

Lord remembered the cruelty he'd discovered hidden deep within Anja when he'd allowed her to top him. There was a vengeful spirit inside of her that had threatened to consume them both. It had come boiling out of her in a savage fit of sadistic violence. He'd been chained helpless to the bed when all the years of abuse had erupted. Lord saw the hatred and pain roiling in her eyes as she pulled out the cat o' nine tails with the razor barbs at the end. He dropped the bell that he'd had clutched in his hand to signal Anja to stop but she was too far-gone. Ignoring the signal, she continued to flail and slash at his flesh, lost in her hatred for her father and uncle and every man in her life who'd followed their pattern. Including Lord himself.

Lord had not allowed himself to cry out. He'd withstood her wrath in silence. Penitence. He would give Anja her pound of flesh but his dignity would not be part of the bargain. He had lost about half an hour before she realized that he'd blacked out from the pain. She patiently revived him. Then she began to cut on him. He still bore the scars from their play.

They tried switching several more times and each time Anja had lost control. Then, when Lord again topped her, he would punish her for her transgressions. Their S&M play soon began to resemble a war of spite. It wasn't long before Anja left him, saying she could no longer be his slave and knowing that he would never submit to being hers. Still they had remained passionate for each other; a passion that had warped into a friendship based on mutual lust, envy, and resentment.

Lord's mind was working overtime. He didn't believe in Heaven or Hell except where they could be found in the pleasures and agonies of the flesh but he could think of no other explanation for the horrors he'd witnessed down in that basement and Anja's disappearance. Lord knew that if Anja had somehow found the key to The Book of Sins and made her way to hell, she would be waiting there for him. He shuddered, imagining what she would do to him once she had him in her grasp with an eternity to devise new ways to make him suffer. He had to make sure that when they met again it would be on equal terms and that meant unlocking the secrets of the book himself. Only he was in no hurry to go to hell. God or Devil, Lord wanted his reign to be on earth.

He stalked out of Anja's home and back to his car; a sleek black Mercedes owned by one of his closest friends and wealthiest clients, a photographer by the name of Jacque Gabriel Willet. Jacque was renowned for his disturbing photos of human oddities, freaks and perverts, mostly nudes, mostly in bondage, mostly procured and posed by Lord. In San Francisco he was more famous than Warhol and his photographs cost nearly as much. He was in love with Lord.

Lord raced through the streets with a sense of urgency speeding him toward his destination. He feared that Anja might not be content to wait for him to join the ranks of the damned via natural causes. It was probable that she would want to drag him down to hell with her right away, before he could unravel the mysteries of The Book of Sins. Lord knew that if he wanted the power of hell he would have to do something more spectacular than merely aping the acts described within. He had to take the book to the next level. He would translate Le Livre Des Péchés into English.

Lord's ego swelled as he imagined linking his legacy to those of the book's past translators. Damien Augustus had gone on to found a religion. De Sade had become one of the most infamous writers in history. Before dying alone in an insane asylum. Lord imagined himself the head of a new religion or an artist whose name would forever resound through the chronicles of history. His translation had to be so grand as to eclipse those that had come before it. He decided to not only translate the decadent tome but to capture each act described within on film using live subjects. Each gruesome contortion illustrated by black and white photographs to replace the crude sketches penned by De Sade. Lord's ego roared like a conquering lion as he gunned the engine and sped off toward Jacque's studio, his destiny calling out to him in chorus with his ambition.

Anja did not know what she'd been expecting but this certainly was not it. The Hell into which she'd tumbled was an endless night of fire and flesh, agony and the screams of the damned. The lake of fire overflowed with more bodies than lava and flame. Anja panicked as she felt herself being crushed and suffocated by the naked weight of innumerable sinners writhing in agony. These were not the ethereal disembodied spirits she'd been expecting. They were physical beings of living flesh, their corporeal forms restored so that they might suffer forever in nerve searing anguish.

Anja was surrounded on all sides by a running river of meat and fat. Endless legions of the damned grabbed and pulled at her in an ecstasy of terrifying agony as molten earth pored over them, turning their meat and bones to a thick sludge, a boiling meat pudding. The press of millions of pounds of corpulent matter smothered her. Anja was drowning, swimming through fathoms of melting skin, muscle, and fat, a sluggish lard running like taffy under the fierce heat of myriad sins. Their blood, sweat, and liquefied flesh dripped into her eyes, nose and mouth, down the back of her throat gagging her.

The damned were pulling her down into the lake of fire in their own efforts to escape. The flaming lava washed over Anja and her own screams joined the terrible chorus of mortal shrieks and cries. She knew that God could not help her here. So she called out to a different master.

Jacque was a short anemic-looking Parisian who wore his hair pulled back in a ponytail despite the fact that much of it had abandoned the top of his head. He had frightened eyes that darted about as if he suspected some predator was lurking just out of sight and he was preparing himself to run for his life at any second. His smile would burst onto his face beaming like the sun for no apparent reason and then just as quickly die away into a fit of nervous grins and ticks or even a scowl. His most annoying habit was that of screeching like a skinned cat when angered, his eyes watering up as if he was about to burst into tears as he berated the victim of his wrath in a shrill falsetto. When his tirade was over his face would relax back into its normal pattern of ticks and grins. He looked like someone who had spent much of his life getting his ass kicked and was still waiting for the next blow to fall. Even his expensive suits and manicured nails could not hide the fact that he was a victim. It had not surprised Lord one bit the first time the man took off his clothing and revealed the lace panties and bra he wore underneath.

Jacque knelt with his nose inches from his model's genitals as he carefully posed him for the next series of photographs. He had tied the young model's genitals up with dental floss so tight that it bit into his skin and drew blood in places. The boy's testicles turned blue from the blood restriction and the tip of his cock was already turning a purple that was nearly black. Jacque was having a difficult time figuring out what to do with the rest of him. He had enough pictures of the boy's genitals in various states of torture. Now he needed a full body shot. He needed the inspiration of his lord and master. As if on cue the phone rang. Lord was on his way and he had some good news. Jacque squealed like a girl. He loved surprises.

Lord knocked on the door. When the door flew open and the ecstatic photographer spilled out into the hall, Lord had to slap him to the floor to get the fawning little queer off of him.

"Stop pawing me and listen! I have news that will shape both of our destinies forever."

Lord had to concentrate all his will to keep from strangling Jacque when the girlish squeals and endless chatter began to tumble out of the man's thin-lipped maw in an inarticulate jumble. He growled out his words slowly.

"Shut the fuck up and listen before I cut your fucking tongue out!"

Jacque abruptly snapped his mouth shut. He had seen enough of Lord's handiwork to know better than to take the man's threats lightly.

He quivered with excitement at both the sound of Lord's voice and the content of his words as Lord relayed his intentions in graphic detail.

"How will we get the models? Even your clients won't go for this. Those sick enough to get off on this type of thing certainly won't want to be photographed."

Lord reassured him. There were ways of acquiring anything in this town. San Francisco was a haven for the perverse.

"I'd like to be in it."

Timothy's meek and tender voice startled both of them as the effeminate young model tiptoed up between them. Timothy was Jacque's flavor of the month. He was one of the prettiest boys Jacque had ever had. As pale as fresh cream with long slight limbs, big trusting eyes that seemed to brim with pain and sorrow, and full bow-shaped lips, like a gangly adolescent girl. Timothy looked every part the willing victim and it was far more than an affectation. He was the star of Jacque's most recent photographs and as such had already been subjected to horrors that would've turned the stomach of even the most debauched masochists. They had both nearly forgotten he was in the room.

"You have no idea what you are getting into little boy." Lord replied staring at the kid like the world's biggest fool.

Jacque rushed to Timothy's side and draped an arm around his shoulder as if to protect him. He tried to turn the boy and lead him away from what could only lead to his death in screaming anguish. Timothy shrugged him off and approached Lord. His body shook as he stepped directly into his shadow and the voluptuous power that radiated from Lord's flesh washed over him. With a Herculean act of will he managed to hold Lord's fearsome gaze with his own. His knees shook but still he did not blink.

"It might kill me? Is that what you are thinking? Do you think I care whether or not I live or die! Fuck, I don't matter! Don't you think I know that? The only thing that matters is the art. Art is the only thing that has made my life worth anything. Until you and Jacque found me I was selling my ass on the street and getting high everyday. I'd have died out there before the end of the year. Either some trick would have killed me or I'd have overdosed or caught AIDS or something. Now I'm fucking immortal! My life has meaning. I am living art now and that's how I'd like to die." Finally Timothy dropped his eyes. Exhausted by the effort required to maintain eye contact.

Jacque smiled, brimming with pride. Even Lord nodded his head in admiration of Timothy's courage. The boy understood. He knew the significance of their art, of what they were about to do. The creation of art was the closest man came to godliness and being a part of that art was the closest this boy would ever get to heaven. Though Lord wondered how long Timothy's conviction would last once the pain began; pain many times worse than anything the boy had yet experienced at their hands.

"Then help us recruit more souls for our little journey to hell and you shall become a part of something that will last forever."

Timothy stared at Lord the way a child would look up at priest or pastor during a sermon, his eyes filled with awe and reverence. Jacque shuddered, imagining what horrors Lord had in mind for his young model. Before they left, Lord called a few of the slaves he knew would be up for this type of thing. Trying to select mostly the ones who would not be missed if they were to inexplicably disappear.

His first call was to Vanessa, the woman he'd been servicing when Anja had first barged in demanding information on the Book of Sins, info he now regretted having given her. Vanessa answered on the first ring.

"Yes Lord?"

"I need you tonight."

"I'm still sore my Lord."

"Are you refusing me?"

"No . . . uh . . . of course not my Lord."

"Then go to the dungeon and collect my toys. Gather everything you can carry."

"Where would you like me to meet you?"

"I'll call you and let you know."

He made three more phone calls and got commitments from each to stand by the phone. Then he told Jacque and Timothy to get dressed and they all went out to troll for rough trade in the leather bars, fetish dance clubs, S&M clubs and swingers bars that proliferated in the City of Sin. They were confident that Jacque's money, Lord's physique, and Timothy's beauty would be all the bait they would need to procure the subjects they needed for their art.

With Book of A Thousand Sins in tow, tucked firmly under Lord's arm, they piled into a limousine Jacque rented for the evening and sped off into the night. As they rounded the corner, Lord spotted a woman standing across the street and gasped. She looked just like Anja. They sped past and she disappeared behind them before he could be sure, but the woman had looked exactly like his former slave and sometime mistress. He shuddered, imagining what she must have come there for. He knew that time was running out. He would have to work quickly.

Anja watched the limousine cruise by and growled low in her throat. She could still feel the flesh and sweat of a million damned souls like an oily film on her skin. She clutched the cat o' nine tails she'd fashioned of their hair, bone, and sinew and imagined it cutting into Lord's back. She imagined flaying the skin from his magnificent body and finally hearing the screams he jealously held within him.

Lord was off to assemble his slaves presumably to mimic her own journey into hell by way of the Book of Sins. If he was successful he would escape her punishment, deprive her of the chance to ever hear the love pour out of him in tender shrieks of mortal anguish. He would never belong to her.

She knew that there was no way she could love him, no way that he could love her, unless she made him bow and crawl, beg for her mercy and her love. Only as his mistress, only as his dominant superior, could she allow herself to love him, would he ever allow himself to love her.

Lord remained the only man she'd ever topped who hadn't screamed for her. She'd whipped, cut, and burned him until he passed out and still he endured his torment in stoic silence. He'd refused to scream for her in life. But now she had many more ways to mine his flesh for the screams within each tender nerve. So many more devices at her disposal.

She stroked her pets as they groaned and complained, uncomfortable with the flesh she'd made for them from the protoplasmic soup and lava that had filled the fiery lake. They gnashed their terrible claws, and bared their terrible teeth, and stroked their long, throbbing, razor-barbed cocks. Anja gazed upon their ghastly ramshackle bodies and imagined what Lord would look like as one of them.

Their bodies had long ago disintegrated in the lake of fire so she'd fashioned them new ones, twisted flesh sculptures each in the form of her own nightmares. The tortured souls within still shrieked in rage and pain as she pointed them in the direction of their prey.

Jacque led them to a dance club in the South of Market warehouse district, where the bondage and fetish crowd mixed with the rave club scene. Lord doubted that there would be any reasonable prospects among these "Fetish for fashion" types, but it was early so he was willing to be open-minded.

The dimly lit club was packed with latex and leather-clad gothic types gyrating to the pounding thrum of a frenetic techno-beat. In every corner of the darkened club, partially illuminated by the electric blue flicker of strobe lights and lasers, pseudo-sadists whipped and pierced their tender-skinned half-committed subs. Lord passed amongst them, inhaling their perfumed and liquored pheromones. He appraised their pale anemic bodies, each with a profusion of superficial welts and scars, most appearing to be purely decorative, looking for one with scars deeper than the rest. One whose flesh bore the marks of a stronger commitment to pain and pleasure than the average horny club-goer looking for a safe alternative to casual sex.

Jacque and Timothy were both staring around the club with eyes wide and glossy with lust. The proximity of young flesh driving them into a feverish state of arousal. The crack of whips echoed throughout the club as wannabe doms whipped their slaves for the amusement of the other patrons. Lord was disgusted. This entire scene was a mockery of his profession.

A sign by the stairway announced a body-piercing booth upstairs. Lord decided to check it out. If there were any true masochists in this funhouse that was perhaps the best place to look for them.

Lord shouldered his way through the crowd ignoring the leering stares and not-too-subtle come-ons from the make-up masochists, drawn to the furious heat of his passion which blazed like a sun in this dark pit where everyone else seemed only slightly more passionate than the average married couple. They drooled over his powerful musculature imagining the intense agony and fathomless pleasure such a body would be capable of meting out. Other doms looked upon him with envy and some dared to imagine what it would be like to top such a man. Lord looked upon them all with a disdainful sneer, meeting their eyes until each one bowed their heads and looked away, subs and doms alike. To call Lord a dominant was like calling a tsunami a wave. He was so much more than that.

Timothy and Jacque watched him with possessive admiration as he disappeared up the stairs. They continued to wander among the dancers and leather-clad pretenders orbiting the dance floor with whips and cats they'd probably never drawn blood with. Some of them had their "slaves" on leashes and both Jacque and Timothy noticed the absence of scars or welts on their backs and shook their heads in disappointment. Timothy thought about the symbol of Lord, a closed fist squeezing a serpent to a bloody pulp, which was branded onto his left ass-cheek. He reached over and patted Jacque on the ass where he knew he'd been branded as well. They belonged to a true dom. Lord had been right. These were all a bunch of poseurs. Not one of these charlatans understood pain. Not one of them understood the artistry of flesh. The multitude of layers that existed beyond the limits of ecstasy, where orgasm became agony and agony the most powerful climax.

Timothy shrugged off the attentions of a tall athletic-looking dominatrix, with skin the color of fresh cream and large lips that were a perfect argument for the idea that oral sex was not an unnatural act and that sometimes nature indeed seemed to favor it. Her ass was full and plump just the way Lord liked it. Too bad she thought herself a top.

The woman was trying her best to look sinister in a black latex Bettie Page get-up as she dragged her whip between her teeth and glared at Timothy. She had cold eyes but they were obviously hardened by pain and sorrow rather than cruelty. She was beautiful. Her voluptuous body was like a modern statue of Venus. Aphrodite in a latex nightie. Timothy had the urge to take one of her massive breasts in his hands to see if they were real. Jacque was imagining stabbing them with a dagger to answer the same questions.

Growing tired of her ridiculous attempt at seduction, Timothy lifted his spandex shirt to show her the runes and hieroglyphics carved and branded into his flesh along with the profusion of other scars, which were the results of Lord's passion and Jacque's art. Her jaw dropped and a shudder went through her. Laughingly her eyes teared up and her lips trembled.

"Would you like to see more or have you seen enough to know that you're out of your league?" Jacque said to her stepping up and throwing a protective arm around Timothy with a cruel smile scarring his face.

The woman opened her mouth to speak but they turned their backs on her and headed up the stairs to find their Lord.

When they reached the top of the stairs they had no problem spotting Lord who was at least a head taller than nearly everyone else in the room. He stood at the piercing booth with a bemused expression on his face. The other club patrons were alternately looking at him and whoever was sitting in the piercing booth. Jacque and Timothy began to squeeze their way through the crowd trying to glimpse what it was that had captured Lord's attention.

When they reached the booth they were greeted by the site of a scarification. An overweight woman with massive breasts whose bra size lay somewhere in the middle of the alphabet, was letting some bumbling buffoon carve a design onto her breasts. The man, who looked like a middle-aged Hell's Angel was hesitating with each cut and every-time she winced he would pull away and wipe sweat from his brow. The woman was growing impatient.

"Fuck, I can't do this. I'm just a piercer. I know I said I could, but I'm sorry." The man said in defeat. "I'll give you your money back."

"Give me the scalpel." Lord interrupted and now everyone turned to look at him.

"Uh, I don't know." The biker stammered.

The woman looked up at Lord as if he were indeed her savior.

"Do you know what you're doing?"

"Trust me." Lord replied slipping the scalpel from the biker's limp grasp and taking his seat in front of her.

He reached out and caressed the woman's massive breasts, pinching each nipple causing her to squirm and squeal. He leaned forward and kissed her on the earlobe and she seemed to melt in her chair.

"Play with your pussy. You'll enjoy this more that way." Lord grabbed the top of her skirt and pulled it out stretching the already taxed elastic waistband. He grabbed her other hand and slid it down between her thighs. Then he began to cut.

She started to wince and moan but her voice was low and smoky with desire. When Lord looked up at her face, her eyes were half-lidded and staring down at him. She was licking her lips and furiously fingering herself. Lord drew the scalpel through her flesh in long sweeping strokes carving what looked like a huge scorpion across one breast and a hawk on the other. The two were engaged in battle. The woman shook and moaned as the scalpel danced through her flesh. Then her entire body began to convulse as a powerful orgasm rumbled through her. Lord backed away with the scalpel as the climax took her and her enormous breasts flopped and jiggled. When she finally collapsed back into the chair, Lord continued cutting on her.

The woman said she was too sensitive to touch herself anymore but Lord had more work to do on her. He never left a masterpiece incomplete. He reached down her skirt and slid his fingers up inside her dripping wet snatch. He found her clitoris and began to circle it with his thumb as he jabbed his remaining fingers up inside her. With his other hand he resumed carving the design, finishing it just as a second orgasm rocked her corpulent form.

When Lord looked up, the crowd that had formed around them began to clap enthusiastically in appreciation of his skill. Lord leaned forward and spoke into the woman's ear dragging his tongue along her neck and the underside of her jaw as he spoke.

"You've passed the audition my love. If you would allow me I can show you ecstasy like you've never dreamed."

The woman's lip quivered and she looked into Lord's eyes with an expression still humid with lust.

"Oh my god yes. Take me!" She collapsed into his arms and Lord lifted her from the chair. Jacque and Timothy stood staring at them both, their faces beaming with excitement.

"My Lord you are truly a marvel! These philistines have no idea what a rare treat they have just witnessed." Timothy reached out and caressed the blood soaked design on the woman's naked breast. She winced and batted his hand away. She'd forgotten that her blouse was still open and immediately began to button it up.

"I was just admiring them. I've never seen breasts so big. They're fucking marvelous!"

"They're truly beautiful." Jacque agreed smiling and scowling alternately in his nervous quirky way.

"Play nice my love. These are your brothers in pain and pleasure. Jacque and Timothy." They both bowed before her with a flourish.

"Jacque Willet? Jacque Gabriel Willet the famous photographer? I love your work!" She beamed. Then she turned toward Timothy appraising him with a new interest.

"I knew I recognized you. You're his model. The one in that picture with the fishhooks and sewing needles piercing him all over."

"That's me." Timothy beamed.

"Would you like to model for me?" Jacque asked, feigning modesty.

"Oh my God. I would love to!" the woman cried out, her massive breasts jiggling with excitement.

"We never say that name. If you must exclaim like that than say 'Oh my Lord'." Jacque corrected her.

"Why? Why 'Lord' instead of 'God'? What's the difference?"

"Well, I believe you've already met Lord . . ." Timothy replied gesturing toward the massive black man whom she was still clutching as if afraid he would disappear if she released him. ". . . and there simply is no such being as God except for our Lord and master." Timothy replied, gazing at Lord with a religious rapture brimming in his eyes.

"I'm not so sure Timothy." Lord replied turning away from them and heading down the stairs with his new prize in tow.

"Lord?"

"Yes my pet?"

"Are you my master now? I mean, am I your slave?"

"I am your savior my love. You are now a child of Lord."

Timothy and Jacque skipped down the stairs after them, giddy with excitement. Lord reached the lower level and was headed for the exit when a tall latex-clad woman stepped in front of him with her head bowed. Lord bumped right into her, knocking her over and Jacque and Timothy rushed to help her to her feet.

"Sorry about that lady. You should have watched where you were going."

"I knew exactly where I was going. Exactly where I wanted to be."

"You!" Jacque exclaimed. It was the Bettie Page wannabe they'd met earlier.

Lord turned to see what the commotion was about and then paused when he saw the beautiful woman with the voluptuous body and the hard tragic eyes of an abused child.

"What do you want?"

"I want this!" She said, ripping Timothy's shirt up revealing his innumerable scars. She started to say more but realized by the look in Lord's eyes that nothing more needed to be said.

"Are you sure you know what you are asking for?"

207

"Yes," she said shuddering inwardly as she stared at Timothy's love trophies, "I know."

Lord reached out and snatched the whip from her hand tossing it to the floor. "Then come with us. But from now on only one hand holds the whip. Mine!" His eyes flashed with a passion so dark and terrible that the woman dropped her eyes and shuddered again. Lord smiled, aroused by her sudden timidity. He wondered how such a woman could have ever imagined herself to be a dominant.

"What is your name?" Lord asked, reaching out to caress her cheek and then sliding his hand down her neck, between her breasts, reaching inside her latex bustier to pinch a nipple. With his other hand he reached around to caress her large round ass pleased with its fullness. He released her just as she started to enjoy his touch.

"Lana," she replied breathlessly.

"Welcome to the family Lana," Timothy chimed in.

"And what's her name?" Jacque asked, pointing to the obese woman still clinging to Lord like a symbiote.

"My name is Sue."

"Welcome Sue."

"Are we going back to your house now?" she asked Lord.

"Not yet. We have more recruiting to do. Jacque and I are going to create a masterpiece. You all will be a part of it. But it requires a few more models."

"Jacque Willet?" Lana chimed in with a star-struck look. They all ignored her question and spilled out of the exit into the night air. The limousine pulled up to retrieve them and they sped off down the street.

Again Lord thought he saw Anja standing in line outside the club. He stared at her features as they sped past, trying to positively identify her. It was only after they were well past the club that Lord noticed something wrong, something not entirely human, not quite alive, about the other club-hoppers standing in line. He could not be sure because he'd been so focused on Anja that he hadn't really paid much attention to them, but he had the vague impression of tusk-like fangs and jagged pieces of shattered bone sticking out like horns and spikes, ill-fitting mis-matched limbs, several different faces grafted to the same head. Demons dressed in the flesh of the dead. Time was running out.

"Shackles" was a leather bar notorious for its rough trade. It was not entirely uncommon to see an ambulance pulled up in the alley beside it or even the coroner's van, the illicit sex acts that took place in the men's room having ruptured one artery too many and left some poor slob in a pool of his own blood, shit, and semen. It was a perfect spot to recruit more subjects for the book.

The limo pulled up in the alley beside the bar and Jacque and Timothy stepped out first, looking like just the type of meal the sharks in this place were used to dining on. Then out came Lana and Sue and finally Lord himself. A bald fat guy with absolutely no muscle tone but with hair growing down his chest like a wool sweater, wearing a leather vest without a shirt, chaps without pants, his pierced and perforated genitals hanging free in the night air, and police issue riding boots identical to the ones Lord himself wore, stared right through Lord's entourage of slaves and right at him. It was a challenge. Lord spotted the swastika on the man's arm and bared his teeth in an evil grin. He locked eyes with the man and walked toward him.

A cold fury burned in Lord's gaze as he strode toward the bar, toward the burly bear in the leather chaps. Lord's eyes were filled with the blood and screams of his many past slaves as well as the terrified and agonized cries of those he'd been paid to torture by his friends in various crime families. Friends with an appreciation for those talented enough in the art of pain to extract information from men who'd learned not to fear death. Cruelty and power radiated from him as he approached the man with every intention of walking through him, staring the man down until he was nearly on top of him, his shadow falling upon him blocking the moon and stars. The man lowered his gaze and slid quickly out of Lord's way. The leather-clad queens in back of him did the same. Lord stepped into the bar while his entourage followed.

The bar was half-empty. It appeared the handful of guys standing outside represented nearly half the bar's occupants.

"Fuck. This place is dead," Lana said.

"Sit at the bar," Lord replied, "I'm going to the men's room."

Lord walked into the men's room and the smell of blood and anal sex wafted up into his nostrils. He'd anticipated the smell and had long grown used to it.

Every stall was filled. Grunts and moans echoed in the bathroom along with the sound of balls and coarse hands slapping against bare asses. Against the sink, three men who had been unable to find an empty stall, were engaged in a furious ménage à trois. Two of the bar's more typical clientele were savagely fucking and abusing a guy who looked more like a businessman who'd been caught in the wrong place at the wrong time than the normal trade this place attracted. A muscular black guy dressed similarly to the guy Lord had met outside, was fucking the guy's throat with a dick roughly the length of an infant's arm. The man gagged repeatedly but never choked even when the black guy's semen erupted into his throat. The other man, who was even larger than the first, the rough leatherman biker type, a combination of muscle, hair, and fat, had his entire arm shoved up the guy's ass and was sliding it in and out, punching up into his colon like a heavyweight boxer. Far from being distressed by the unnatural distension of his anus, the victim of this bizarre prison rape fantasy was vigorously masturbating, each thrust of the man's arm into his rectum eliciting a moan of profound ecstasy. He flagellated his own miniscule erection until his cum shot out onto the piss-stained floor.

Lord smiled. This guy would make a welcome addition to their little menagerie. He thought about the woman back at Anja's little dungeon who'd had the corpse's head crammed into her ass and marked with satisfaction that this guy would have no problem accomplishing that feat. He wondered how long Timothy could hold his breath.

The black guy who'd just shot his load down the little businessman's throat, turned to face Lord with a courage born of both the normal male post-coital over confidence left from his recent sexual conquest, and an unnatural stupidity.

"'Da fuck is you looking at bitch? You want to suck this dick too?'"

Lord wished he had more time to enjoy killing the man. Instead he simply thrust his fingers through the man's eye sockets and into his skull, settling for the satisfaction of watching the man's death convulsions as his fingertips pierced his brain.

The huge biker dude cried out as his partner collapsed to the floor and abruptly wrenched his shit and blood covered arm from his bitch's anus. Tears were streaming down his face for his fallen lover as he started toward Lord.

He lasted a few seconds longer than his partner had. Lord drove his fist into the man's solar plexus, crushing his xiphoid process and collapsing his lungs. The guy slumped to the floor gasping for air as his lungs filled with blood. The little businessman started to scream and Lord silenced him by slapping him hard to the floor.

"You like pain little girl?"

The man nodded his head "Yes" then quickly changed it to "No" recalling what had just been done to his recent lovers. Lord smirked and whipped out his own enormous cock.

"Not that kind of pain. This kind of pain."

The little businessman's eyes widened with hunger.

"You want to be my bitch? My little slave boy? Or do you want me to leave you here? With them?"

The effete businessman looked from Lord's impressive organ hanging inches from his face to the two corpses lying on the piss and cum stained floor in a growing pool of blood. He nodded his head.

"Say the words," Lord commanded.

"Yes. Yes, I want to be your slave. My Lord." He reached out and took Lord's organ into his hands as if he were holding a sacred object and began kissing all along its length with eyes filled with love.

Lord smiled, pleased.

"You've heard of me?"

The man paused still holding Lord's massive cock and gazed up at him.

"Of course I have my Lord. My name is William, William Gray. I paid for your services once. I was inexperienced then, practically a virgin to the scene. You'd been too much for me then but I'm better now. I've striven to make myself worthy of you. I'm willing to try again if you'll have me?"

Lord smiled in reply. He drew his cock out of William's hands and back into his pants noting the man's sorrow at the loss. As they left the bathroom, Lord noticed that the sounds of sex from the other stalls had not diminished for a second during the entire encounter. The people here were used to minding their own business. Getting fucked was far more important to them than getting killed.

Even William felt it the second he stepped out of the restroom. There was something violent and malevolent in the air, something dark and unnatural. The air was charged with hatred and lust. Fights started to break out in the back of the bar and the sounds of passion from the restroom they'd just left turned to shouts and screams of rage and terror. Beyond the front door, the screams were even more agonized. Lord recognized the sounds of ripping flesh, sinew being torn from bone, bones crunching. He knew what was coming. He grabbed his small coven and headed for the exit at a dead run. Timothy and Jacque followed without a word, knowing better than to question his actions until they were all safe at home. The rest of them followed cautiously, shouting questions at their backs. The little businessman was at Lord's side when they burst out into the alley. He assumed they were fleeing the scene of the murder before the bodies were discovered, attributing the pall of death and madness that had settled on the bar to the ferocious black man at his side.

They spilled out into the alley and tumbled into the open door of the limousine as savage guttural roars, barks, and howls echoed from within the bar accompanied by agonized shrieks and the smacking and sucking sounds of someone enjoying a grand feast. Lord looked back just before the exit door slammed shut, just in time to see the half-human creatures spilling into the bar. A gangly mob of vaguely anthropoid monstrosities with a profusion of asymmetrical arms and legs, fanged mouths, eyes tucked in places that would grant them no advantageous views, jagged bone protrusions from which the living flesh of their victims already dangled. They were ripping the place apart, killing and fucking anyone they could catch.

The smell of blood, smoke, burning flesh, and internal organs reached Lord's nose as he slammed the limousine door shut behind him. Luckily he was the only one in the car who would have recognized the stench.

The man who'd first confronted Lord as he'd stepped from the limousine, spilled out the front door as they flew past the bar, out of the alley, and into the street. His face had been slit down the center, peeled back away from his skull, and pinned back behind his ears with nails driven into his skull. His ass had been so savagely fucked that it appeared to have exploded. His ass cheeks had been ripped apart so viciously that they were nearly falling off and his anus was now a gaping maw. It looked like a flower in full bloom. Lord recognized the technique immediately. This was Anja's handiwork. Anja and her new pets. They were getting closer.

Lord's heart beat against his ribs like a captive beast pounding the bars of its cage for freedom. Anja was coming for him. She knew that he would soon finish his work of art and secure an honored place in hell. Which meant that he would escape her torture.

213

There was no way he could complete the translation before she caught up with him but perhaps he could finish the photographs. He looked over his growing tribe of deviant misfits. They had no idea what they were getting into. This was so much more than just an orgy of deviant lust caught on film for posterity. It was even more than the pivotal act of sexual and artistic sacrifice that Timothy and Jacque believed it to be. Not just sacrificing their bodies or even their lives for art but sacrificing their immortal souls, condemning them to eternal torment at the hands of Mistress Anja.

With Anja on his tail, Lord couldn't risk another close call at a nightclub. He had to keep moving. That meant his only option was to pick up some street meat. He told the driver to head toward Polk Street, ignoring the frantic questions from Jacque and the others who'd all heard the screams and animalistic growls coming from the bar and seen the faceless death rictus on the dying leatherman. They were starting to piss him off. He didn't have to explain anything to any of them.

"In for a penny. In for a pound," Lord growled at them. They would all soon know what he meant. They belonged to him now, body and soul.

"Who's the square?" Timothy asked, poking William in his soft little tummy.

"William this is everybody. Everybody this is William."

Sue and Lana welcomed Lord's latest acquisition with cool suspicion. Sue was already growing jealous and snuggled close to Lord for reassurance. Timothy rolled his eyes and laughed at her insecurity. Secretly growing jealous himself.

"So what's your trip William? What are you into?"

"I found William in the restroom with this big muscular dude's arm halfway up his ass."

"Impressive," Jacque squealed, already thinking of the perfect pose to take advantage of his unique talent.

"So what happened to the guy who had his hand in your ass?" Timothy asked.

William looked over at Lord who smiled back at him and winked. William lowered his head and fell silent. Everyone noticed the exchange but said nothing. Each of them filling in their own blanks.

Lord turned to the Bettie Page wannabe who'd joined them back at the nightclub. He reached out for her throat and pulled her close to him, dragging her across Sue's lap and onto his. He ran his hands over her body as he growled in her ear.

"And what exactly is your specialty Lana? What is it that brings you into our demented little family?" Lord questioned.

"I'm . . . I don't know. I saw Timothy's scars and I somehow knew what it was that I'd been missing. I'm sure you could tell that I was a submissive before I decided to make the switch to a dom. I was sick of all those bumbling tops that were even weaker than the bottoms they were trying to dominate. When I saw Timothy, I knew that whoever he belonged to was the man I'd been looking for."

"And what if you can't take it? What if a real dom is just too much for you?" Jacque chimed in.

"Then I'll suffer," she said solemnly. Lord nodded his head in approval and sent her back to her seat.

"That you will dear Lana. That you will."

"Hey Sue! Show William what Lord did to your tits! This is fucking great! You're gonna love this!" Timothy was trying hard to hide his nervousness behind a veil of cocky self-assurance and puppy-like enthusiasm.

Timothy started unbuttoning Sue's blouse and this time she allowed it. Anything to erase the memory of the man with the missing face. William leaned in close to gawk at the design carved across Sue's massive breasts.

"Beautiful," William marveled.

215

"So what the fuck was going on in there?" Jacque asked, voicing the concern etched into all of their faces just below the surface of their forced smiles.

"I could show you if you're curious," Lord replied, leaning forward until the heat from his eyes threatened to sear off Jacque's eyelids. "Are you curious Jacque?"

Jacque's eyes began to water and his face broke out in a riot of ticks.

"N—n—no. I'm not curious. I don't give a fuck."

"Good," Lord replied, leaning back into the plush leather seat as the limousine hurtled through the dark deserted streets like a black submarine in the open sea.

Anja was livid. Lord had escaped her again. Her meat puppets had gotten overzealous and started ripping apart the drummer boys outside the club, fighting with and fucking the bouncers with their long, lethal, prehensile phalluses, making them scream for their lives, ruining any chance they'd had to catch Lord unaware. They'd wasted time and alerted Lord to their presence, allowing him to slip out the back.

Withstanding the urge to tear the idiotic creatures apart, which would only have wasted more time, as she'd have had to reconstruct them, she let her pets vent their frustration on the club patrons. Anja stared listlessly at the blood-soaked walls, the ceiling fans strung with human intestines and flinging viscera around the room, the heads lined up like empty beer cans atop the bar, and the few patrons still alive and gagging on demon dick, dripping scalding semen down their chins, out of their distended rectums, waiting for their turn to die. She tried to block it all out and concentrate on where Lord might be headed next.

Her hell-spawned Frankenstein rejects were starting to go mad in their makeshift bodies. Their souls were still human beneath the layers of tortured flesh and they were rejecting their infernal forms with an instinctive spiritual revulsion. Their egos rebelling against their own hideousness and driving them insane.

Her pets were turning on each other, ripping and clawing at their own bodies and those of their demonic brethren as they fought over the heart and sexual organs of their victims. Anja had to use her whip to restore order. But even still they shambled about as if in a daze, shrieking and convulsing like severely retarded children.

Both the pain of manipulating their ill-crafted muscles and the affront to their vanity at having to exist as these repulsive abominations, was taxing the limits of their sanity. Soon they would be no good to her. It took yet a few more cracks from the whip to get them moving again.

She hadn't yet figured out Lord's destination. He still didn't have enough slaves to reenact even those positions described in the first chapter of the Book of Sins and she didn't dare take her pets wandering from club to club with their bloodlust steadily growing and Anja just barely managing to control them. She had to figure out exactly where they were going. Anja sat back and tried to remember the names of his other slaves; his repeat customers. She'd met a few of them back when she was one of them and he'd even slipped and told her one or two of their real names once while bragging. Anja grinned malevolently and picked up the phone book in back of the bar. She sifted through the white pages trying to locate those slaves whose names she could still recall. She had an idea where he might turn up next.

"Fucking Anja!" Lord thought to himself as he stroked Sue's long curly brown hair as if she were a lap dog. "What the fuck does she want me so bad for? It was her dad and her twisted uncle that abused her. All I did was show her a way to enjoy her pain. Why isn't she going after them? Why me?"

Sue felt his body tense and looked up into Lord's dark fearsome eyes. Shadows swirled deep within those sunless pits. It was like looking into hell. She imagined she could see the souls screaming in agony, burning in indescribable anguish on the surface of his retinas.

"Is there anything wrong Lord?"

"We are almost here."

They cruised up Polk Street appraising the rows of drugged out prostitutes and transvestites. Jacque pointed out a young slender Filipino boy with wounded eyes and a face even prettier than Timothy's. Timothy countered with a tough-looking teenager with gang tattoos and hard vascular musculature. Sue and Lana were tittering over a black transvestite with breasts nearly as big as Sue's and an ass like an inflatable beach ball. She had big seat cushion lips, a dick-sucker pucker, and eyes delirious with a cocktail of drugs. Lord ordered the chauffeur to drive on.

They pulled up alongside a thick-muscled Latino leather boy, wearing tight denims, a leather vest, and a police hat. He had a thick handlebar mustache and handcuffs and a police baton hanging from his belt. William rose up excitedly, pressing his face against the window and almost drooling. Again, Lord ordered the chauffeur past.

Lord was considering going back for the transvestite when they passed a Filipino woman with a slight build and fierce eyes. She had a small firmly muscled frame with a tight muscular ass like an Olympic gymnast. She wore a red latex miniskirt similar to Lana's that just barely covered her superior posterior and a latex halter-top that revealed her rippling abdominal muscles. There were welts on her thighs and she had scars on her back that had obviously come from a whip. Lord licked his lips appreciatively, ignoring the jealous sneer that tore across Sue's features.

The limousine slid up beside the delicious Filipino and Lord rolled down his window. The woman leaned in and then quickly backed out and started to turn away when she spotted the carload of misfits.

"How much do you want?" Lord offered.

"You don't have enough. I don't do groups."

"You wouldn't have to do all of us. These guys don't even like women. But they do." Lord said gesturing toward Sue and Lana who were suddenly very interested.

"How do I know you're not a pimp?" She asked halting in her tracks and looking Lord over suspiciously. She pointed to a livid purple bruise around her throat. "I've already got a pimp."

Lord smiled at her without answering.

"What's your specialty?"

She turned so Lord could get a better look at the welts on her back. "I like it rough."

"So I see."

"But it costs more."

"Not a problem. Get in."

Lord opened the door and she hesitated a moment, looking in at the bizarre menagerie seated inside the limousine.

"Hurry up will ya! I'm paying this limo by the hour!" Jacque squealed. "Oh for fuck sake! Here's $500; now get your sweet little ass in the car!"

That decided the matter for her. She slid across Lord and Sue's laps into the car. Lord found himself immediately aroused by her slight sensuous body as she crawled over him, sliding her tiny breasts over his throbbing erection. He rubbed his hand over her rubber-coated callipygian buttocks and had to restrain himself from taking her right there. Her ass was a marvel of nature.

She snuggled in between Lana and Sue and began stroking their bare thighs.

"My name is Pinay," she said as she slid her hands up between their thighs. "So which one of you am I fucking first?" She asked, glaring lasciviously at them with her hard eyes that seemed to hold the same combination of wrath, lust, and sorrow that Anja's had. Lord would regret seeing her die.

Lana pulled the girl onto her lap and began stripping off her clothing, kissing her beautiful face and sucking on her tiny breasts.

219

Sue rolled over to join in, leaving Lord alone with his thoughts for the first time since she'd joined their little party.

"Save some of that for the camera. Do you think we have enough models now? I know there are a lot of poses but we don't have to use a different model for each shot do we?"

Lord didn't want to tell any of them that they would probably not survive more than one or two of the sexual acts he had planned. The agonizing postures and positions in The Book of Sins did not really allow for encores. He knew Timothy was dying for a peek at the book. Even Jacque had not seen it yet though he'd heard of it and Lord had tried to prepare him as much as possible for what horrors it contained. Lord held the malevolent tome close to him. They would all know its contents in time.

"That's okay Jacque. I've got my other slaves waiting."

Sue, William, and Lana all bristled at the news that there would be still others joining their party. They each wanted Lord to themselves.

"Do not worry my pets. You shall all get more of me than you can possibly handle. No one shall be deprived this night. That I promise."

Lord picked up the cell phone and called his slaves to tell them to meet him at Vanessa's loft. His first call was to Alex, a young doctor with the pain threshold of a fakir. He agreed, brimming with excitement. Lord was getting excited as well. The anticipation of sex and the fear of his own death and eternal torture combined into a powerful aphrodisiac. He dialed his other two slaves and listened to the whine of a dial tone. They both had call waiting and they'd both been told to expect his call. There was no reason for their phones to be busy. Cold fingers of dread creeped over Lord's shoulders and raced down his spine.

Bob and Alice had been with Lord for years, long before Anja. They had been two of his first slaves. They'd both assisted in educating Anja in her duties as one of Lord's chosen people. He hoped that they were still alive even though he'd been planning on killing them anyway. There were always more slaves to be had. The world was filled with men and women in need of a master, in need of a Lord. He turned to watch the three women beside him as they licked and caressed each other, already planning around his two absent acolytes who he knew were probably lost forever.

San Francisco has a surprising number of bars for such a small city. Lord watched the lines of enthusiastic club-goers with mild interest as they cruised past on their way across town. There is so much beauty and diversity in the human form that Lord wished he could fit thousands more into the limousine, lose himself in their flesh, wash himself in an ocean of blood and sexual fluids.

They were passing a lesbian leather bar when Lord's eyes widened in shock. There stood Anja, in the flesh, her posse of disfigured zombies ripping apart dykes right there on the sidewalk. She spotted him seconds after he spotted her. Her face contorted into a smile that closely resembled a snarl and she pointed her demons toward the speeding limousine.

Lord quickly looked around the limousine to see if anyone else had noticed the on-rushing horde of the vengeful damned. They were all engaged in their own conversations or absorbed in their own fears. He turned back just as a man with the faces and breasts of at least three different women, the arms of a weightlifter, and the genitalia of at least seven different men in a seething nest between his mismatched legs, caught up with the car. He was moving much faster than humanly possible and his muscles were almost falling apart under the strain, breaking free of the tendons and bone and bunching up under his skin. The creature raked a hand, spiked with shards of protruding bone that appeared to be ribs, across the vehicle. The screech of bone grating metal was just barely audible over the chatter within the limousine.

The chauffeur spotted the shower of sparks that flew up from where the thing was slashing its claws across the rear fender. He looked into his rear view mirror, right into the face of the ghastly demon/corpse, and punched down on the accelerator, speeding them quickly around the corner and leaving the nightmarish thing behind.

"What-tha-fuck! What was that?"

The chauffeur rolled the partition halfway down searching the backseat for anyone else who may have witnessed the horror that had nearly overtaken them. Lord caught his panicked eyes before he could spread his fear to the rest of them and silenced him with his own stern gaze.

"Shhhhh." He said and the man turned back around with his eyes still wide with terror. Lord tried to hide his own mounting fear as he turned to find everyone looking at him with concern. He stared them all down without offering a single word of explanation for either the chauffeur's sudden panic-attack or the fact that the limousine was now on its way to breaking a land speed record. The less they knew the better.

He smiled malevolently and they all found better things to look at. Lord went back to looking out the window. Keeping an eye out for Anja and her pets.

The ride across town to Vanessa's upper Haight Ashbury District apartment was filled with a combination of Timothy's exuberance, Lana and Sue's lustful anticipation, Pinay's coy sensuousness, Jacque's tittering, and Lord and William's stoic introspection. William was afraid Lord would kill him and Lord was afraid he wouldn't have time to kill him before Anja killed them all.

They pulled up in front of an old Victorian house painted in garish yellow and red and piled out of the limo in a disorderly mob. Lord was in no mood to correct them. They would not live long enough to be trained.

222

He knocked on Vanessa's door just as another vehicle pulled up and one more guest arrived to join the party.

"Welcome Alex."

Alex was a tall, slender, athlete, doctor, and extreme masochist with lean wiry muscles. He ran marathons and pierced and branded himself for fun. He had a huge python draped around him and there were several other cages filled with various exotic animals in the back of his Honda Civic hatchback. Lord and Jacque smiled. They now had everything they needed.

Timothy and William helped carry the cages out of the car as Sue and Lana fawned over the snake. There were two more smaller snakes in the other cages along with several rodents and weasels. William's mind raced over the possibilities.

"Lighting! I didn't bring any lighting!" Jacque whined as he fitted the expensive telephoto lens onto his Nikon 35mm and stuffed rolls and rolls of film into his pockets.

"Make do." Lord commanded, leading his entourage into the house in a procession as dichotomously solemn and joyous as a New Orleans funeral. He grabbed Alex by the arm halting him in his tracks and whispered in his ear.

"Where's Bob and Alice? I tried calling them after I called you to tell them where to meet and they didn't answer?"

"I tried calling them too, just before I left. I couldn't get them either. I talked to them earlier after you called me and they were excited about coming. I thought maybe you'd gotten a hold of them and they were here already."

Lord relaxed his grip and his eyes went dark and ominous. He knew that neither of them were coming. They were probably dead already. Anja would have remembered them from when she was part of Lord's circle of playmates. She would have assumed that they would be part of the party. She'd probably already tortured them both to death trying to find the location of the party. Unfortunately she'd jumped the gun. Neither of them knew.

Worry was slowly giving way to dread but Lord was determined not to let his mounting fear ruin this crowning moment for him. Once he had the illustrations and he'd secured himself an exalted place in hell, he could take all the time he needed to translate the book and secure his place in the annals of human history. Once he'd surpassed even Anja's own feats of deviant perversion not even she could touch him.

Vanessa stood at the top of the steps wearing only a robe, which was wide open and catching wind, as she greeted her guests with nipples erect and pussy freshly shaven. She smiled at Lord and held out her arms to welcome him and his menagerie into her home.

The room had already been rearranged to give them more space to perform and candles filled every available surface; window ledges, tables, chairs, art niches, the fireplace mantle, everything except the floor. The fireplace was lit and a flame raged inside, warming the room. Everyone immediately began to disrobe without needing to be asked. Lord peeled off his own clothing and opened Le Livre Des Péchés, the infamous *The Book of a Thousand Sins*.

"Time to play."

The first screams belonged to William. Predictably Lana lost her nerve and fled the house without a word. Sue once again snuggled tight to Lord for reassurance as she watched Alex lubricate the eighteen-foot python with peanut oil and attempt to ease the entire thing into William's rectum, which was stretched far beyond its capacity.

Alex was struggling with the thing as it resisted being forced into such a confined space. The monstrous serpent nearly crushed him before he managed to get the head inside. After that it began to slide in fairly easily.

Blood flowed from William's anus in a steady stream as the thing writhed its way into his lower bowels. Nearly five feet of reptile was slithering around inside of William before it got stuck. Its panicked undulations tickled William's prostate and he abruptly ceased screaming and began to coo delightedly. He took his miniscule penis in his hand and began aggressively masturbating, tugging at himself so hard it looked like he might rip the tiny thing right off.

Jacque had placed an iron helmet with spikes inside it on top of William's head and the weight of the thing was slowly driving the spikes into his skull. A sheet of blood poured down his face giving him the agonized and rapturous look of Christ on the cross.

Jacque flitted around him snapping pictures as the python wound the rest of its body around poor William and began to constrict. All the blood rushed to William's head turning him purple and blue and causing more blood to pour from the wounds in his scalp. Lord rushed in to rescue him before his bones started to snap. He wrenched the python from William's ass and strangled the life from the thing. William collapsed into Lord's arms gasping for air. Everyone began to clap, awed by the fact that William had survived. Now it was Sue's turn.

Her breasts had scabbed over with blood from Lord's earlier scalpel work and after tying her down, he reopened the wounds by whipping her breasts with a cat made of leather, knotted and braided and embedded with shark's teeth. Jacque's camera clicked steadily as Lord tore the scorpion and hawk design to shreds.

Sue screamed and cried out, tears streaming down her face. Lord paused to lick the blood from her lacerated and mutilated breasts sending shivers all through her. She began to plead with him to stop. He kissed her deeply silencing her and then sent Pinay to calm her by burying her head in her pussy as he continued to whip her.

Pinay misunderstood his command and began to lick Sue's sopping wet vagina. Sucking her clitoris and nearly bringing Sue to orgasm.

"No! That's not what I meant!" Lord grabbed Pinay roughly, lifting her off the ground. Vanessa rushed over with some barbed wire to bind the poor girl's arms behind her. They tied her up in barbed wire from her shoulders to just above her calves leaving only her luscious ass unscathed. She cursed and screamed as the sharp barbs punctured her skin drawing blood from dozens of wounds. A curtain of liquid red rained down her body covering even her ass in a slick crimson sheen. Lord lifted Pinay up and shoved her entire head up Sue's snatch, ripping her wide.

He used the blood dripping from her punctured flesh and Sue's flayed mammaries to lubricate his own erection and then slowly inserted himself between Pinay's golden brown buttocks parting those perfect globes with his massive organ and then aggressively thrusting into her anus as he resumed whipping Sue's breasts. Lord came with a roar and a shudder watching the little street hooker suffocate within the torn and ragged hole between Sue's massive thighs. Sue came as well . . . just as Pinay stopped breathing.

The rest of his little assemblage stood in shocked and horrified silence as Lord continued to fuck Pinay in her ass, quivering with the last tremors of his own little death, while her body convulsed in its death throes. Her spastic movements sent yet another orgasm ripping through Sue's rotund body. Lord withdrew himself from her corpse seconds before it voided its waste fluids all over the floor.

Lord dragged Pinay's lifeless carcass out of Sue's vagina just as the huge woman collapsed into tears. He leaned over and kissed her deeply on the mouth and then licked the tears from her face. Sue smiled even as the tears continued to fall. Her breasts looked like raw hamburger and her hideously distended vagina looked as if she had just delivered conjoined twins.

"In for a penny. In for a pound," Lord declared glaring at his remaining playthings and wiping the blood and excrement from his cock, daring any of them to back out now.

He kissed Sue once again, grateful for her sacrifice. Then he picked up The Book of Sins and turned the next page. It was Timothy's turn.

Knowing that Timothy's contribution would be particularly gruesome, he decided to chain up his remaining lovers so that none of them would suddenly get second thoughts. He knew that their enthusiasm had probably weakened seeing him truss Pinay up in barbed wire and shove her up Sue's snatch. He could sense them wanting to follow Lana's example and flee screaming down the street when Pinay's muffled screams had started to die down and her chest ceased its rise and fall. They had only found the nerve to stay by reminding themselves that he had saved William and she was, after all, only a prostitute he'd purchased for their amusement. Though none of them had found her death particularly amusing.

Vanessa brought Lord the scalpel she'd retrieved from his dungeon. At his command she rushed to get him a needle and thread and two of the animal cages. Then she allowed herself to be tied up as well. Now Jacque and Lord himself were the only two in the room who remained unbound.

Lord began his cutting starting with Timothy and working his way around to all of them, cutting into their flesh and fucking the new orifices, sewing animals up inside them and sewing sexual organs to mouths. He skinned Timothy alive, and cut a hole in his abdomen for Alex to fuck with his tremendous cock, which was nearly as large as Lord's. Lord then cored out Timothy's asshole with a paring knife and ordered Alex to fuck that as well before he finally popped one of Timothy's eyes from the socket and pierced his brain with the tip of his dick. He finished by coating Timothy's naked muscle and fat with his semen as Jacque shot off one roll of film after another.

Just before he perished, Timothy smiled over at Jacque with Lord's dick in his eye-socket and asked if he had gotten it all on film. Jacque smiled and a tear rolled down his cheek.

"Yes Timmy. We got it. We got it all. You're going to live forever."

Next Lord found further use for both William's peculiar talents and Pinay's still lovely corpse, amputating her lithe and delicate limbs and fucking William in the ass with them. As both his own passion and the savagery of the acts depicted in the book increased he sliced off and ate one of Sue's breasts and then sewed a muskrat up inside her vagina. He slid one of the smaller boa constrictors up into Alex's rectum and sewed it shut before taking the scalpel to the young doctor's penis. After he'd skinned and bisected it he ordered William to give the doctor a blowjob. Jacque zoomed in for a close up as William stuffed both bleeding halves of Alex's cock into his mouth.

After Alex reached a bloody screaming orgasm, Lord cut him up the middle in the "Y" incision used by coroners, peeled back the layers of skin, muscle, and fat covering his rib cage and nailed it to the floor. He then drove penny nails into his body all over, ripping pages out of the bible and sticking a page on the head of each nail. He used up the entire bible before he ran out of places to drive nails in. He then laid a crucifix inside Alex's exposed ribcage, right beside his heart, and then pissed on it as Alex drew his last anguished breath.

Lord could barely keep track of where he was in the book. The pages were almost turning themselves and inspiration far beyond anything contained within its pages flowed into him.

He composed a symphony out of their flesh. Twisting and shaping it into fluid shapes like sound from an instrument or colors on a painter's palate rather than the skin, muscle, and bone of sentient human beings. He sculpted nightmarish works of living art from their writhing shrieking bodies, carving into them to reveal the masterpieces that lay hidden within, waiting to be uncovered. A chorus of anguish rang out as the screams reached a crescendo beneath his scalpel and his whip.

Jacque could hardly keep the camera still, this was so much more horrible than he had anticipated. Still, it was beautiful. This was indeed a masterpiece. It would however, have to remain anonymous until after he was long dead and beyond man's ability to prosecute. No way could he put his name to this now. Even in the photos it would be obvious that the models could not have survived these poses.

Both the temperature and the occupancy of the room suddenly began to increase. Others guests, not of earth, were coming to join the party. Demons of every description, not the tortured meat puppets that Anja was dragging around in search of him, but fallen angels grown hideous during their aeons of infernal incarceration, had come to play. They scooped up Lord's slaves like dessert on a buffet table. Those not already dead soon found themselves praying for death as appetites and imaginations even darker than Lord's consumed them. Long phalluses many times larger than a man's ripped into them and slavering mouths and tongues tasted them in places they would have thought unreachable until the demon's claws and fangs granted access to them. Lord and Jacque were the only human beings in the room not being fucked, tortured, or eaten alive. Lord ordered Jacque to continue shooting and he did. Whatever was going on, they were apparently not on the menu.

Anja heard the shrieks and knew she was heading in the right direction. She'd had to cut a swath through half the deviants in town to get this close and her pets were now crazy with bloodlust. They streamed along ahead of her, snatching innocent pedestrians off the street and raping and mutilating them. She had given up on trying to control them. She just hoped they wouldn't be spent by the time they reached Lord.

It had been a stroke of luck that she had spotted the girl in the latex fetish gear weeping her eyes out at the bus stop. She'd seen the woman earlier that evening being led around by the nose, following Lord and his little entourage from one pick-up joint to the next. Anja noticed, just before she set her pets on her, how much she truly did resemble Bettie Page.

The woman did not hold up for more than a few seconds with Anja's hideous pets savagely fucking and torturing her before she'd given them the address to Lord's little party. That was another stroke of luck for Anja. Had she held out longer she would not have had time to tell Anja anything before the vicious beasts ripped her to shreds. They were now well beyond Anja's ability to control. They had gone completely mad.

Her pets were not merciful with Lana and neither were they very respectful of her corpse. They tore her head off her shoulders to allow for two more holes to insert their engorged cocks in. Four of the beasts latched on to her decapitated head and fucked her skull through the neck, the mouth, and the empty eye sockets. Cocks punctured her body from every angle.

They tore her apart completely as they each reached orgasm. Her steaming viscera was left to decorate a street sign, and the rest of her was strewn from one end of the block to the other. Except her breasts, which one of the mad little beasts kept as a snack.

Anja quickly made her way to the house she'd described and was pleased to see the limousine parked just were Lana had said it would be. The driver spotted them right away and took off quickly down the street without bothering to alert his passengers inside.

When she started up the stairs of the little Victorian with the Sesame Street color scheme, Anja's pets suddenly fell back, quivering in fear. Anja felt it too. The place reeked of hell. They were too late. She darted up the stairs, taking them two at a time, and burst through the door in time to see Lord, exultant like the god he'd always believed himself to be, watching his lovers being torn apart by the infernal lusts of the minions of hell.

Lord smiled at her in that superior way she'd come to both love and loathe and scooped her up into his arms. She melted there, suddenly powerless. He tore off her clothes in rapid gestures and began to make love to her. He still had the scalpel in his hand and it joined in their foreplay, adding a searing contrast to his loving caresses. He entered her even as he continued to cut into her. Anja felt the love pour out of her in liquid waves as his blood and gore soaked organ pounded up inside her. He bit her several times, his eyes glazed with lust, and his blade bit even deeper. Even after all she'd experienced in both her life and her afterlife nothing compared to the love of Lord. The voluptuous pain and torturous ecstasy he was capable of had no equal on earth or in hell. Anja screamed in torment as her every nerve sang out in salacious agony and a massive soul-consuming orgasm built within her. They reached their climax together, an earthquake that shook the room. Anja felt as if she had died again.

As the screams, and shrieks and sounds of animalistic torture and murder surrounded them, Anja looked into Lord's eyes and finally admitted to him the source of all her rage and hatred.

"I love you," she said with tears welling up in her eyes.

"I love you too," Lord replied brushing the hair from her eyes and kissing away her tears. He smiled as he stared deep into her eyes which had now softened with love then he lifted her off his cock and flung her into the midst of the demons.

"Did you get that on film?"

"All of it," Jacque replied.

As Anja was torn apart and raped from the inside out Lord and Jacque gathered up all their film and left, *The Book of a Thousand Sins* tucked under Lord's arm. A fiery lake rose in Vanessa's living room and all its occupants joined the inferno seconds before the two artists left the house. Lord's head was still swirling with inspiration as they walked down the darkened street. He stroked the cover of The Book of Sins and grinned happily. He had a lot of writing to do. With the book's help, he would write a new bible, a bible for a new religion with him as the central deity.

He imagined his word spreading across the globe as millions of sensualists and thrill seekers flocked to his temples in search of an experience that would transcend life and give meaning to their mundane existences. And he would gather them all to his bosom and grant them the ecstasy they seeked. He would free them from the mores, traditions, and societal, moral, and cultural restraints that have for so long fettered the development of the human spirit and show them how to suck the marrow out of life. He imagined the worship of Lord replacing Christianity as the world's dominant religion. He imagined a world where passion reigned, where lust was canonized and abstinence abhorred, where his name was sung in hymns and whispered in prayers. By the time he died, he'd be more powerful than Satan, larger than God.

Lord began to hum to himself as he turned onto Haight Street. Then he began to sing, making up lyrics as he went along, composing the first hymn in honor of lust and desire; in honor of Lord. The words spilled out of him as if he'd opened an artery and was bleeding it out.

"*. . . And I will love you in my dreams and with every conscious breath/ And I will take you 'tween my thighs and hold you to my breasts/ and I will drink your semen down to commune with you my Lord/ Give my flesh to your whip and blade to prove my love to you oh Lord/ and let my blood pool at your feet as I drop down to my knees/ and give you my beating heart for you to do with as you please . . .*"

Jacque looked over at him.

"Those are some pretty cool lyrics. It sounds like gospel music. What is that you're singing?"

"I just wrote it. It's called *Giving Your Heart to Lord.*"

"I like it."

"Good. I'll teach you the words. I'll teach everyone."

No Questions Unanswered

My jaw hung open in awe as I watched the blood spill through the gaping wound I'd somehow ripped in the fabric of creation. I saw his face then, contorted in agony. I recognized him instantly, as I knew I would. I watched him writhe in indescribable pain as the explosions tore through him with a sense of profound dread descending over me like a dark shroud. It was like watching the universe grind to a halt and expire, and at that moment that's exactly what I believed I was witnessing. His death throes, I was certain, would mean the annihilation of all that existed. I watched him perish screaming and convulsing, meeting his end with as much mortal terror as any man, staring me directly in my eyes, knowing that I had murdered him.

In my mind I had committed the greatest sin imaginable. In my mind I had doomed us all. I knew—I hoped, that my punishment would rival any torture ever imagined by man, that I would suffer as no one ever had before. That's how it should have been.

I didn't mean to kill him. That was not my intention at all. I guess I wanted to know the truth. I knew there would be a price for that. We all know it and that's why most people are comfortable just adopting the beliefs of their family and culture rather than seeking true knowledge. Knowledge always comes with pain while ignorance does provide a kind of bliss. Besides, if we have faith that our beliefs are correct then it almost feels like genuine truth. But deep down we know it isn't the same. And being a man of science I had to know, not just believe.

You can build consensus around knowledge. Knowledge has predictive power. It allows you to accurately predict events that logically follow from that truth, e.g. gas is combustible. If this is true than it follows necessarily that if I touch a lit match to gas it will combust. This is a sound theory and if this theory is correct then it is a fact. We can create experiments that will confirm or refute it. Such as actually placing that lit match into a gas jug and watching the ensuing conflagration. Belief has no such capabilities. No predictive power. Since it is not based on any genuine facts you cannot set up an experiment to confirm or refute it. How would one set up an experiment to confirm or refute the statement that God loves us?

"If God loves us then He won't allow innocents to suffer." Yet, innocents suffer everyday by the millions and it does not impact faith one iota. "If God loves us then He wouldn't allow evil to overcome good." Yet, everyday the pious fall prey to the wicked and the faithful explain it away. Because the statement "God loves us" isn't based on empirical evidence, it cannot be refuted by it. Therefore we can't build consensus, hence, the multitudes of different faiths and beliefs.

"But what if I could set up an experiment to prove it? Not to the world. Just to me. What if I could prove that God did or did not love me? Did I say me? I meant us. I meant the world."

Of course I'd said exactly what I meant. I didn't care if God loved the world. I wanted to know if He loved me. I wanted to know why He allowed my parents to be murdered by that burglar when I was eight-years-old, leaving me to be raised by the State in one foster home after another. I wanted to know why He allowed that wrinkled old septuagenarian who reeked of Ben Gay and gin to beat me with his cane and lock me in the basement with his dogs every night. Why it took the State so long to finally discover it. And why, when they did, they just shuffled me off to yet another foster home, this one the home of a sweet, loving, overweight woman who'd previously been accused of sexually abusing the two foster kids already in her custody. Why I still can't get her sickening perfume and pastry smell and the squishy feel of her flesh out of my mind. I wanted to know why I'd never married or had kids. I wanted to know if HE gave a fuck about me!

I sound angry, don't I? It almost makes me sound like I did this on purpose. But I assure you that what happened was an accident. Not that you'll believe me. In fact, I'm pretty sure that you won't believe any of this.

That's okay though. I know what happened. And I know why it happened. There was no revenge or animosity involved at all. It was just a simple miscalculation. Even geniuses make those, you know.

Anyway, that's how the idea to use the Ion Engine got into my head. I needed to do something bigger than anything anyone had ever done before. Something that would decide the question of God's love once and for all. If He loved His creation, would He let one man destroy it?

The Ion Engine works on the principle of quantum acceleration. Electrons traveling many times the speed of light, punching holes in the fabric of time and space. I knew I could build such a thing. I'd been commissioned by the government to do just that in the hopes of creating an engine powerful enough to take a spacecraft to another galaxy. The problem was containment. At that speed, a single electron would acquire so much mass that it would hit with the force of a nuclear bomb. And this thing would fire millions of electrons! Launching it would annihilate everything surrounding it for miles. Of course, we could use standard thrusters to lift it into orbit and then fire up the accelerator once it was safely in space, but an entire ship propelled at that speed would be hit with specks of dust that would likewise have the impact of nuclear explosions. What kind of shielding could withstand that? So the project was scrapped. But, I still have all my notes and all the knowledge. I even have access to all the equipment courtesy of Uncle Sam and Lockheild Aeronautic Industries. I could do it. I would do it.

"Would God let me, though? Would He let me destroy the world?"

If He loves us, than I guess He wouldn't. I had to find out. That is both my greatest asset and my greatest weakness. Once a question comes to my mind I cannot rest until it is answered. It's what led me into quantum physics in the first place and from there into quantum mechanics. It's what led me to the Nobel Prize as the first man to discover the Higgs boson, the particle that gives rise to a field through which all other subatomic particles, quarks, gluons, photons and electrons, must pass and explains on a subatomic level why matter has mass. They called it "The God Particle" because figuring out how it works would give us the answer to how the universe itself was formed. It was only a theory until I isolated one in a fission reactor right here in my laboratory at Lockheild. Proving theories is what I do. It's what my mind was made for. It's why I can't let this question rest.

"Does God love me?"

They, Christians that is, say that one shouldn't tempt the Lord. I'd always been willing to risk hell for the sake of knowledge. I guess you have to be. I wasn't even sure that it was the Christian God I was after. I rather doubted it. I was almost certain that our concept of divinity was flawed by our own fears and desires as well as our vanity. The idea that we were made in God's image was almost definitely another of man's egocentricities. But, whatever God was, I meant to find Him to isolate His love the same way I'd isolated the "The God Particle."

The principle of the ion generator is simple. It works like a modified particle accelerator using an electromagnetic field with an alternating current to propel negatively charged electrons at protons with an antithetical charge. This creates a snowball effect as the collision of the two oppositely charged particles causes an explosion that propels those protons into other electrons which hit other protons and on and on building up speed with each successive impact until you've got those babies traveling faster than they did at the moment of creation. Well, it's simple if you're an award winning physicist, like me.

The problem is that nobody knows how big this snowball will get and if it will ever stop. It could be the answer to perpetual energy or the end of all creation, possibly the end of the entire universe. I knew that it was both. And that's why I knew that a just and loving God would never let me create such a thing.

I woke up that morning drenched in sweat and shivering despite the humid temperatures outside. The fading echo of a nightmare still cast its pall over me as I struggled from sleep like I was swimming to the top of a great pool of mud. I was thankful that I couldn't remember the dream, but suspected that I'd be having it again soon if I was still alive. Knowing what I was about to do, I was surprised I had survived the night. I half expected to be murdered in my sleep like my parents or to suffer a stroke or a heart attack, anything that would have kept me from getting into my car and driving to Lockhield Laboratories. But the sun smiled down through the broken slats in my wood blinds just as it did every morning. Squinting against the sunrays, I rose from my bed and dragged myself into the shower.

Even as I bathed I kept expecting to slip in the tub and crack my head on the tile floor. I could almost see myself lying there with bright red arterial blood spurting from a gash in my skull, looking up into the light with my soul being drawn heavenward. It's what I wanted to happen. Disappointingly, I finished my shower without incident.

My legs wobbled as I walked to my car. I looked at the neat rows of identical stucco homes with their identical red clay roof tiles and their identical drought-friendly rock desert landscapes, wondering if any of this would still be here after today. I watched the paperboy meander up the street, peddling his mountain bike in a slow leisurely motion, a comically large satchel of newspapers slung over his arm. I watched my neighbor, Mr. Green, walk out to meet him wearing only a housecoat, blue corduroy slippers, and red and white Fruit of the Looms, his graying chest hairs forming a trail down over his protruding stomach as it parted his housecoat, his ratty little Yorkshire Terrier "Skippy" yipping at his heels. I waved to them both. I watched lights go on in kitchens up and down the block as one by one my neighbors rose to greet the day, and I wondered if any of them would still be here.

The drive to work was uneventful as was the walk from the underground parking lot to the elevator and from the elevator to my lab. But there was still plenty of time to stop me.

I lined up the powerful electromagnets in a machine that looked like a gigantic centrifuge with a gun turret attached to it. Some of the magnets were almost as large as I was and I fully expected one to topple over and crush me, so I had my two young lab assistants help me lift them into place. They had questions of course, but they were used to me ignoring them and weren't surprised when I sent them away. I transferred energy from the fission reactor I had used to find The Higgs boson to give power to the magnets. They would be the most powerful electromagnets ever. I sat back and looked at what I had built, daring myself to turn it on.

I searched my mind for one memory that would sway my decision and it was only then that I remembered the good times, before my parents' deaths. I remembered birthday cakes, Thanksgiving dinners, Christmas trees and Easter baskets. I remembered throwing Frisbees in the park with Dad. Sitting in the kitchen licking spoons clean of cake batter as Mom laughed and wiped the excess off my cheeks. I remembered being tucked in at night with a bedtime story from Dr. Seuss and a kiss on the forehead. I remembered hugs. Then, inevitably, I remembered the gunshots and the screaming. I remembered the smell of sulfur and blood and the insane grinning face of the crack-head as he ran past my bedroom door and smiled at me with his hands full of blood-soaked money and jewelry. He had looked happy, almost proud.

I tried to shake the memory out of my head. I tried replacing it with other happier ones, recent ones, like giving the valedictory speech in high school and again in college. Then I recalled going home afterward to an empty apartment and crying myself to sleep. I thought about standing up on stage in Geneva receiving the Nobel Prize for Science and how proud I had been until I looked out at the audience and remembered that there were no loved ones out there to share my joy. Even my colleagues were not my friends, barely more than acquaintances, and some were almost strangers. I had never learned to form relationships.

I reached out to the keyboard and began to type in the formula that would initiate the ion engine's electron accelerator and launch an endless explosion that could recreate the Big Bang and destroy all matter in the universe. I wondered if trillions of years from now the explosion would reverse itself, as Einstein predicted, and collapse inward again. I wondered if the universe would ever possess life again.

There was a bible in one of the desks. I went looking for it, knocking over chairs and spilling papers everywhere in my haste to find it. I couldn't locate it, but I did find a copy of the Koran. I wondered whose it was. With today's sociopolitical climate, having an Islamic text and a security clearance would have made many people very nervous. It was not surprising that whoever owned it had attempted to keep it hidden. I looked for the bible a while longer before contenting myself with the Koran. I held it tight to my chest and prayed.

"God, if you can hear me now, then You know what I am about to do and why. You know what will happen if I go through with this. Everything that You have created will vanish. If You value us at all, You will not let me do this thing."

239

And with that, I threw the switch. Or rather, I pressed enter.

I had pointed the barrel of the accelerator upward as a final precaution, just in case the magnetic field failed and the electrons flew out of the vacuum tube. Immediately I heard the explosions going off in the tube. At first I could count each individual one. Then they came so fast that there seemed to be no break between one and the next, just one endless roar. Then the tube exploded. I braced myself, as if you could anchor yourself against the force of a supernova. I saw white hot light explode from the accelerator and I was certain that the end of the world had come. Then the hole appeared.

The six-inch thick glass that enclosed the chamber where the ion engine sat did not as much as crack. In fact, there was no damage to anything at all except for that gaping hole in the ceiling that seemed to have ripped open the sky but had done more than that. It had torn open reality the way you would tear a Polaroid. There above me was the sun and the clouds and the faint ghost of a moon, yet between it was a gaping portal the size of a shopping mall and within that portal I could see HIM and He was hurt, mortally wounded—by my machine.

His blood was the blackness of space dotted with starlight and his eyes were like suns growing dimmer as I watched. His flesh was night and day and ocean and sky and seemed to have no end to it. His face was human. Or at least that is how I perceived it. But it was that horrible rictus of pain that struck me most of all and that look of surprise. The same look I'd seen on the face of my mother and father when the bullets punched through their bodies as that crack-head emptied a stolen nine-millimeter Berretta into them. He was surprised that I had hurt Him. He was not omniscient after all.

His eyes became human then. The fire in them extinguished and they were the green of the earth with a halo of brown orbiting the pupil, like a volcano amid an island of verdant flora. Tears filled them and I knew they were not for his own physical pain. He wept for the loss of the creation that he would never see again. He wept for me.

I maintained eye contact as galaxies yet to be born spilled from his wounds in a premature birth that would no doubt doom them all. I could feel my soul diminishing, growing cold as I stared deep into those tremendous orbs that had witnessed everything I had spent my career trying to understand. He began to dissipate as his essence spilled out into the void and became new universes.

"Perhaps this is how it is done? How it has always been done? Maybe I was meant to kill him so that the next universe could come forth? Maybe the death of a God spawned our universe?"

The theory brought me no comfort. I couldn't prove it and neither could I believe it.

Despite my guilt and shame, I could not look away from that mournful stare. He looked so lonely. So helpless. I felt like He needed me there, to watch Him die. Like, perhaps, He had made himself visible to me just so I could see His pain. I wanted to reach out for Him and hold Him, to comfort Him in His final moments. But it was impossible. He was so vast. I was not even sure how I was able to comprehend His size or even to see it all through that one portal that should not have been large enough to encompass His infinite image. So I just watched with tears streaming down my face as He died and the portal closed again.

I walked out of the lab with my legs even more wobbly than when I had entered. My eyes would not close or blink. The image of His death was branded onto them or rather through them onto my spirit. I reached for my car door and fell to my knees. My stomach churned. My sorrow roiled there indigestible until it came boiling back up and I regurgitated the few morsels I had managed to ingest in the last day or two.

I was expecting the earth to up heave, for fire to rain down from heaven, the oceans to flood creation, perhaps the Angle of Death with his flaming sword of vengeance. But instead, Barney the chief of security just waved to me and told me to drive safe as I drove out of the parking lot.

I watched the news carefully in the days that followed. The same wars still raged. The same criminals still got acquitted and the same innocents persecuted. The same half-off sales and two-for-one sales and this-weekend-only sales still flashed their commercials every eight minutes in between. The same church scandals, political scandals, celebrity scandals, blockbuster concert and movie premiers, football, basketball, baseball, and hockey stats and figures still dominated the newspapers. I started going to churches, mosques, temples, and synagogues looking for some awareness, some indication that anyone had noticed. The sermons had not changed and neither had the responses or lack thereof. TV evangelists still claimed to hear his voice. God was dead and nothing had changed. God gave His only begotten son and it changed the world forever. He throws himself in front of an electron accelerator to prevent the destruction of all creation and the Super Bowl makes the headlines.

At least I had answered my question as well as so many others. Man was so far from the divine. Our illusions and our faith kept us from ever knowing the true God when eventually science would have allowed us to discover him. Instead we filled the gaps in our knowledge with belief, fantasy, faith, lies! So, I jumped the gun and forced the meeting. Now the creator's death is on my conscious.

I looked at my hands expecting to see blood. Not the sticky red ichor that humans and animals bleed, but that cold black blood filled with sun and stars that leaks from the wounds of gods.

"If God is dead, then what happens when we die?"

The question burst into my head unbidden and I knew immediately that it would be my demise. It was the logical question, the only one I had yet to answer and it worried at me until finally I devised the perfect experiment. I bought the gun today for two hundred dollars at Super Pawn. Tomorrow, I go to join Him.

"... You have to come to him and beg forgiveness. God is all loving, all merciful, but if you do not ask for his forgiveness in the name of

Jesus Christ our savior then you will die with those sins on your soul and you will burn in the inferno. You have to be baptized in His holy name and accept Jesus Christ as your Lord and savior."

I laughed. I couldn't control it. The unrelenting hypocrisy of those who had "received the calling" never ceased to amaze me. This should have been a funeral for the Lord of Creation, this entire sermon his eulogy, yet instead it was just one more opportunity to scare the God-fearing into filling the collection plates. I laughed until tears wept from my eyes.

The young preacher shielded his eyes from the lights and looked out across his congregation as the laughter grew louder, echoing from the back of the cathedral where I sat.

"Is something funny my son?" he asked with exaggerated annoyance thick in his pompous voice.

I looked around the immense cathedral marveling at the time and money that must have gone into constructing such a monolithic temple. All the craftsman and artisans who had carved the ornate statues, placed each stone one at a time to build the tremendous thirty-foot walls, painted the stained glass, fashioned all the gold and silver into crucifixes, all paid for by scores of the faithful on the hopes that it would bring them closer to heaven. Yet, none of it had anything to do with God. I knew more about God in that instant that I watched him suffer and die than any of the endless stream of charlatans that had stood on that pulpit. They didn't even know he was dead.

"I'm not your fucking son, Padre."

He blanched and then his face turned red with anger. The entire congregation gasped.

Several men stood up and shouted angrily at me. They began moving towards me snarling and waving their fists. I guess they were going to show me a little bit of Christian love. I smiled and showed them my Tech. nine millimeter as I rose from the pew. That silenced them. I turned back to the pastor who had lost the color in his face again when he saw the automatic pistol.

"Who the hell am I supposed to be asking forgiveness from, Padre?"

"You are supposed to ask for the Lord's forgiveness. Now please, do not bring that weapon into God's house."

There was a quiver in the pastor's voice now. His eyes darted nervously around the church looking for help as I walked towards him.

"Don't you know shit, Padre? The Lord's house is empty."

"God's house is always full. Full of the holy spirit."

"God is dead, Padre. I killed him. Shot him down like a dog in the street. I'm probably the world's greatest assassin, but no one even knows who I am because no one knows he's dead. And no one knows God's dead because no one ever knew God. All of this . . ." I waved my arms gesturing widely at the ornate stone statues of Moses, and Mary, the stained glass depictions of the birth of Christ, the Last Supper, Moses parting the Red Sea, The Crucifixtion. I still had the gun in my hand so half the room ducked as I gestured towards them, ". . . is bullshit! You are full of shit!"

I was halfway down the aisle and the young pastor who had probably fucked half the single women in his congregation and a quarter of the married ones, was looking more and more like a caged animal. Every one wants to go to heaven, but no one wants to die. Not even a preacher. That alone should have been a sign to any reasonable man that the whole religion thing was a scam.

"I want you to tell me, Padre, how I am supposed to ask God for forgiveness when he's dead? Who is going to forgive me for what I've done? I mean, God was already in heaven so it ain't like he goes to heaven when he dies. So who's doing the forgiving now?"

"I—I don't know what you are talking about. Now, please, leave this church. You are scaring all these good people." Sweat was bulleting down the pastor's face and his heavily moussed, gelled, and sprayed, perfectly styled hair was beginning to frizz.

I looked around the room and no one had moved from their

chairs. They all sat riveted to the front of the room like they were watching a soap opera on television. Their faces were both sad and horrified yet all of them looked curious, like rubber-neckers straining to spot casualties as they cruised by a car accident.

"You're the only one that looks scared to me, Padre. Your flock just looks a little nervous, maybe even excited. This is probably the most memorable time any of them have ever had at church. Now, please, answer my question. Who forgives the man that murdered God?"

"You cannot murder God! This is blasphemous!"

I walked up to the pulpit and shoved the Tech.9. right into the pastor's pretty young face. The man was rubbing me the wrong way.

"Who the fuck am I blaspheming against? God is dead! Haven't you been listening? I killed him! And none of you so much as noticed! You still stand up hear preaching your lies, claiming to have a direct pipeline to God, and yet you don't even notice that he's gone? You say you talk to him? You say you know God? That you've got a personal relationship with God?"

"Yes, I have a personal relationship with God. I talk to God every day."

"Well, what's God's favorite color? What's his favorite type of music? What's his favorite movie?"

"I—I don't know? What does that have to do with anything?"

I was so angry now that I was snarling.

"Because I can answer those questions about all the people I know. I know these things about all the people I have a personal relationship with. Yet, you speak to God everyday and you don't even know whether he likes James Brown or Green Day? When was the last time you spoke to him?"

"This morning! I spoke to him this morning at my bedside!"

I looked into his eyes and the belief was as clear as day. The man was not lying for whatever reason he thought he was telling the truth.

I almost lowered my gun. I almost walked out of the church. But then I saw it. I saw him doubt.

"Careful, Padre. I know you couldn't have spoken to God this morning because I haven't slept in over a week. Not since the day I punched a whole in the Supreme Being with an electron accelerator. I'm telling you that I killed him. I watched him die right there in my lab. So I know that you didn't speak to him yesterday and so I'm pretty sure that you've *never* spoken to him. I'm pretty sure that you don't know shit about God. But I do have one more question for you."

"What's that, madman?" the young pastor's eyes blazed defiantly as he finally found his guts.

"Careful, now. I'm not in the mood to be challenged. All I want to know is what happens now?"

"The cops come and you go to jail and then to a hospital where you can get some help."

"No! I mean what happens to all of us? I mean how does this work? Is it like a gang thing? I mean do I become God now that I've killed him?"

The sirens came exploding out of nowhere. Suddenly they were all around the church. Red, blue, and white lights flashed through the stained glass casting a kaleidoscope of colors around the cathedral. The front doors opened and what looked like half the police force spilled into the already crowded church.

"Drop your weapon! Drop it! Drop it, now!"

About two dozen guns were now pointed my way. I smiled at them.

"One more question, Padre. It's been worrying at me all week and I just can't seem to find the answer. I hate unanswered questions. That's how all this shit got started in the first place. I keep trying to leave it alone, but it's just not in me. I have to know."

I looked at all the guns again. The cops were still shouting at me, but I couldn't hear them. One officer was walking towards me with

246

his palms facing me talking in calm soothing words that sounded to me like jibberish. It was like I was in a dream.

"If God is dead than what happens when we die?"

The pastor smiled at me. The expression was about as far from holy as you could get.

"Why don't you find out?"

"You first, charlatan." I pulled the trigger and so did they.

ABOUT THE AUTHOR

WRATH JAMES WHITE is a former World Class Heavyweight Kickboxer, a professional Kickboxing and Mixed Martial Arts trainer, distance runner, performance artist, and former street brawler, who is now known for creating some of the most disturbing works of fiction in print .

Wrath's two most recent novels are THE RESURRECTIONIST and YACCUB'S CURSE. He is also the author of SUCCULENT PREY, EVERYONE DIES FAMOUS IN A SMALL TOWN, THE BOOK OF A THOUSAND SINS, HIS PAIN and POPULATION ZERO. He is the coauthor of TERATOLOGIST cowritten with the king of extreme horror, Edward Lee, ORGY OF SOULS cowritten with Maurice Broaddus, HERO cowritten with J.F. Gonzalez, and POISONING EROS cowritten with Monica J. O'Rourke.

Wrath lives and works in Austin, Texas with his two daughters, Isis and Nala, his son Sultan and his wife Christie.

deadite press

"Brain Cheese Buffet" Edward Lee - collecting nine of Lee's most sought after tales of violence and body fluids. Featuring the Stoker nominated "Mr. Torso," the legendary gross-out piece "the Dritiphilist," the notorious "The McCrath Model SS40-C, Series S," and six more stories to test your gag reflex.

"Edward Lee's writing is fast and mean as a chain saw revved to full-tilt boogie."
- Jack Ketchum

"Bullet Through Your Face" Edward Lee - No writer is more extreme, perverted, or gross than Edward Lee. His world is one of psychopathic redneck rapists, sex addicted demons, and semen stealing aliens. Brace yourself, the king of splatterspunk is guaranteed to shock, offend, and make you laugh until you vomit.
"Lee pulls no punches."
- Fangoria

"Slaughterhouse High" Robert Devereaux - It's prom night in the Demented States of America. A place where schools are built with secret passageways, rebellious teens get zippers installed in their mouths and genitals, and once a year one couple is slaughtered and the bits of their bodies are kept as souvenirs. But something's gone terribly wrong when the secret killer starts claiming a far higher body count than usual . . .
"A major talent!" - Poppy Z. Brite

"The Vegan Revolution . . . with Zombies" David Agranoff - Thanks to a new miracle drug the cute little pig no longer feels a thing as she is led to the slaughter. The only problem? Once the drug enters the food supply anyone who eats it is infected. From fast food burgers to free-range organic eggs, eating animal products turns people into shambling brain-dead zombies – not even vegetarians are safe!
"A perfect blend of horror, humor and animal activism."
- Gina Ranalli

"Squid Pulp Blues" Jordan Krall - In these three bizarro-noir novellas, the reader is thrown into a world of murderers, drugs made from squid parts, deformed gun-toting veterans, and a mischievous apocalyptic donkey.

". . . with SQUID PULP BLUES, [Krall] created a wholly unique terrascape of Ibsen-like naturalism and morbidity; an extravaganza of white-trash urban/noir horror."
- Edward Lee

"Apeshit" Carlton Mellick III - Friday the 13th meets Visitor Q. Six hipster teens go to a cabin in the woods inhabited by a deformed killer. An incredibly fucked-up parody of B-horror movies with a bizarro slant

"The new gold standard in unstoppable fetus-fucking killfreakomania . . . Genuine all-meat hardcore horror meets unadulterated Bizarro brainwarp strangeness. The results are beyond jaw-dropping, and fill me with pure, unforgivable joy." - John Skipp

"Super Fetus" Adam Pepper - Try to abort this fetus and he'll kick your ass!

"The story of a self-aware fetus whose morally bankrupt mother is desperately trying to abort him. This darkly humorous novella will surely appall and upset a sizable percentage of people who read it . . . In-your-face, allegorical social commentary."
- BarnesandNoble.com

"Fistful of Feet" Jordan Krall - A bizarro tribute to Spaghetti westerns, Featuring Cthulhu-worshipping Indians, a woman with four feet, a Giallo-esque serial killer, a crazed gunman who is obsessed with sucking on candy, Syphilis-ridden mutants, ass juice, burping pistols, sexually transmitted tattoos, and a house devoted to the freakiest fetishes.

"Krall has quite a flair for outrage as an art form."
- Edward Lee

AVAILABLE FROM AMAZON.COM

Printed in the USA
CPSIA information can be obtained
at www.ICGtesting.com
LVHW012346150324
774600LV00002B/289